KAWHOCUMDIA
a novel by
Donald Henson

ISBN 978-0-615-43082-9

A list of Characters and points of interest

Zadator (Leader in the programming and Sam's hero when his kidnapping became too dangerous).

Belsha (is wife of Zadator and biological mother of Samuel).

Sam Orrington (pronounced Warrington, he is also the Captain).

Jimmy (befriended by Sam and becomes close friend and crewmember).

Danny (befriended by Sam and becomes close friend and crewmember).

Manny (Danny's Aunt who raises him as her own, he calls her mama).

Alicia (is Danny's real mother who left him at a very young age).

Miss Linda (is Jimmy's mother).

Bo (is Jimmy's dog but his real name is Junior; given to him by Jimmy's real mother).

Harlan (is Sam's father).

Maggie (is Sam's mother).

Samuel (is the son of Zadator).

Peace (becomes Samuel's wife but is his girlfriend first. She is also a prehistoric woman, programmed).

Obit (is a prehistoric man who becomes empowered through the mistake of a brain plug transfer).

Lore (is nicknamed Fly by Obit).

Older men in town (spread rumors around, smoked cigarettes and some chewed tobacco).

The Zorvirax people (seldom seen and only here in a multitude on Veltrax Eta).

Whittle Cove (is a small town where Sam, Jimmy and Danny are from in the south).

Jess (is Jimmy's daddy, his nickname is Mr. Jeff).

Rick (is an old High School mate of Sam known during the time of Sam's first head injury).

Sector 18 (is Ioliau entry into Zorvirax homeland).

Karole (pronounced Carol is the name of the ship and the ship's individual that comes alive and takes part in life. She likes the nickname Mo).

Julie (is the receptionist and secretary in Masujue's office).

Marcie Halund (is an old friend of Sam's from college).

Masujue (Sam's dream girl and what Zadator has said was his fate, also she is a psych owns and runs her own office).

Officer Wolf (an investigating officer on Sam's car break-in).

Tamajue (is the grandson of Masujue's brother and became an inductee into the programming).

Lalah (is the daughter of the chief of Obit's tribe).

Belshala (is the territory most of the people of Veltrax Eta Live and work).

Faith (is Masujue's mother).

Aukiauk Guard (they work and live on fueling station, and take care of security for entry into Veltrax Eta.

Don (is a musician with his own discipline and almost famous but a man of vision and clarity, he becomes one of the programmed).

Baxter (is the bar owner hitting on Don who is also the brother of the woman bartender. The brother is a well-known gay in his circle of friends. Don is unaware but not totally and has a hard time enduring the passes made by the man).

Tre'gic's (is the band Don has worked with for years. They are almost famous too).

Cocktail server (Baxter's sister).

Cat (woman police officer in the cocktail lounge on the call Don made for the possible dead man).

Jack (is the male police officer on the scene of the shooting in the men's room with Don and the police officers partner Cat).

Monday (was the shooter in the men's room at the lounge where he shot Don and the two police officers as they entered. Don was not in as much danger as the officers).

Men with hats and trench coats (are the council from Veltrax Eta; considered the antagonist).

Cabbie (hired to find Jack and Cat felt a connection with his character of the big city).

Daddy (is Don's dad).

Elaine (is Don's mom).

The red barn at Elaine's house (is the vehicle's hovering spot, it later becomes a historic place where aliens were reported to have been seen, hence the famous picture in the paper).

Jeux (is Don's daughter).

Law (is Don's son).

Mack (is a police officer that works with Don's wife, and thinks he knows Don well).

Ra el (is the mad gunman that attempted the Presidential assassination stopped by Don).

Huang He (is the river in China Zadator and the crew went to explore and work on to save millions of lives).

Yevbalcavna (is a planet named by a Russian astronaut because of a signal he kept getting from the pod. He did not really know how he was getting the signal but claimed it was the advanced Russian technology).

Faiocak (is the father of Peace, wife to Samuel son of Zadator).

Khrami River Valley (is located in central Georgia near Russia).

Dunk (is the FBI agent that worked with Don, he did not like Don).

Cheyenne (was the reason for Dunk's name, septic tank dunk, nasty mess, get the picture).

Lance (is Don's boss while at the FBI).

Artifice (is Don's own ship created by Don's mind witnessed by Ra el).

Zorvirax (they are the people of Veltrax Eta).

Anna (Lore's mother; died in childbirth).

Virgil (Lore's father swore a curse on the baby boy).

Minnie (is the midwife that brought Lore into the world and raised him as her own).

Keeper (is from the future and programmed with the power, has fallen in love with Lore, Fly).

Sue Lee (is Keeper's mother and she was born in China, she became a traveler with a crew on a spacecraft but does not have programming or the power).

New York sky city (is the floating city on the outskirts of New York City; Keeper's home now).

Leonardo Pelter (developed New York sky city).

Emily (is Don's Spacecraft's name. She has her own personality).

The Church of the Holy Sepulcher, Bethany, Golgotha, and all of Jerusalem are some of the places Keeper wants to see while she is there.

Nado (is the young boy rescued by Obit in the village).

Definitions

1."the Dor'enavant a un autrui et arri' ere" meaning, transformation of the Universe.

2. Tetibreaicula- is formulated elevation of the heart rate and creation of a chemical that accelerates the healing process. This process stays thousands of times faster than normal also unknown to the human race except for those beings programmed with the power.

3. Brain plug removal- is the removing and transferring of one-person's brain plug to another person's whereby secrets are stolen from one person to another or so it is told. This is what was done to Samuel son of Zadator and Obit son of a higher tribesman.

4. Yat gooed- is a good day greeting usually used in the morning but can be used in passing as a greeting of the day. Yat gooed, nahae is usually the reply given to show the

speaker brotherhood. Some used it as kindness back to the greeter for him speaking in the first place.

5. Ba-gee-bers- anything that has the potency of something scary that makes stuff come out of you, be careful.

6. Kawhocumdia- spirits from the sky that fly or God like.

Dedication

This book hereby dedicated to the V shaped lights that led me home that night in August; will forever stand, remain and exist, be it present meet future or otherwise. They are what brought this book about. The whole night of terror, and each stop that I made, made a difference in my life. The failures that I went through after that night, the un-relentless-pursuit they gave me out in front of me, to show me they knew what they were doing, and I didn't. Then even more so, leading me every inch of the way, and luring me out into open waters where the sharks live, metaphorically speaking of course. Knowing there was no other way except for me to face my fear, and grow. The many-many nights I waited for them to come and take me away in my sleep. The knowing it would only be just one more night and they would come; only driven as if possessed they permitted me to ponder my thoughts, and their deeds.

They took me down that highway just as if they were driving my car. They knew they did that. We both left at a snail's crawl. The crafts were easing off just as I was easing off in my car. They just would not leave me alone. I know they knew me somehow but they sensed I did not want to know them. Therefore, they did it from afar.

At another time-period, they were watching and waiting to see where I would go. Taking control of my car lights, flashing them off, then on again, then off again, repeatedly, maybe to see if it would drive me crazy. However, it did not. I made it through. Somehow, I made it through. In addition, this was another time after my first encounter.

This time I was sure of being harassed. It was our first encounter. Mile after mile I played along. What do you want from me, I would ask them? Of course, there was no comment, moreover any response at all. I still waited for them to reply. They never did in words. However, it was the test; the test that I put them through that settled it for me. It was I they were after trying to have some effect on at least, something they could witness. I would stop even though it was late at night, and I was alone on the deserted highway. They would stop and wait for me to start back again. I even go out and relieve myself in front of them. I was trying to show them what a barbarian I was, and for them to come on if they wanted a piece of me. How stupid I was. They knew what they were doing. I moved on, and they moved on in front of me. I would say to myself, "I'll lose you on my turn up ahead, I know I will." They made the turn ahead of me, and it made me stop to get myself together again, because I lost it.

After three or four times of letting the breath out of my mouth in the most unusual way that I had ever done in my life. I moved on slowly. I feel the fear coming back right now, as I write this. Just as if it was that night, I must do, as it is this night, and move on. I must always move on. That may be the lesson here. Never give up. Never be defeated, move on, no matter what it is up ahead on the road in front of you.

I do not think about that night anymore, much but I remember the whole way, there were seven lights in a V formation. There was one point, and three lights each side just behind the front light. I would imagine they were about a half mile ahead of me. This was simply because of the distance away it seemed. This was at the point they were when they stopped at the turn to my mother's house. It just so happened that I was staying there for a short while or so I thought. There was a streetlight at the crossroads. It was just a caution light, yellow from the direction I was traveling, and the other way it was a red stop light. The V formation of lights, or crafts, or ships, whatever, now headed east when I got close enough to see them clearly. I was a block away from them looking up at the unbelievable sight, when they moved with such speed toward the east, the ocean; they literally disappeared into thin air. This is the truth the whole truth and nothing but the truth so help me God.

Foreword

Dear Mother,

I arrived in New York yesterday and it is more than I imagined. When I got out of the taxi from the airport, the warm breeze was hitting my face; the commixture was perceivable even to Buddy. He barked so loud it was as if he were saying, we are here we are here.

I cannot tell you how the title of the book came to me; it just came unexpectedly. It was as if the prehistoric tribesmen that captured Samuel were looking over my shoulders as I wrote. They were saying the word almost at the exact same time each time I would write Samuel's name, or even when I would think it. Finally, when I focused on his character and what he must have looked like to these prehistoric tribesmen, the word they were saying in unison was Kawhocumdia, Kawhocumdia; meaning God like or spirit from the sky.

O.K. mother, I have to go, someone's at the door, give Dad my love.

Your son,

To

Jean

"Chapter One: KAWHOCUMDIA"

HOW DO YOU STOP DEGENERATION OF THE HUMAN CELL? IT IS NOT SIMPLY BUT BY CREATING A PERFECT SYSTEM OF REJUVENATION, AND REGENERATION; *OR BY RECEIVING THE PROGRAMMING.*

SAM WASN'T SURE OF THE PROGRAMMING and what it all meant. He wasn't-sure about much of anything except the facts that lay before him. He knew strange men or creatures of some type had kidnapped him. He knew he had taken a shot in the back of the neck, and then was hustled off to some unknown location. In addition, they put him in a vehicle; his eyes were covered and then he was dragged

24

out of the vehicle and pulled along the ground like a sack of potatoes. Now, he knew he was getting far away from his home. In the norm, this would have been a monster's deed, vile in every sense. The things that were going on in his mind were convincing him this was a good thing coming from something bad. It was really an amazing thing, this power and all that it entailed. He did not know he was in for a long haul. For him to receive all of the programming he needed, it would take at least five or six days. He knew time was running out. There was something or someone telling him, there was not enough time. It whispered to him like a cold chill in the night, something unwanted. In Sam's case, it was something he knew he should pay attention. His sense of fear, coupled with his urgent need to escape, came back again, and again. He knew his escape, when he was ready, would be imminent.

THAT VOICE, WHO DID THAT VOICE BE-LONG TO, AND WHY WAS IT SO COMPELLING? The voice was telling him the same thing.

"When you are ready, you must escape, and I will help you. Do not worry; I am on your side. It will work out O.K."

While the voice was-speaking to Sam there was a sense of security surrounding him, his worries would go away for a short time but then return, and the fear was there, undeniable fear.

The power was the knowledge. The knowledge of the formulas that had advanced a small part of a civilization that was far beyond just super beings. It was a powerhouse, truly a powerhouse.

Sam was telling himself over, and over.

"It must be real, it's happening to me. It must be re-al."

Then, the humor kicked in,

"I'm beginning to understand math better than ever before."

Sam could only laugh slightly because of the drugs that kept him partially unaware, and unconscious.

Alien beings with super powers, and human beings through programming could have super powers. It came to him, the unbelievable things they could achieve. Sam was in a state of shock, he could not believe the programming, but it was true. They could do anything you could imagine. Now, they were programming Sam. He knew this was a gift greater than anything in his world was and, greater than anything or anyone in the human race had ever seen. There was also another world, still unknown.

Torn between what he knew was in the good old U.S., and what this alien intelligence was showing him, Sam had but one choice. He tried to hold on to what he had learned in college but the power was too great. It was a gift. The farther they took him, the further he wanted to go. His degree in computer science was nothing compared to the degree his knowledge was increasing and soaring past anything he could have ever dreamed or imagined.

Sam had always been a hard worker. He simply let it go when he would overhear some of the young boys saying things about being spoiled, and from a rich family of lawyers. The older men in town would sometimes look at him, and gesture with a lit cigarette in their hands, as if to point and say,

"there he goes again. That's the rich lawyer's son; he's just plain lazy, I guess he'll just become a lawyer too, someday."

Sometimes he would fire off a shot at them about their smoking.

"You boys are going to kill yourselves smoking those things."

The usual response was for them to spit on the ground in Sam's direction. He did not care; but he cared if they hated him, and they really were punks. He still felt sorry for them because of their ignorance and lack of education.

He just smiled, raised the first two fingers on his right hand, like a cub scout, and gave them a polite wave and went on his way. Even though his parents wanted him to become a lawyer, he had his mind set on computers, and going into business for himself. The newest thing in business was the computer. He already knew his music was just a part-time thing. Maybe someday he might think about a group again.

He had a sense of pride about himself-and-where-he-was-from. Now he was getting a sense about his-captors-and what they were-about. The information came to him in the middle of his thoughts. The thoughts came without warning. It is what is actually possible with the right information. He had no idea where things were coming from, it was starting to come as a system of filing, organized as if it were easy accessing. His visuals started at first, and led him to, wanting to experiment. It did frighten him where his mind was going. Not all of the conventional wisdom he had-been-taught about but some were underlined as overrides or deletes. New information to contradict the old is careful with debate. "Debate is a good thing but-don't-forget the proven facts. Everything being-given to you now will be backed up in your experience in life. You have many things to your advantage now. This will be a new way of life. Take your time with this even though it is moving fast into you. Learning is a process, and this process is like none other."

Sam heard it but still wondered where was it coming from, and how he could retain this new knowledge. No sooner than he had the thought, a visual came to him from a place not yet understood by Sam. Bits and particles only with shapes in the forms of letters, and numbers, and symbols were spewing at a high rate of speed. Only by Sam forcing himself to try to recognize the particles for what they were, was he able to tell. He then realized he was looking into his own brain. The falling pieces of data were falling in a tube shape as if they were flowing down in a pipe. When they reached the bottom of whatever, it seemed to loop back up toward his vision close to his eyes again. Then without warning, the loop disappeared and the flow was as in the beginning. Each time it would loop again, and repeat itself once again, the loop would disappear again. When he agnized all that was happening, the storage of information was in a flow to-be-filed, he snapped back into his normal vision. This was a time of relief, the good feeling that he had control of the stopping the unusual event that was taking place in his mind. A stream of air came from inside his chest, leaking out of his lips where it made a slight blowing sound. He sensed the release of pressure from his being, and it was good. Then another release of air spewed from his mouth, which came just as reassurance that it would be O.K...

Sam thought to himself, human beings would never evolve this far in intellectual advancement. Not in billions of years would human beings reach his intelligence at that very moment. How could this be? He was alone in his thoughts, thinking of his family, friends at home; wondering what was going to happen to them. A peace came to him at that moment that made his life worthwhile. He realized he had already had the peace of believing in the Creator, no matter what.

Sam wasn't-sure if this was in the beginning of his programming or if it came later, just before he-was-released outside the door of the hanger. Then it-happened… For a second or two, he had a vision of himself and the woman of his dreams. They were talking in a parking lot somewhere near his home. He knew he was in love. When the vision went away, a voice came to him and assured him he would see her again. Remember the voice said; it would be the first time that they had met. This was only a vision of the future.

Zadator planned for Sam to escape. All of the details are still a bit sketchy, and now we may never get it all from Sam. He is still the old-fashioned-guy that believes in a little privacy. Of course, there is still the mind reading thing. I can hear Sam's voice echoing in my ear.

"That-can't-be-done, you know the formula, and it can't be beat. No one can enter without permission or without legal reasoning."

I said, "I know, I know." There was more echoing of Sam's voice.

"You know you're the best lawyer I have."

"I know, say I adding, just kidding."

Sam said,

"No, you are the best."

Sam was feeling the depth of his perception of his mind and wandering into the walls of his confinement, and reaching the outside visually with only his mind. He quickly reeled back into the confinement. He was able to send a message to his brain to take-a-look. He thought to himself, how unusual this was. A small puff of air that was a release of pressure came from his mouth again and he shook his head slightly. Conclusion, thinking he might be going mad. Sam then returned to reality. It was true he could really do that.

He wondered how thick the wall would have to be before he-would-be-stopped from getting through visually. He did not pursue any information beyond this quick visual that sent his mind reeling but blocked out the outside world so he could gather his thoughts. As before, he went out of consciousness again.

When he awoke, he reached further into what he already knew. Finding answers to questions that had been unanswered to the human race for thousands of years. His crying out, "oh my God," was only internal, like some nightmarish dream where screams are never heard, and you are trying to wake up but you cannot.

Not one peep came from Sam's tries. He realized the only thing for him to do, was to wait. He had to try to get all of the information he could yet not cause any trouble. Not hard, since they had him drugged. Revealed to Sam later was all of the information he would ever need, including updates on the new, evolution of it.

The keys to the Universe are the formulas, and it-is-written, that in the beginning, God created the heaven, and the earth. This world was-created so far away in the heavens its creation took place billions of years ahead of earths; The-formulas that were created in this world; were-created-before-earth was flung-into-a-little-ball. This planet was so far away that it would take earth's human beings traveling at the speed of light three hundred and sixty nine billion years to reach its soil. Throw out the calculations that are-derived from the formulas for time travel because they did not work, and could only work with the beginning of the programming. This leads back to the time travel formulas that were-used to reach earth. Time travel formulas are the most complex. The amount of measured space that can-be-reached with time travel is much faster because of the advances in the future. These advances have been learned and taken back to the present. Mind or ship can move to a space in time travel, in-stantly-be-updated on information in that time, move again in space, and still be-filled-in again on newer information. Movement in space or any open area where their space ships travel speeds in enormous proportions are-reached. Once you reached a new dimension a co-ordinance can-be-changed to set a new location with the relevancy of the formulas provided. When the creation of the time travel formula was first used everything changed. This shocking revelation of this new unimaginable information was more than Sam's mind could comprehend. With the programming, it was starting to make sense, except on a level he had never known before. You could not call this making sense in Sam's world. Human beings would have a zero rate comprehending the smallest amount of what Sam was going through. Now Sam was starting to understand more about himself.

My experience with Sam was much later in his life where I spent enough time with him to learn first-hand of his transformation. He was the first to make it possible for all that followed. Now, he was receiving more than programming. He was getting a message that came to him on a screen inside his mind's eye. He knew it was possible he could be hallucinating but even his common sense told-him-different. Sam had always had a good mind.

To explain the facts of what just happened to him, would be to say, that it was as if a computer screen suspended in front of his face, with only a slight green haze or whatever color you wanted to set it for background coloring. It could be with words or pictures, or movies, or mathematical equations on it, and other images brought to forefront by super vision; the movement of the head left or right would bring on a two-second delay in its moving to catch up. Then, it would be set in its proper position again, which would be in front of the face, it read, time travel will be a must if you are to get back to your planet, and your people. Sam thought about what the message meant. He knew he needed more information of what was to come, he would think about it again later, and worry about it later. What he needed was more time. His eyes closed, and he was out again.

Before I explain about Sam, you must first know at least a slight sum about the planet from whence these powers come. There are many unbelievable things with the right information happen and Sam was getting just that.

A magical civilization that was on the other-side of our solar system, and beyond several, maybe many solar systems was far from the reach of the people on earth. This place with the species of Zorvirax beings, could read minds, see into the future, and fly with the greatest of ease, these three were among many other super-feats. It was only with their thoughts that this-magic-was-performed. Their looks were that of human beings but that was one of the few similarities. Time travel and space travel without a- space-craft. Things we would actually see if they were of a mind to let us and still us as human beings could not or would not believe it was happening. Our minds under normal circumstances cannot even handle the reality of what they are capable of doing, thus we see but do not believe. Our acceptance of them would have been impossible but the Zorvirax knew this. They kept themselves hidden, even with their own people. This was- done by cloaking. The power to become invisible is still part of the fable told about them in some parts of our world. It is-said that there are unexplained visitors in the night and sightings of human beings flying in the sky, as if they were angels watching over us.

Not all of the Zorvirax people were worthy of such power. Most of the population on the planet was just not qualified mentally, their capacity to understand would not have been possible, and not to say they were not intelligent. They were much more so than the people of earth were.

Some of the human beings on earth had something different going for them that was better than the others that they tried to program. There were special chemicals that they found in their bodies. This made it better for the recipient of the power. It was an enhancement for receiving the pro-

gramming. This led to better results, which far exceeded everybody's expectations. The results were so much better, even
more so than on the Zorvirax.

The Zorvirax also could pass their knowledge onto
other minds by touch. This was through secret formulas that
only a few knew. It was their opening of a door to the Universe, and the power of learning, as well as, progressing to a
super being with this wonderful, highly developed intellect.
They were learning a way to live together in peace, much
more so than earth beings, and the other species of the Universe.

Still, not everyone will want peace. Not knowing
what programming could do for the world of human beings
is the biggest undiscovered find of all. The Zorvirax people
were programming, and re-programming to advance in powers. They created super powers beyond the human imagination long before earth's creation. One of their secrets was the
development of a formula to reverse the aging process. How

they stopped the degeneration of tissue, and old beings became young. They had developed a procedure that would enable them to memorize, and never forget. They found undiscovered resources in the brain following these formulas, and the power that they had developed. Once it started, things just began to evolve in all areas of the mind. The mental research started to grow, and developed with overwhelming progress, and success. They were mystifying themselves in research. Many of the Zorvirax gaining these super powers started coming together for the common good of all. The most advanced would share knowledge. Each individual had his or her own talents so after they-got-programmed they could create their own particular formulas for even more advancements.

"Chapter Two: KAWHOCUMDIA"

Sam was a very handsome, strong young man. Small schools did not accept other students if they were different and Sam was a leader and the prize of the bunch for being different. All of the girls liked him and were always putting him on the spot with invitations to all sorts of social functions. There were plenty of invites to some private affairs too. He was always the-man in every aspect of the term. The men and boys of the small town were always catching the corrections he would give them and as nicely as he could, yet the poor results were not from Sam's nice way of doing things. He worked for his parents around home on the weekends and after school. It was his way of showing Harlan and

Maggie how he appreciated the support they gave him in every way. It was the cutting the firewood they really could not stand. It was Sam's responsibility to keep the firewood cut and gathered from the woods and that kept him in good shape physically. The men were the worse. Most were just plain jealous of his abilities at most things. It was his character that the good people of Whittle Cove worthy of respect themselves, admired. He was actually the hero of the town in some areas. He often spoke of Christ in crowds and gatherings in town or in church. It would be his opinion that most of the people lack constructive things to do, so they were always trying to oppress anyone with excellence. Hence, mediocrity always criticizes excellence. Even before in my mind Sam was destined to be a great man. He tried with great effort to keep his powers a secret. To stay in business with the computers was his dream before, now he knew he assumed these powers to help the world to become a better place. He will always be my friend, and I will cherish the time that we have had together. I only hope he remembers me with a fraction of as much honor and respect as I have for him. He truly is deserving of all the blessings he gets. Sam was different very different and Sam's town was on the Zorvirax's to do list. It was in Sam's town, they thought that whatever was in the water affected the mental makeup of all of the people. This ingredient made Sam's chemical make up in his body a better choice for programming. The smell of the water was very bad. The sulfur in the water made the smell. For a long time the Zorvirax people wondered why anyone would live near such bad smelling water. It took them many generations to learn that it was not a bad smell after the local people got used to it.

Not just the water in Sam's world that was interesting to the Zorvirax but actually the location of an expedition. The son of the great Zadator was lost on that expedition. Left on earth as a child, he was to bear the burden alone. Zadator was a new leader in the programming of Zorvirax beings.

What was in Sam's world was the end of life in the future. Without the help of the Zorvirax the planet, earth was surely doomed.

The laws of their planet, Velterx Eta, were changed, and there could be no more experimenting with human beings. This law was put into effect and the capturing, and taking of human beings ended. There was one exception to the law. If they could find someone to volunteer, then after they were tested the programming could begin.

Sam knew about their spying, their mind reading, and that they thought they had a perfect human specimen. The Zorvirax people were right. He was a perfect specimen but not for capturing. Sam was a free spirit as a small child. He had no idea of the power of the Zorvirax. He had no idea that day when he-was-taken-by-them what was to come. His parents had taught him to pay attention to his instincts. There were many things the child of parents that were well to do could learn, when taught with the highest ethics, and of course skill. He feared very few things, and could sense danger in an instant. Sam's past few days had revealed some of the things that the Zorvirax had done, and he would have to keep the knowledge of this to himself. The powers were right out of a superman comic book, and even more than that. He knew it was true but at the same time could not believe it. Sam knew this secret would not be easy to keep. He had always been honest to everyone he had ever met or known. Now, Sam thinking of having to lie would be almost too hard to accept; Things were different under these circumstances. His powers would put him in danger 24\7. How would he ever sleep?

Sam was still in the first stages of his transition, he trembled with a cold chill. He had to get it out of his mind. He shook his head trying to shake it out. Sam again thought could this really be happening.

These things, to Sam, seemed to be playing again, and again, over, and over in his mind. He was remembering being here at this same point in time, and thinking the same thing.

The change that he had already gone through was hard and there was no one to explain the entirety of this to Sam; it was just the way of the programming. Even though it was almost impossible for a human to grasp these concepts for the development of the mind, his human side was still clinging to sanity. While the programming was taking him further and further away from being a normal human being, Sam realized what a gift this was. It was the greatest gift ever given to man, scientifically.

He stopped and thought to himself for a few seconds, there was a pause in his movements. The momentary silence was an overwhelming space in time. He thought that this was not about him, at least not all of this, but then again, he was what it was about to him. He was not a pauper or the aristocracies who seem to be-chosen for obvious reasons in things like this. This was about a power unknown to man, or at least to Sam, that is what his thoughts were. He was very confused but knew God was in control. God was for, and of everything good. This set Sam's mind at peace for a moment.

Sam knew he had to write down his thoughts. This needed articulation before it was too late. He wrote on a small scratch pad that he took from inside his wallet. It read,

Jesus Christ is my Lord and Savior through the Grace of God. I believe in Him for all things that are-given to us with grace. It is with His love and kindness we learn His saving grace for the good of all-mankind. His love is forever and is everlasting through all time, with His promise of our place in heaven with Him, and, our everlasting life with Him. In the name of the Father, the Son, and the Holy Spirit, I write this for my Love for Him and the things that He has done for me, and for the things, He has in store for me. Each day from now, and here to come, He will be my guide, my teacher, my friend, and the pen will never leave my hand. I am His servant, and He is my Master. This humble path and these few but simple words are the things that must-be-said:

before it is too late. I praise His name, and give Him the

praise, and credit for all things, in Jesus Christ's name I pray,

Amen.

He put his pen back, folded the paper, and put it in

his wallet.

"Chapter Three: KAWHOCUMDIA"

Harlan, Maggie, and Sam were three loves in my life that will always transcend the words of love I express. Harlan loves Maggie as much as he loves life itself, but he is still the kid in the house. Sam is such a wonderful son, and has a forgiving heart of the saints. Maggie loves Harlan dearly but she holds on to the hope, and faith, that God will someday turn him around. It is through the visions of faith many things have been settled. They were married when Maggie was almost twenty-one. It was the promise of the good life, two story houses, double-car-garage, and the sweet sounds of pitter-patter of little feet running through the house. Their tries would leave them silent for a day or two, then each saying, "let's try again." Maggie would say, "Sure, we'll just have to try again later," adding, "Sweet darling Harlan." It brought Harlan closer to Maggie. He became an even sweeter, sweet heart. He lavished her with affection, and love. He would bring her bouquets of flowers in the middle of the day. His considerations for her were unbelievable to their friends, and family. They just seemed to make everyone around them even happier. Harlan was always her hero on any given day or night.

It was a surprise, and a shock, when they got pregnant. Maggie had always wanted a boy first. Sam was their dream-come-true. Harlan thought he was the best thing that had ever happened to him, except meeting Maggie. Harlan had gotten her to do a little lighter work out, and jogging routine during her pregnancy. She was so thrilled with Harlan. She said she loved him even more than she thought possible. He smiled, and said,

"I love you even more Darling."

Sam had gotten the best of both worlds, having two

lawyers as parents. As a kid, he did not always think so but now that he was an adult, it was great. It was even super. Sam's strong features and handsome looks got him into a lot of challenging situations. He always used his head, and came out all right. There was only one thing that gave him any problem, and that was his memory. He handled it by training himself. His singing and playing guitar helped. His long walks and running daily kept him going during the week. Sam thought the jogging was necessary. Bringing in the wood for their fireplace was excellent exercise. His bad memory came from a bump on the back of the head during a wrestling match. It was Sam's opponent he was worried about, that was a mistake. They later teased him about it calling him "Sam the Slam." It did not last long. They stopped as it became apparent he was growing in size. He was also gaining respect as the battles he won mounted in number. Sam was much, much more than any of his classmates. He realized that at an early age he would be the caretaker with his friends, if he ever had them. In his heart, he cared for everyone.

Sam's nightmare first started on a long walk through the woods. As he had done many times before, he walked the hills, and many trails. This made his walk a great workout. As he turned where the trail made a bend, the group of men came from out of the bushes. They had been hiding, waiting for Sam to come along. He saw them as they came out of their blind too soon. It gave away their position. He turned to run when his instincts took over. Their suspicious nature forced Sam to make his move. He only got a few steps when the shot hit the back of his neck. Sam heard the shot that sounded like a muffled gun. His first thought was they missed. Seconds later, he was on the ground going into unconsciousness. Before going out he heard the men talking in a strange language. Even stranger were the trailing sounds at the end of their words. Sam decided later that it sounded much like the sound effects machine he had bought. He also found out later these men had many tricks up their sleeves, and they used them on Sam. The shot in the neck rendered him unconscious. This was where Sam's memory test started. He started to make mental notes of everything. His semi-consciousness, and in and out of awareness was to be the way he stayed for the next few days. He felt their presence during the time he was captive.

There was a slight chill at times. It was almost perfect weather. The beings around him were in, and out always rushing. However, the fuzziness made it impossible to know what was going on at first. He remembered the voice that said he was there to help him.

Sam had escaped, after coming to, and finding himself in front of this large door. He feared for his life and fled. He did not understand his memories at all at this time. Sam's capture made him very unhappy. He felt a huge disappointment.

When he got to the chain link fence that surrounded

the compound, in seconds, he was over it. He slipped past the security system using his new unbelievable gift, hoping he was not going to lose his life. He knew he was going back, and nothing could stop him.

It was like magic, he disarmed the sensors with just a thought. He went through one section to the next. He was safe, and he knew it. Even though Sam was new to this kind of power, he was going to have to face it; it was time to get on with what he had to do. Each step he took was getting him closer to his objective. Getting back to the place, he had escaped from a few days before. It would get him the answers he needed to complete his mission. Alternatively, so he thought. Sam did not realize he was not through with his programming. The final segment would reveal something so magnificent; it would make the rest of his days, exciting, and unbelievable.

He was sure when he reached his destination, he was about to embark on a journey of huge proportion. He believed it would take him to where this began. Sam knew he had to find a way out of the mess. As more and more of the information entered his brain, Sam began to put it all together. He became deliriously happy. He began to chuckle, he started to laugh. He became so filled with joy the only way for him to control himself was to let loose with laughter. Once he realized how loud he became, he started to scan the area for life. This made him grasp his situation again, and it brought him back to reality.

He was now by himself in the dark, as he had been before, only this time he had a power that none of the old neighborhood would ever believe. The power he himself had not recognized or used yet was flight. This thought troubled him. He did not want to attempt what he was feeling. He sensed the danger in being in midair without something to catch him, if he fell. Then, it all seemed so easy; he wanted to try it with all the forces of nature against him.

He first focused as hard as he could to make sure he

wasn't stepping into a sensor, and then out of the shadows, and as quickly as he stepped, and thought, he felt his heart pulsing. Then the doorway in sight, the place he fled from, and up and flight accomplished. The doorway, seventy-five, maybe eighty yards away, built inside of the mountain was right in front of him. It had only taken Sam a few seconds, and he dropped to his feet just as if what he had seen Superman do in the movies. This was terrific. Now he could repeat himself this way every time. There was enough light to see clearly. The whole area glowed brightly with light. There was no moon in sight so it must have been artificial. Now, he was done. He was there at the place to enter the door. He saw himself automatically cloaked when he left in flight. He answered his own question,

"Automatically done for you sir, standard flight procedures".

"Nice," Sam said to himself.

Realizations started popping into his head one right

after another. Sam began a chorus of OH's like nothing you ever heard. Then it was back to business. He looked at the massive door with no visible way to open it. He saw a hand print on the rock wall beside the door. Sam put his hand up to fit into the imprint. Magic, it opened easily. As the massive door started to rise, Sam noticed something he had never seen before. His arm's bicep was larger than before. Both of them now were bulging out as if he were an athlete. Not just in shape but in dynamic shape.

Inside the huge confine, the surprise of his life awaited him, a space ship a futuristic flying machine. Sam composed himself. He said softly,

"Like something right out of a science fiction novel."

"Chapter Four: KAWHOCUMDIA"

There it was the unbelievable, right in front of his eyes, a space ship or spacecraft, whatever. The size of it nearly scared Sam out of his wits. There was a lot of room. Its lines were the smoothest of any plane or craft he had ever seen in books, movies, anywhere. He still goes on about the looks of his machine. It also had the wings of a sparrow that were very small compared to the size of the craft. Lights ran the distance of the wings, and across the center of the ship. It would have made a half moon. He ran forward toward the ship. There was no one around.

Sam reached the craft, and stepped up to the ladder on the underside of the ship. The ladder could have been thirty feet to the craft's entrance. Sam made it up the ladder, and through the entrance door. To his right was a closet filled with uniforms. The door was standing open so that anyone entering could easily see inside. The uniforms were not all his size but he did not stop to count them. Something told him to put the uniform on that best fit. He did it very quickly. It fit perfectly.

He moved to the pilot's seat. Sam found the release lever for the craft's ladder he flipped it. The door closed right behind the ladder. He took his seat, the expression on his face was a settling calm, and he is in. There was no one to witness this but Sam felt it all over his face, his body language was cool, he was in control.

The inside was so quiet and not to mention the design. It was a beauty. The room behind him was the body of the craft. To Sam it was so spaciously neat, and cozy. It fit him. He looked over the controls and realized he knew how to fly the craft. He had been in this one or one like it before. It must have been when he went through programming during his half-conscious state. He knew then, that must have been when he learned how to fly. No doubt about it, he could fly his ship with no problem.

Sam still feeling confused about the why and bewildered said to himself,

"I've got to get back. I am only getting part of what has happened, and is happening to me. It reminds me of the day when Tommy Underwear, yep, that is what the kids called him. He forgot he was just in his underwear. Nice person, I just felt sorry for him. All of the kids laughed at him."

The memories and missing pieces not filled in yet were confusing. He dropped his thought, and said to himself again,

"I've got to move on and get-out-of-here."

At the most, it would take Sam five days before he would reach earth. He plotted the course and checked the fuel. It is time. He looked at his watch. It was late but Sam kept his confidence up, and said,

"I hope my watch is right. What would everybody say? What would they think?"

Sam hit the button. Now he had fifteen seconds to strap himself in. He knew in a flash the giant door would close automatically behind the ship. In a few seconds Sam would be on his way home. He stated again to himself.

"What a nightmare. Will I make this trip?"

Sam tried to figure out what he would say. He would explain, and it would be O.K. The numbers started to roll out of Sam's mouth 10-9-8-7-.......2-1...

While Sam was in count down, he started to think about Whittle Cove and what was in the plan to be; it was not going to be easy. It would take magic, and more magic. Sam was up for it, he just knew he was. He had to be, Sam was going to be Super Man. Only time would tell what his fate would be. If Whittle Cove was-in trouble, Sam would have to help. He was still thinking about his super strengths, traveling from one time to another. To change people's lives, it would have to be-done with a lot of consideration.

Blast off.

Sam could see the things he was leaving behind, there was not much of a connection in reality but the ties would bind him forever. He only wanted to get out of there and get back home. Some place he knew as home. A place he could feel some since of safety.

"Security, I don't know why we take advantage of it."

Sam spoke it out-loud, but no one was there to hear him. He was feeling his father's presence but Sam knew it was only a feeling. His eyes clouded up. Sam tried to get-control-of-him-self saying,

"I've got to stay in control,"

He clenched his teeth, his jaw flexed with tears running down his cheek. He grunted with only a slight noise in his throat. There is no one there. He felt the distance he was from home and the-loneliness-in-his-heart.

After fifteen seconds in darkness, he is on his way. Sam checked the speed of the Craft that was light-years-ahead of anything his world ever experienced. His instruments were all good. How the time travel worked was still unexplained to Sam but he knew it did. It was in the sense of knowing that the formulas worked that gave him the peace of mind that he needed, time would reveal all that he needed to know.

His body settled back into his seat. His hunger and light-headedness were still there. He had started thinking about it earlier but felt nothing. For days, he had not stopped but to barely think about food. They must have given him something to sustain him through his I.V. tube. Sam pulled on his sleeve to look for a needle stick but found nothing.

"Maybe it was put in somewhere else,"

Sam wanted to say it out-loud but kept his mouth shut this time. He was sure now that he had flown his craft before in some kind of training. His senses were picking up the smells in the cockpit. He noticed the scratches from when he was there before. He simply could not put it all together. He was sure he would in time. The guide who had talked to him promised, and that was good enough for Sam.

There is very little light in space, so the view was of the stars, like a canopy pulled overhead for his entertainment but real, and now alone he saw the beauty. It was in this moment, he wished for another person to be there now but alone he experienced this star-packed-beautifully-placed-surreal-scene. He was experiencing the amazement of it all. He kept trying to hang on to every moment. Thinking now that he might find someone someday, wondering about the vision he had during the first part of his programming and to feel-every-feeling with the girl in the parking lot. How could he tell her about it?

Sam's whole life had been about communication, and memory. Now the insecurity seemed to disappear as he flew across space. Time was now a bigger problem with time travel capability hanging around his brain mixing in his thoughts. He wondered how many people would give it all up to be doing what he was doing right now. He thought,

"God only knows."

He was thinking about the space program on earth. How far behind from this new-found-world-were-they and how slow will earth go on the development of the program? They had only started two years earlier in '58. How long would it take to catch up?

Sam spoke it out-loud almost humorously,

"I don't want to even speculate how much time."

Sam's further thoughts on the subject came without sound, but weighted heavy in his heart.

"Chapter Five: KAWHOCUMDIA"

Lauws hav mercy chil, Manny said to Danny, "why do you's wants to go swim mins' in dat snakes filleds pond?"

The force of Manny's language runs deep in the south, only sometimes her dialect is barely understandable to the outsider. Anyone that knew her understood that she meant the Lord would have mercy. She said lauws for Lord, and chil, for child, which was her favorite to use when she was around children. Sometimes she would use the term chill'ens, meaning children. It just depended on how she felt. Manny did-not-misuse these words on purpose, or at least she did not some of the time. This was some of the funny parts about the south, sometimes put on, and sometimes not.

She did miss the education that she so desperately wanted Danny to have. She did not want him to learn the way she learned, the hard way.

Manny was Danny's grandmother but was-forced to raise Danny after his natural mother took off for parts un-known: His mom was-never-heard-from-again. Manny just figured Alicia was too young when Danny was born; and that she just was not ready to be tied-down to a child. She felt shame in that but Manny could not hold anything against her daughter. She remembered when she was younger her-self. It was the reason for her drinking whiskey, to bring back that wild feeling of her youth.

There were certain tempos, and rhythms to the way Manny spoke. It also had an up or down tone on each word, depending on where she placed it and that made the empha-sis on her words more dramatic. Manny was the perfect 'sto-ry-teller.' No matter how insignificant the story was to her young listeners, she made the lines full of drama, and held their attention with excitement galore.

She continued.

"It runs right to da swamps, and you knows what Miss Linda said, you knows, and what's happened to her. You knows."

Manny did not have just a southern drawl, but a mixture of slave talk from the old days, and a-snappiness-in-her-speech. It must have come from the years of her ironing clothes, and chewing gum telling her stories. The children would stop their playing, and listen sometimes for hours. In her stories, she would talk and pop her gum, talk and pop. It was her custom to make a bubble in the side of her mouth, and pop it with her teeth. The continuous popping of gum came from the way she would fold it, as she would chew. It would explode in between words, at her discretion. She did not chew gum when she drank moonshine whiskey.

Danny said,

"what mama, what happened?"

Manny continues with her story as she sipped out of the tall glass of moonshine she had filled earlier, clear-white-lightning, pronounced whyit-lite-nin.

"Well, Miss Linda,"

Manny said cautiously,

"done wents to da flowing well."

Manny hesitated, to draw out the drama in what she was telling.

"To to,"

she stuttered,

"gets a jug of wa-der, when da snake,"

she stopped, and hesitated a while.

Manny stuttered.

"It it it was…"

It was impossible to tell if she was faking the stutter or not, but it was good.

"And, ah wha-der-mocks-a-cun, it it it crawled,"

She stuttered again.

"it it it crawled outta da wha der, yeh sur."

She wanted to assure respect to the boy, who would be a man soon.

"I-believes it was a wha-der-mocks-a-cun, and-it-slips-under-her-foots-to gets-by.

What Manny lacked in education, she made up for in her ability to-dramatize-what-ever-she-was-telling. As long as she was not too looped before the story was finished.

"I don'ts know wheres dat snake was going, but he didn't pay much mind to Miss

Linda is screaming. She jumps thre____,"

she chuckled between words,

"__e," "feet."

Manny's laughter is getting more delightful in be-tween sips of her whiskey, she continues but with slight chuckles between some of her words.

"It just keeps right on going outta dat-wha-der and under her foots, and on outs to cross da hi-ways. I guess. Un huh."

Manny made it plain that she did not know where the snake was going, and did not care. She shrugged, shook her head furiously, and made faces, disapproving of the snake. This meant she made it clear she did not like snakes. Manny thought seriously about

the snake as she sipped on her whiskey.

She said to Danny,

"no sur, absolutely not."

Her English was improving inconsequentially, nevertheless improving for the

dramatization and emphasis, just to get her point across to Danny.

"You cannot go in dat snake filled wha-der-hole, period. And dats da enda it."

There was a pause as Danny held his head down looking at his feet.

"I don't wants to hear any mo abouts it."

Manny keeps talking as she continues to tell Danny the story, and starts fussing about his hair.

"Yo hair done got pickeyed up. You needs to fix dat mess."

Manny takes another sip, and continues,

"Miss Linda done yelled at her little boy Jimmy, and tells him to runs get the hoe.

Wells now, we alls know how fast little Jimmy was at running, he was in second place ats da grade schools track meets. And dems-boys-from-out-der-on-da-farms-was-fast, um huh, you know dats right."

She slightly sings it as she finishes her sentence.

"Well, Jim, dats whats I calls him now dat I nos better dan to calls him Jimmy. He don't like it much any mo since he turned sixteen."

Manny call out loudly to Danny,

"Lordy, would you please takes dat dog back outside, he's driving me crazy just sittin there staring at me, like he

wants somethin alls da time. Please Danny! Please do somethin wit dats dog."

Danny got up, and took Bo by the collar, and said,

"come on Bo."

Even though his name is Junior, Danny did not like
the name Junior, so he called him Bo. Bo had been Danny's
dog since he was born. His mama is the one that named him
Junior.

Danny got Bo to go outside through the back door.
He came back to his
chair he had taken from the kitchen, and sat back down. He
barely prepared himself
to listen to Manny's story but somewhat receptive.

She looks over at Danny to see if he is still listening,
and starts.

"Let's see now, where was I? Oh yea!"

She exclaimed with loud laughter coming from deep
down in the bottom of her midsection.

"He says Jimmy was a little boy's name, and he wasn't a little boy any mo, a specially since he was able to tote da gun, and goes squirrel huntin.' He says he's a pretty good shot too."

Manny laughed ridiculously. When she recovered from her laughing episode, she continued.

"He also said he would have to be more careful than usual, cause he done lost the safety on da 22 rifle but he wasn't going to tell his daddy. I show axed him why. He said, because his daddy would probably beat the crap right outa him. And we know dats right."

"Mr. Jeff is a mean somebody. We done heard he made the remarks that he would likes to kill somebody."

Manny knows that Jimmy's daddy is- really-named- Jess but everybody else calls him Mr. Jeff, so she does too. She finishes her comments.

"That'd be because of them snitches dat done went to the cout house." "Yea, and told the FBI about something.

Like somethin he ben doin wit moonshine whiskey."

"I done taste me some of dat."

She woo-hooed with a high-pitched screech, and laughs ridiculously again.

"They say, Miss Linda ain't afraid of him but you know dats not right. She's bound to be afraids, or somethin's done wrong wit her. Um huh. Bad wrong."

Manny could not talk anymore, the outbursts of laughter left her throat so dry she started to cough, and her voice was getting hoarse. She began to speak some of her words so low that they were almost inaudible.

She said to Danny,

"bring me dat jug-a-shine over here."

By this time, she had a vile sound to her words, and the smell of the moonshine filled the room. Danny had enough; he was starting to feel the embarrassment. If she had not gotten drunk, it would not have been so bad. However, she did. She forced herself to finish her statement to Danny, "dats it, dats it sitting on da floor over dare."

Danny looked at her, shook his head as if in a reply of no, not actually meaning to say no. He was just thinking of how pathetic she was when she was like this. She slapped him behind the back of his head. He was not being defiant but Manny was too drunk to know that. Danny quickly got up out of the hand-woven kitchen chair, and went to the jug he could clearly see from where they were sitting. When he picked up the jug, he said to Manny.

"Are you going to finish this story?"

It was with a look that he might have given her when he was eight or nine years

old. He knew back then he could have gotten away with it. Only if he was far enough away, she sometimes got too violent.

Manny replied,

"yes, now brings me dat whiskey or I'll knock you

cross dis house."

It was too late. Danny walked over, and handed Manny the jug. He said,

"I don't want to hear this stupid story anymore, anyway!"

Still he stepped far enough away that Manny could not hit him again.

"Those stupid white boys don't care anything about me, so why should I want to hear anything about them, anyway? He is just some stupid white boy! He's probably getting his butt whipped about something, right now."

Manny just said,

"huh."

It was a grunt. She shook her head wiping her face in dismay at what Danny had said. Danny took off out of the house through the back door. It slammed a little louder than usual but not loud enough for Manny to say anything, especially with the buzz she had going.

Manny's thoughts about Danny were as if he was her own son. She did have mixed feelings about raising him alone. This was something Manny thought about all of the time because she felt she was forced to do it. When her daughter left, she did not know what else to do. Her grandson would have been homeless, and he was her only grandchild. Manny **had** to take him after her daughter ran away to the city. She stopped to reflect on her life, maybe think about what she could have done differently, also, about where she had gone wrong in her own life.

Manny never knew where Alicia went. She heard from some of the folks that hung around the bus station, say, they saw her buy a ticket. In addition, she got on the bus.

It has been fourteen years now, and Manny has not gotten a letter or a phone call. Danny will be sixteen this Friday, October 24.

"That boy hasn't even seen his mama that he remembers,"

Manny said it aloud Even though she was trying to say it to herself she said it aloud. Now Danny had run away. Manny felt things it was a sign from God.

She said over, and over,

"Oh my God, what have I done, Oh my God what have I done? Oh my God, what have I done?"

"Chapter Six: KAWHOCUMDIA"

Danny had left Manny's for good, with just the shirt on his back. What he did not know was what was about to change his life forever. Now, Manny was alone. What she had said after Danny went out the back door was something she would never forget. The pity of it was there was no one there to hear. Tears rolled down her cheeks as she started to sob. Danny was far gone, and out of ear shot by now. Manny just had to let it out.

"Oh God," she cried, "What have I done?"

She could not have stopped the flood of tears if she had tried. The whiskey had only made things worse. She did not know what was to become of Danny, "he was a good boy."

As she said it aloud to herself, she added,

"but without a father and only a grandmother what chance does he have?"

Now, with her sobering thoughts she said to herself again,

"Oh Lord what have I done? Please dear Lord, help me, what have I done?"

Manny was very poor, and had little if any education. She was determined, that, was not going to happen to Danny, but what chance did he have? She was thinking solemnly. Manny knew she could not have helped him much. In some things, she might even harm him. This was something Manny hated to admit. She knew her drinking had gotten worse. She had only had an occasional drink before Alicia left home. Now, Manny blamed herself for Alicia leaving. Manny's only income was the ironing and what little housekeeping she could get. In addition, the word she hated to hear, *welfare* the small amount from the government.

Her friend down the street had an uncle that made the moonshine whiskey. He let Manny have it free. Free as long as she treated him right a few evenings along during the month. That was something they had to keep from his wife. Manny knew it was wrong but could not help herself. He helped her with a little bit of money when she asked for it. It was not much her pride, her pride she always had her pride. It got in the way too many times when they needed things, and she just could not ask. Manny really liked him; he was the best-looking man she had ever seen. He had muscles that made him look very interesting. Nobody cared if he was part white; he was still a black man.

Somehow, Manny stopped her sobbing, and put down the glass of whiskey. She knew she was wrong for slapping Danny. She stopped and prayed for forgiveness, this took a while. She made a vow to her God, and a promise to herself, she was going to tell Danny she was sorry. Manny wished he were there right now, she would tell him she loved him very much, and that she was sorry.

Manny spoke aloud talking to herself again,

"I hope he don't go to Sam's again. That boy, I hope he do not go back. I know they'll put him in jail for sure this time."

The trouble with Manny's promise was that it was never going to happen. Her chance with Danny was over, at least for many years to come.

Jimmy was the same age as Danny, and lived just a block down the street. They were never friends. Danny never thought white boys would like a black person, no-way, no-where. Danny just stayed away from white boy's period. There had been times when he saw Jimmy coming down the street but Danny just hid behind a tree. He watched him walk on pass. Jimmy never looked Danny's way, so he did not know why he hid. Danny's thoughts about himself were, I am just a kid, and kids do dumb things. Before today, Danny thought he might stand out in the open, and just watch him, as if he knew him. Maybe today Danny would wait for him to look, or speak.

Therefore, Danny was just standing there near the street, thinking about where he was running to, maybe Sam's, maybe Jimmy's this time. He was waiting in anticipation so he could speak if Jimmy came by and looked, or spoke. Then, in all the amazement Danny had ever had, Jimmy just appeared, and disappeared into thin air. Danny's mouth dropped, and it sucked the air right out of his lungs. He could not breathe. His eyes were about to pop out of his head. He stood there wondering while he tried to get his breath back. Had he lost his mind or was this some spiritual thing happening? Maybe he would be the next to go. Danny looked to the sky, and started to pray to God.

"Lord, if I got to go right now, take me take me I'm ready. It'll be alright Lord, just take me."

He knew he had just witnessed the impossible, but it

was true. He just witnessed a human being disappear. Danny was feeling something for the first time in his life. It was the feeling that something far greater than he or anyone else in his town knew. He felt now he was a part of it. Was it something from God or some evil trying to take him some place he did not want to go? Then Danny spoke it aloud, like a wave of electricity surging through his body, I am smart. I am not stupid; I am a thinking feeling human being.

Danny walked out into the street. He decided to jog down toward Sam's to see if anything else was going to happen. Consequently, Danny took off running in a trot. He headed the same way Jimmy went when he disappeared. Danny had been jogging for some time when he realized that he was at Sam's parents place. It was Sam's place of residence. Danny saw this sprawling homestead with beautiful shrubs, and lush flowers. The trees were huge, and they created this serene landscape. Danny's eyes always opened wide every time he saw this place. There was too much for him to take in. Each time it got him a little excited. There was no time for site seeing. If he tried to enter without permission, his situation may turn out to be trouble. He remembered the last time. Sam had saved him from being incarcerated. Danny stopped to think things over this time. When he found Sam, he would tell him about Jimmy. His disappearing act, would be detected if he continued to do that in front of people. If he were going to pull it off, he would need some help from other people.

"Like me and Sam."

Asking himself the question,

"how am I ever going to find him? He is never going to believe me anyway. Nobody's going to believe me."

Danny fixed his eyes on something high up in the trees near the back of the place. He could not really determine what he was seeing but it looked like a reflection of a mirror. He could not believe what he saw.

"It's an opening in the sky. There are steps; no it's a

ladder going up to the opening in the sky."

Danny was baffled. He knew he was going to get into trouble. Something was going to happen to him. Something bad was going to come of this for him seeing Jimmy turn into the invisible man. Then he remembered he could trust Sam. Danny was feeling the frustration not knowing where Sam was and now this strange event, or aberration.

Danny saw a trail that led to the back, and he started to run. It must have been one of Sam's jogging trails. It was perfect. It led back closer to the spot where Danny saw the alleged opening in the sky.

"Where are you Sam?"

Danny said it to himself.

"I sure need to speak with you."

Danny got back far enough he could see the top of the tree. There were no steps or lights, no mirror, nothing.

What is going on here?

Danny becomes even more frustrated. He did not see

anything leave the place, not a motion of anyone in sight. He stepped back behind a tree to get his thoughts together. He reached in his pocket to pull out a cigarette. As he was reaching for a lighter or a match, he finds that he has none.

"Now this is bad. This is bad."

Danny did not smoke cigarettes many times before, just times that were stressful and sometimes just for fun.

He observed that nothing seemed to be happening at the house. Danny spoke aloud to himself in a very low voice.

"I'll wait for Sam."

With his back up against the tree, he slides down, and his bottom touches the ground. The temperature was perfect. He felt himself getting sleepy and cannot help it he falls quickly asleep. A half hour passes.

Sam was gently shaking Danny's shoulder and saying wake up, Danny, wake up. He realized Danny was in a deep sleep and shook him harder, Danny wake up.

Suddenly Danny woke, jumped to his feet, and almost yells,

"Sam, where you been man, I've been looking all over for you?"

Sam interrupted Danny, and said,

"Danny listen, we don't have much time. You have to swear to me now that you will do whatever I say. It'll be just the three of us."

Danny said with hesitation in his voice,

"us, who is us?" Well, sure, whatever you say Sam, I'm in."

Sam said,

"Jimmy, Jimmy will be with us. I've got some fantastic new information you're going to love it."

Danny holds his tongue, and thought to himself,

"I'd better listen up and get myself together, and be prepared."

Sam says right back to him,

"That's a good idea, hold on to that thought; I'll explain when we get inside the ship."

Danny held his curiosity but is about to pop.

"Chapter Seven; KAWHOCUMDIA"

Sam saw the curiosity in Danny's mind as it turned with wonder and excitement. Sam reached for Danny's hand, and asked,

"are you ready?"

"Sure."

Of course, Danny could not have been ready for what happened next. Sam's hand touched Danny's as he tightened the grip on his hand. Within a second, they were inside the ship. Everything around Danny was whirling at the speed of light. In an instant, Sam stopped all of the action for Danny to catch up.

"How was that ride,"

Sam asked.

Danny's mouth was still partially open but said,

"good, that was O.K."

Sam saw the bewilderment on his face, he said to
Danny,

"good."

"Go over to the closet, pick out a uniform that fits
you, I'm sure your size is in there. We will start programming immediately. I will be talking to you with telepathy.
You'll understand, I promise."

Danny walked straight to the closet. He saw the uniform, and grabbed it. The changing room was across the
floor, he headed toward it. Sam called to Danny, and he
stopped, turned, and faced him.

"Danny, I want you to meet Jimmy, Jimmy Danny,
now that's taken care of, back to work."

Danny looked at Sam to ask the question, and suddenly Jimmy appeared, and Sam started to explain telepathi-

cally. When Sam finished, Danny turned back and went into the dressing room, and put on his uniform. Jimmy stayed visible, and returned to the helm. He carried on with checking the ship. Sam continued to fill Danny in on the details of what had happened to him. They discussed Jimmy, and his invisible incident out in the street in front of Danny's place.

Danny came out of the dressing room, and headed toward Jimmy. He had a slight smile on his face. He said to Jimmy,

"when I saw you disappear back there on the street in front of my grandmother's, I didn't know what to think."

"Yea, Sam and I thought you might be curious, and would come find us.

Danny responded as cool as he could,

"I was staying cool until I got what the word was."

They are all cutting in with chuckles, now. Danny looked over at Sam, and said,

"that's why I came looking for Sam."

Sam stopped his laughter, and began to tell his story in more detail about his abduction. He stopped for a second and told Jimmy,

"we are going to have a seat while I tell my story, prepare for takeoff."

Jimmy said,

"aye Captain,"

He spoke with a more mature voice than the voice for his age.

Sam seated Danny in the programming recliner, he is now continuing to explain programming, and finish telling his story.

Sam asked Danny again,

"are you in?"

Danny does not hesitate,

"aye Captain."

Sam gave Jimmy the command to start count down. Jimmy started by flipping the switch. Count down began.

Jimmy said in a whisper to Sam,

"countdown started."

Sam locked himself in; he showed Danny the button to press for his lock-in. As Danny felt the ship moving, barely, he settled back with a feeling of confidence knowing that he was a part of something magnificent, and exciting. He is sure Sam will explain more after takeoff. Danny knows something is up but he is ready. Sam looked at Danny with a slight smile, and Danny felt better. Now, safe with his thoughts, he said to himself,

"a white boy taking me on as a friend. This is something, and me a crew member."

A few seconds went by and only the thrust from the speed of the craft hit them. There was no noise heard except for the faint sound of the ship moving through cosmos. As it reached outer space, dead silence covered the outside of the ship. Danny loved it. He too could not believe it was happening. As the ship leveled out to a speed unfamiliar to either of the young men, there was a peace among them. Sam is the first to speak. He said to Danny,

"do you know why you are here?

Danny answered the Captain with,

"yes sir. I want to be a part of this."

"Good."

The Captain was pleased with Danny's answer. He continued,

"with deep concern I am sorry about the trouble you had at your grandmother's, she will miss you greatly."

"Now I have briefed you with the story of the power, and you know that much. You are starting the programming in just a few minutes if I have your consent that this is what you want. You can answer me with aye, if you give your consent."

Danny, more resolute to be a part of Sam's mission, became unwavering at that moment, and replied his most sincere, "aye sir."

Then Sam said,

"then I want you to know you can read my mind. You have my permission, and I will be your guide. If at any time you need me, I will be there for you. The process will start when I give you the signal. I will give you instructions. The programming procedures will start now."

Sam's commitment to Danny was genuine. The look on Danny's face was the look of amazement, and then disbelief. The understanding had already started to come through. Matured in seconds he had control in his eyes with the knowledge of many things. He said to Sam,

"thank you Captain, I understand.

He leaned back in his seat, closed his eyes, and like a child expecting Christmas he fell asleep.

"Now that he's asleep I'll give him the temple touch, and start the full programming."

This gave Danny the complete programming, Sam

was sure of his choice, and felt it was his wisest of decisions. Since Jimmy already had the power, he replied to the Captain's thought command to stand guard over Danny in case he needed anything or incase anything should happen to Danny. Jimmy replied,

"aye Captain. I'll take good care of him."

The goodness in Jimmy's voice pleased Sam. He turned to Jimmy and said,

"good, that's good."

Sam's estimate on the time it would take for Danny's programming was five maybe six days. He did not know how long the process would take exactly, because Danny had special talents. Each day would tell, and Sam would watch Danny each day no matter what it took.

"Now we wait."

Sam's mission would only be able to start when the crew was complete. Since Danny was convalescing, he felt he should turn his attention back to Jimmy.

Sam was ready to take over the helm, so he spoke to Jimmy aloud instead of using telepathy,

"get some rest; I'll stay up in the pilot's seat."

Jimmy said to the Captain,

"aye Captain but I would like to stay with you a while, and if you don't mind, I'd like for you to read something I've written."

Sam took his seat and turned to face Jimmy. Jimmy handed the Captain a piece of paper with something hand written. Sam noticed the perfect appearance of the writing by Jimmy. He said, "this is well written Jimmy."

"Chapter Eight; KAWHOCUMDIA"

Sam began to read:

Please forgive me Sam. I am sorry I did not tell you this before. My dad was an unholy terror. His return from India was a horror. He made moonshine whiskey, created illegal gambling houses, drank like a fish, had many, many affairs with women. He did many countless things that were illegal, not to mention the bad vulgar language he used every day, all day. He crashed his hot rod Ford after getting out of the army, nearly killing himself. They took it to the junk yard. He was guilty in a court of law to have been drunk, nice first day home. This was after walking into his superior officer's office in India, and telling him if he did not get a plane or a ship home, he was going to swim. After the car crash, he then caught a bus home to the restaurant called the Pena Restaurant. This was where my mother met Dad. He was in a partial body cast after the wreck. There was something said about him sitting on a bench waiting for the bus, and some woman being afraid of him. I guess this was because of the way he looked.

When I was a young kid I would listen to the adults tell these stories. You are not supposed to let little kids hear, is what I would hear some of them say. This one I was not supposed to hear. I do not think I was supposed to hear any of the bad ones about my dad. My mother Linda would always change the subject if I or anyone else asked questions about them. Like if it was true or not, I do not know, maybe it was. I think about this now and I do not know why I wanted to hide it from you. I think I am a little ashamed.

My dad was not a tall man; he was actually short, five feet eight or so. The more of this I write the less I like it, so I am going to stop now. Thanks for reading this, your friend, Jimmy. P.S. I had a lot more saved in my head; I think I will trash it now.

Sam folded the paper, and put it in his pocket. Sam could not catch his eyes. There was a loud explosion; the craft went into a spin. The Captain hit his head. Jimmy grabbing hold of Sam saw stars with him. Jimmy slid under a seat near Danny. After more spins, and several more crashes, the ship came to a stop. Jimmy looked for the Captain but all of the lights were out, everything went dead.

There was nothing but silence. The Captain lay still. Jimmy heard the groaning sounds coming from the ship. The rocks the ship was perched on made a crushing sound that sent chills down Jimmy's spine. He wondered if movement from the inside would cause more damage. Therefore, he lay still thinking about his next move. The cabin started to fill with smoke. He now realized he could not see the Captain.

Jimmy strained trying to move and said aloud almost

yelling,

"I can't move I'm stuck."

He growled trying to free himself, and once again failed.

Jimmy stopped his straining, and called, "Captain."

Quietly he called again, "Captain."

Trying to free himself again, he made a loud groaning, this time even louder. With all of the ship's power down he started to wonder if all of his powers had left him too.

"That's impossible according to my programming, he tried again, and he snapped free.

Now trying to reach the Captain through the smoke, he used his super vision to locate him. He said using telepathy,

"Captain, can you hear me at all? I cannot get through, something is wrong with your _____ He stopped and used his own sensors to detect where Sam was, and what he thought was wrong with the Captain. Jimmy said,

"Oh no."

He scrambled to get to the Captain. He continued to call,

"Captain, can you hear me?"

"Chapter Nine; KAWHOCUMDIA"

Sam's eyes opened, the dirt from the hole leaked in on them. He quickly shut his eyes keeping most of the dirt out. There was a foul smell coming into his nose. He spoke,

"what is that horrible smell?"

The next thing he noticed was the unmistakable burning electrical smell. It alarmed him, and he sensed danger. With this warning, he himself seemed to be short-circuited. He tried to look around. There were flashes of things going on in his head he did not understand. He knew his memory was failing. What was all of this confusion? He could not believe what he was seeing. A room full of high tech instrumentation. Smoke filled the air. The pain from the back of his head hit him hard leaving him almost unconscious.

"This couldn't be,"

he said to himself.

All around the room were emblems that Sam was sure he had no clue what they meant. The craft was not small and withheld no expense. Sam was a space buff in his younger, and his adult years. This was nothing like anything he had ever seen. The seconds that had gone by since the crash seemed like forever to Sam. Someone calling Captain, can you hear me? The noise coming in his ears was coming through the smoke and unrealities that were ringing in his ears. His confusion was too overwhelming. Sam slipped into unconsciousness. Even though he was unconscious, the inside of his mind was working on a solution to the problem.

The lights were all down but his sensors were finding the circuitry to the ship. Sam's rehabilitation had started. His brain reconstruction was in regeneration. Cells were finding placement. The defining key was his programming. He felt himself answer a question.

"What do you remember?"

He thought he said,

"Remember? At this point I don't remember anything."

Then someone called out Captain.

He responded internally, it was to himself,

"who are they talking to, calling them Captain?"

An alert flashed in his brain over, and over, beware
consciousness dangerous, stay calm. The Captain smelled
something again, and responded with,

"this place smells like a dump, a landfill. Phew."

The odor brought back all sort of memories but everything going on with Sam was internally. Then the search
formula programmed into Sam hit pay dirt. While Sam's
memory restore process was going on, he had a recall of an
old friend, Rick. Rick's dad owned a business in a small
town not very, far from where Sam lived. Rick was at school

with Sam when he got his head injury. Sam became a good friend of Rick's. His mother helped him repeatedly. He loved her with all the love a human being feels for another. She guided him with her loving way. Now he could feel how the problem had helped him in the present. Somehow, his life meshed back the broken lines from the past to the present, and now to the future. This is where all lines intersect once the human being has gone through programming.

"I knew I had conquered that problem."

As he thought this, it was as if a huge weight lifted from his shoulders. Something was helping Sam all over again every time the pain hit, and every time he started to slip further away into unconsciousness.

There was a light coming from the outside. He could clearly see it coming through the opening made by an unknown projectile. Whatever hit the ship exploded, and turned to dust? Nothing but dirt, and dust were visible.

His connection in his mind came like a gust of wind.

Instead of it slamming the door shut, it flung it wide open. Sam was conscious. He felt some pain, and knew his injury was severe. His feature for analysis, now turned on, started working on his well-being. Programming to reprogram his body and his ship all started visibly all at once. He then heard Jimmy still calling,

"Captain, can you heard me?"

"Yes Jimmy I can hear you fine.

The smoke was finally clearing, and the hole in the hull was closing. Sam jumped to his feet, and he tried to open his mouth, he could not. His jaw was broken. His assessment had brought up a head injury, now almost completely back to normal.

Sam gave Jimmy a telepathic command to get the ship off the rock it was on, and back in flight. Jimmy said,

"aye Captain."

Jimmy heard the Captain's thoughts when he cried out,

"Jesus!"

Not only was the pain still in his jaw, the pain in the back of his head was back.

The smoke in the compartment had all cleared, and Sam, Jimmy and Danny were O.K... Sam tried to cough once but the pain was too severe. He was able to suppress it with out to much of a problem. Jimmy asked one more time,

"you are alright now Captain, are you not?"

"Just a little tight jawed from the break; it'll be fine in just a minute. We are lucky Danny stayed under while all of this was happening. I think he is aware now, we are all fine."

The Captain tells Jimmy to check the rock they just left and to be sure, it is marked, and flagged as a discovery. He also tells him to plot a course for Veltrex Eta. The ships repair should be complete in a few hours, and the timing is just right after Danny's programming. His plan was to get some sleep, and to let Jimmy take over for as long as Sam could sleep. He needed to extra rest for the right healing to take place.

"Chapter Ten; KAWHOCUMDIA"

Jimmy settled back, his thoughts were of the way the ship went down. He wondered what had hit them, and was anxious for the ship's report. He was sure the ship's security system would have the complete story soon. Without five seconds passing by the paper, report came in. He immediately reached for the report. It read, Coded for the Captain.

Jimmy was in charge, so he read on. The ship is back in perfect working order, and back on course. Destination; sector eighteen, Ioliau, plotted by the Captain; Security one, level one. Jimmy did not know how long Sam would sleep, so he folded the paper, and put it in his upper right pocket.

Jimmy thought about what he should do, and said to himself,

"I want the Captain to see it."

He then answered himself with,

"fine." and laughed with a stiffened snort. Jimmy smiled to himself with a sheepish grin and was alone with his thoughts.

He checked the ship's log on screen in the ship's viewer. The ship was now in full control of speed, and on course, moving faster than Jimmy or anyone knew exactly. Suddenly Zadator makes a mental appearance to Jimmy. Jimmy formally welcomed him, and Zadator spoke to Jimmy,

"I have been monitoring the situation with your crash, and Sam's head injury the whole time. You have done well. You are also very capable, and very good.

My message was to your Captain. I named my son Samuel and my wife chose his name.

There was a journey to your planet on one occasion.

My wife had gotten permission from the counsel to be a part of the expedition. This was back in the beginning of earth, in addition, when the counsel was more in control of the programming than they are now. I almost laugh as I tell this story. It is because they have such little control since I took over. She also got permission for our son to come along thrown in the deal.

As we planned, there was to be an investigation into some of the human being's literary accomplishments, that would be, the literature of the times. We had chosen a particular part of the south, near your home. Of course, it was before your time. This was a time when some human beings were starting to advance far beyond their lower developed brothers, I am sure you know they were called pagans. We had wondered about taking someone from the lower walk, and programming him or her. Just as an experiment into something that would have been a sympathy gesture. This thinking led us to the belief that we were right in trying it.

We were just in the wrong time space.

We did go on the expedition, and spent the total of eight months in this one particular area as I told you earlier. However, six months was for search and rescue. The search gave us time to gather more information than we would have normally gathered. The rescue failed. My son Samuel was the one lost. The worst part was the fear we all had started to share, that he could be dead or worse. He could be alive in captivity, maybe taken by some barbaric tribe. We knew they would not have understood him. He could have been helpless after an attack.

Not all was lost on the expedition as far as learning about life on your planet, and with first-hand information, it was wonderful. We will get over the loss of our son because we know that in the future he will return. Not as he was maybe but he is still our son."

"Chapter Eleven: KAWHOCUMDIA"

There is silence, and then Zadator speaks with a thoughtful voice.

"Will you forgive me? I must go now. Belsha, my wife, needs rest. I will be in contact with you and Sam later."

Zadator fades away visually in Jimmy's mind.

Jimmy sits there thinking about Zadator, and then Sam. He got up shaking his head from side to side, with wonderment, and excitement on his mind. He said to himself, in a very low voice,

"this is new; I'll have to think about this. I'll just have to think about this."

Jimmy pondering his thoughts brought to mind, an old teacher of his, Mrs. Dubois. He remembered how smart, and sharp she was in class. He decided to visit Sam's mind to see what was going on. As soon as he made contact, Sam's message to Jimmy said,

"not just yet Jimmy."

Zadator was telling Sam,

"what shapes your future now will be the fact you want to change things like unwarranted punishment to the innocent. Wars caused by one man or many, erosion of the moral fabric of the youth. There are many evil men selling drugs, forcing young women into prostitution. Time travel can change these men forever and cannot be saved is no longer a term we use for anybody. Someday when you are ready, you can have a look at what your life would have been. Now only you can change earth's destiny. You can change the catastrophic phenomenon that will destroy planet earth. Unless intervention takes place that will be the end.

There is nothing else to say except you will not let this be the end. By the year, it is to happen you will be strong enough, and wise enough. You will be the changing element. I cannot reveal it to you but I will be with you, with telepathic communication, and will help you if you need me. You have a crew now, and they will be of great help, you will see. In the future you and the things you do at this time will later be termed, "the Dor'enavant a un autrui et arri' ere" This translates to the transformation of the Universe. Time travel will bring about the changing of events that save the human race.

The eyes of the past have helped to see the future, and now it is up to us to do what we have to do. Sleep now my friend; do not try to speak. I am your guide."

The Captain felt his presence leave but did not stir. Nobody at home knows where they are but each having the same feeling the magic was within them, and Sam and Jimmy more so than Danny but Danny catching up very fast now. Their communication together would be a strange sight to anyone back home and the goodwill and friendship bringing them closer together. They each knowing the blessings that they have, better now than ever before. There is an understanding that there is a greater development of the human race coming and each praying for a part of it in their souls to be with them for as many years as is possible.

Sam suddenly bounds to his feet, and headed into the dressing room, which is for relieving bodily functions also. He returns after a few minutes to his resting place, and back in position falls quickly to sleep again. Jimmy, feeling the Captain's return sighs but not with the usual human concerns. It is with great wisdom Jimmy feels Sam's presence. He too will be alone someday in his leadership. It is the decisions he will make, with no one to help him decide, that will change the greatness of earth. His knowing that Sam had chosen him brought a lump to his throat, and a tear to his eyes.

He suddenly feels the presence of a woman but he

does not know why. Then, there she is standing on the left of him, she said,

"I'm your ship's personality. My name is Karole, sometimes I go by Mo can I be of assistance?"

Jimmy looked to his left but when he saw the woman in uniform, he could not believe his eyes. He opened his mouth to say something but nothing came out. He realized his mouth was open, and forced it closed, and the word,

"what,"

which was in a question, came out of his mouth as smooth as silk. She did not seem frightened but confident, and sure of herself.

"Let me explain,"

she said to Jimmy.

"I am neither man, woman or machine but a combination of all that we are. I being your companion when you are in me, let me explain, me or I being the ship. I thought I heard you say something about being alone, and me feeling you a bit more human than I am. Well, I just thought you might want to meet me. Anyway, if you don't need me, I'll be off."

As she turned her back to leave, Jimmy blurted out, "Wait!"

"Chapter Twelve: KAWHOCUMDIA"

Jimmy's actual age would have shocked anyone, with such a mature voice, he sounded thirty-five at least. It was something he recently acquired after programming. Not just the maturity but also his voice changed too. His experience with the opposite sex was still very limited. This was why he cried out again to the ships feminine image,

"wait. Can we talk? Come back for just a minute."

Jimmy was not shy; his innocence was suddenly out in the open all over the place. He was already asking her,

"what do I call you? Do you have a name? I am sorry if I gave you the wrong impression. I was just so stunned

when you appeared like that. I did not even know you existed. I thought I knew everything about the ship. See, there is
some much I could learn from you. Can't we please start
over?"

Jimmy was almost begging her to come back and talk
but she just turned back and looked at Jimmy for just a second, and said,

"Everything's alright, I'll be back later and we'll talk.
Do not worry so much, we are fine. In addition, I have
known about you ever since you came aboard.

She eased in,

"now get back to work, and quit worrying."

"O.K... Wow. I'm blown away."

Jimmy walked backwards back to his seat at the
helm, and bumped the back of his legs on the chair. He fell
back into the seat just as he said,

"I'm blown away."

He was ashamed of his incompetence. He did not re-

ally know what to call her. However, this time he thought he
had really seen a beautifully developed,

"woman,"

was what finally came to mind.

She spoke softly. The sound came from inside the
ship,

"thank you, for that thought."

Jimmy turned to look in both his left, and right 90
degree angle, visually, and he relaxed, and smiled. He
thought to himself,

"great, you're getting my open thoughts, how exciting."

As the she, the ship, started to think about what Jimmy had said, she said telepathically,

"speaking of starting over, my name's Mo, what's
yours?"

She was just kidding Jimmy about not knowing his
name, of course.

Jimmy almost pig snorted when he laughed, and asked,

"what are you doing later?"

Mo answered Jimmy by supplying the answer telepathically. They spent the next hour with no interruptions, and tried to learn about each other as much as possible in such a short period.

After the hour of communication between Jimmy and Mo, Sam woke up just long enough to tell Karole to turn the ship around, and head for home. Sam was aware of Mo from the day he arrived at the first stop before he headed back to earth. Mo told the Captain,

"aye sir."

That was that, and they headed back to earth.

He did what he could do to keep a low profile on the ship when he arrived home. He wanted to do some things he had already set up. The times were just not set, so he made some calls, made the appointments to install some computers. First, he would have to see what they needed. Then, arrange, hire some installation service men, and that would be it.

The call came in from the office of a psychologist who did therapy for all sorts of people from all occupations. She worked with a psychiatrist to make sure her more severely disturbed patients got the treatment they needed, as well as what they deserved.

Sam was the only one left in the waiting room but a few minutes before a beautiful young woman was sitting across the room. She had gotten a phone call on her cell phone. She then got up out of her seat, and headed to the receptionist. She whispered something to her, and immediately left the building. Sam had not read her mind or invaded her privacy in any way, and was not one to presume much but he thought she must have gotten an emergency call. From the look on her face, and the body language, it gave Sam the impression it was serious. Sam had not made conversation with the young woman but now the silence was deafening. He picked up a magazine from the table in front of him without even looking. He started to flip through the pages, watching his surroundings, and gazing back at the magazine in front of him. Nothing for him to do but look for something to read, or at least something he could pretend to read.

The waiting room door opened from the outside, swinging into the room. A breeze came in with the fragrance of a goddess riding through a place in time where their no foul air zone had any interference or disruptions from a world full of disturbances. There, beautiful flowers grew, and perfumed nymphs toyed with stranger's heads, and dazzled their minds as they sprinkled their fantasy in the air. Somehow, magically put it in all of the places that counted. This done purposely was to make a person or persons go mad, or sometimes fall crazy in love. It slipped into his nose to the top of the nasal cavity, and his olfactory nerves picked it up. It was with the elegance of a ballerina lightly skipping, floating, and dancing through the wind where it must have come from some place magical but powerful. In addition, because of its existence, and slipping through space, and time unnoticed, unchanged, would explode with its powers in an instant, when it arrived to the right senses, surely a potion to entrance a spell on anyone, even the undeserving. It must have been conjured up by noble fairy's that had only one duty, and that was to create the world's most beautiful fragrance, used only in spells for falling in love. The appearance of a pond came as suddenly as the rabbit in the magician's hat, the reeds by the pond were swaying ever so gently, and reality slipped away.

Sam knew he could no longer tell if it was real or not. It made him feel he was there waiting to get in the boat for a ride across the pond.; to ride with a beautiful princess with long blond hair, with nurtured skin since she was a small child. Her complexion unchanged except for the slight bit of tanning from the sunshine. Then, as if he were in a wonderful dream, where everything seemed to be going his way, the rise of more excitement than he had ever experienced in his life, seemed to be walking in the door. The scent of the woman could not have been anymore intoxicating as she made her way into the waiting room. Her dynamics were pushing the walls back a foot from their original position. The room seemed to rumble as she made her line of attack past Sam. She had a very expensive gray suit from one of the shops downtown. This was where all of the beautiful people shopped. It had the look of a million-dollar-baby on this woman. Her class was running over in her cup. She was the most beautiful woman Sam had ever seen. There was no doubt about it she was his choice. You could tell she was in the prime of her life. If women looked, they envied; and it was all God given right down to the beautiful toes and feet, and that she had. He could tell everyone loved her. Sam thought to himself as she disappeared down the hall,

"this could be the therapist. She was perfect. This is

love."

He could hardly believe what had just happened. His head was still spinning. The more he tried to control himself, the worse it got. Finally, the receptionist spoke in a very soft voice, and said,

"you can check out the computers now."

It was almost in a whisper. Sam immediately stood up, shook off the spell he was in, and headed for the door to the receptionist's room. As he entered, he noticed how neat the room was, which he expected. There were three computers spaced with enough room, and each had a very nice chair. Not to mention all of the space on the desk you could ask for. It was clean as a whistle, neat and tidy.

Quietly Sam started at the first computer, and opened up the tower. The receptionist had told him the computers were all to slow, and not much memory. Sam had thought at first to try to save them some money. That he would just replace the hard drive, and upgrade the system's windows.

Now, he wanted to first check for any enhancements made in the motherboard, or anything inside that he needed to know about.

Sam finished with his inspection, and went on to the next, and the next. He finished quickly with his notes on everything, and went into the other rooms, which were empty, and had no sign of life. Only the computers and the office furniture were there. He made the same examination of each computer in each room in the office, six to be exact. He took notes on each one of them, and gave each one the same concern, and attention. He was very thorough. However, his thoughts were on the woman he saw come in the front door. Sam was able to focus on his job and assess the system. He finished with the same speed he was accustomed to performing. He thought to himself,

"this will be a big job. I will have to think this through over several days, just like normal everyday stuff."

As Sam was leaving, he passed by the front desk, and

asked the receptionist,

"what was your name, I'm sorry I don't think I got it?"

The young girl just smiled and said,

"Julie, its Julie Mr. Orrington."

Sam moved his head up, and down in a gesture that he acknowledged he got it, and said,

"thank you Julie, I'll be in touch.

He headed for the front door. He was about to put his hand on the door knob, when he heard someone calling,

"excuse me, excuse me sir."

The voice made the hairs on the back of his neck stand up. He thought for a second,

"could this be the therapist?"

Just as he turned, he realized it was Julie, the receptionist.

"Do you have a card, and I'll put it on file?

Sam replied confidently,

"surely."

He reached in his pocket for a card, pulled one out and handed it to her.

He said to Julie,

"again, I'll be in touch."

Sam was ready to leave. He just was not ready to meet the therapist yet but was very anxious too. He thought it to himself, and nearly said it out loud,

"I want to but I'm going to just let things happen in their own time. Like the vision I had about the future."

"Wow."

The receptionist said,

"I'm sorry, what did you say?"

"It's nothing, nothing at all."

The therapist had disturbed him with an earth-shaking event. Sam's life was now having many of these events. He would have to think this one thru, this had never happened to him before. Was this his true love at last? Like the song at last, he thought his love had come along. Could it be happening to him? He was shook up. He had not gotten over her entrance into the waiting room yet. He needed time to prepare himself.

Just when he put his hand on the doorknob, he felt a tug from the other side. He let go so that he did not interfere with whomever it was coming in. As the door opened, he could see it was an old friend from his college, Marcie Halund. Sam and Marcie made their nice greeting exchanges, and Sam was out the door. Marcie knew Sam pretty well from college, and knew how he was but she knew this abruptness was not like him at all. She had never been around him at work place, she thought to herself, "this is a bit strange, oh well, it's O.K..."

She knew him well enough to know that something had just happened, or something was going on with her dear Samuel being in such a hurry.

Sam just happened to innocently let his mind go back

to see what she was thinking. Just for security, he peered into her mind for a check. He heard what her thoughts were, and put a mental suggestion in, that she should call his mother and talk for a while. She franticly searched for Sam's home phone number in her cell phone to see if it was on the list. Sam had already entered it with his new power from the programming. He got it in ahead of her to give her a-calm-down-mode.

She blew out a puff of air, and said softly to herself,

"that was close, close, close."

She smiled and relaxed, she knew now she was chasing Sam for the first time in her life. She thought,

"what fun, what fun. See mama was right, he did have a job here today."

In addition, now Sam got the whole story by peering just a while longer. He said to himself as he thought about Marcie,

"got ya."

"All he could think about now was the therapist, and how he was going to meet her. His car was three rows over in the parking lot, and he decided to jog to get there. Sam clutched his tool bag to his chest, and started to run with a slow, and easy but steady pace. Sam was a track star in Junior High, High School, and College. When he got the chance, he was always running everywhere he could. The only time he was not running was a short part of his life.

When he reached his car, he could tell someone had broken in. His rear-door-window on the driver's side was completely broken out. His alarm had failed to alert him of the break in. Immediately, Sam used his power to call it in. He was able to do this by sending a mental message to the pay phone across the parking lot. The operator on the other end said,

"911, what's your emergency?"

Sam responded with the news about his car being broken in to. After the 911 operator was sure, she had all of

Sam's information she said,

"O.K. sir, we'll send an officer out immediately, and you are to stay right where you are until we get there."

Sam told the operator he would, and thanked her, and he hung up.

While he was waiting for the police, he said to himself,

"it will just take a few minutes; I'll just take a step back in time, and see what happened here.

No sooner than he said it, a figure stepped out of Sam's body, he immediately cloaked. It was actually Sam as a second self, able to move freely, and be a time traveler. He was able to do this without anyone being aware. Sam was actually going back in time to watch his car being broken into. He figured he had been inside the building working on computers around an hour and a half. His second self would be reporting everything to Sam even while the police were talking with Sam. Sam said to himself, "waiting always waiting, but this is different, I'm waiting on the police because my car is ruined. But, I'm waiting on a criminal in the past, and I'll be able to help the police solve the crime."

Sam was picking up broken glass, stopped to lean against his car. He let out a steady sigh, and spewed air from his cheeks. They were bulging out as if he were Louie Armstrong doing a number on his horn.

Trying to decompress himself, he almost said it aloud,

"who could have done this?"

His second-self-answered-him as soon as Sam had finished his sentence,

"I think I will be able to tell you the answer to that question in just a minute, someone is headed this way from behind the parking lot.

"This person is bold. It is broad daylight."

"Chapter Thirteen: KAWHOCUMDIA"

Sam knew he had nothing of value in the car, so why? Sam's double that had gone back in time to the scene of the crime said,

"Sam he's here. The young man has a tire tool in one hand, and it looks like some type of electronic device. It is lit up quite nicely. Yes, it is in his other hand. He has a ski mask on, black of course. I am not quite sure but I think he is wearing black tights, nice. Oh, my God dude, I think it might be lass; no, I am sure now he is a male. He might be able to give me a good run for my money, if I tried to grab him. I think I'm just going to lay low anyway, and see where he goes after the break-in, is that O.K. Sam?"

Sam quickly replies,

"of course dude, it seems my alter ego has taken on a complete personality of his own, dude, a? Watch out for the time change, O. K.?"

Sam's alter ego replied,

"but of course, dude, chat with you later, telepathically."

Suddenly without warning, the sweet smell of perfume filled the air. There she was the therapist. She came up to Sam with the most concerned look on her face, and said with fervor,

"are you alright?"

Sam responded with,

"sure, I wasn't here when they broke in."

She said,

"thank God. I was worried sick when Julie told me of your trouble. She said someone that came in the office told her, she immediately reported it to me. I was a nervous wreck. Therefore, I had to come see about you. Thank God, for neighbors talking or I would never have known.

Sam could not believe she was here. He could tell her concern was genuine. Moreover, he did not want to take advantage, so he said,

"I was hoping I would get to meet you soon but under different circumstances.

Sam knew he might not get another chance like this, and he put out his hand, and said,

"Sam Orrington, I'm your new computer man. We drop the W on our name."

"Nice to meet you, my name is Masujue. I wanted to meet you this afternoon but I knew you were busy with the computers. I did not want to bother you. You know a man, and his work. Do you work on home computers too?"

Sam started to answer but was to slow he was staring. Masujue quickly jumped in, and finishes with, "are you just a business computer man?"

Sam said after regaining his composure,

"no I work on home computers too, where they have them."

As the police car drove up, Sam said,

"Masujue, would you excuse me while I talk to the officers?"

As he started to walk away he stopped, and turned around to face Masujue, he said,

"my parents are having a small get together for family, and friends. It will be this Saturday, would you like to come?"

Masujue hesitated, and smiled the really cutest smile Sam had ever seen.

She said,

"that sounds nice, O.K...

Sam answered back,

"O.K... I'll call you later then."

Sam turned again, and walked away toward the police car. Before he had taken ten steps, he turned to look back at Masujue. She was standing there looking at Sam; she waved a sweet-woman-wave, and said,

"I'll wait."

Sam nodded his head in acknowledgement, turned, and walked on.

As he went toward the police car, the driver saw Sam approaching, and proceeded to get out of his car. He called out in a loud voice,

"sir go back and stand in front of the car until we are ready for you!"

Sam called back just as loud as the officer did so that he could be heard over the traffic in the area. The officer had already identified Sam as the owner of the car. Sam made a mental check just to make sure these cops were whom they identified themselves as, police officers. Sam turned, and went back to the car he was already thinking about trading in. He got another look at Masujue, and was very pleased with what he saw.

In a few minutes the female officer got out of the car on the passenger's side, and approached Sam saying,

"my name is Officer Wolf; would you please come with me?

At that very moment, he looked back at Masujue just in time to see her wave, and walk away. Sam waved, and she smiled at him, and disappeared from view. Sam walked on with Officer Wolf.

There were four men in the car, and three were wearing suits. The one was in a tee shirt with some weird artistic drawing on the front. He also had on dark pants, and snickers. He was holding his head down but Sam could see he had black hair, and it was long to his shoulders. There was a small bit of a bald spot in the crown of his head. He could have been mid twenty's or late thirty's, it was hard to tell.

Officer Wolf stopped Sam at a distance that he could

visually see the young man in the back seat. She asked Sam,

"have you ever seen this man before?"

Sam quickly answered,

"no ma'am, I haven't."

She said,

"step back six paces, and wait till I tell you to move."

At that instant, Sam, and his second self were reunited, his thoughts to himself were,

"I know, I know.

What Sam's alter ego discovered was that the man in the back seat of the detective's car was picked-up when he followed Sam's second self to a minute-market. After spotting the alter ego following him and was trapped by the alter ego and the police Sam's alter ego said,

"I changed my looks for a little while; I was interviewed by the police."

Sam said it again,

"I know I know dude."

Officer Wolf standing six paces away, turned partially back around to Sam, and asked,

"what did you say?"

Sam did not stammer, he politely stated,

"it was nothing, just thinking out loud."

Officer Wolf turned on around, and walked toward Sam. When she got next to Sam, she said,

"are you sure you don't recognize him?"

Sam spoke again trying to see Masujue as he told the Officer,

"no ma'am, I don't. I've never seen him before in my life."

"Well sir, he's sure saying he knows you from earlier, that is you were supposed to have been following him earlier, and we met the witness that identified him stating he saw him break into your car. Believe me, our witness does not look anything like you. You are free to go. In addition, we will be contacting you in the next few weeks, maybe three. Things have been busy around here. Anyway, we will hold this man for breaking into your car, and keep him locked up in the mental ward at the county jail. So, do not worry we have our man. It will not happen again as far as this man is concerned. Good night sir."

Sam raised his two fingers on his right hand, gave a polite wave, and said,

"good night ma'am, good night sir."

He bent down, and got a good mental picture of the male officer, he knew he did not want to forget this event, ever. Sam turned back toward where he had last seen Masujue walking. It was too late she was gone. He scanned the area to check, and she was gone. That was the last time Sam saw her until generations later. Sam found out the following Sunday, she had mysteriously left town with an old friend that showed up unexpectedly. Masujue's mother gave Sam this message from Masujue,

"sorry Sam, if he hadn't of shown up like this, I

would have gone out with you gladly, again I am very sorry.

Sam did not know why it happened this way but it did. It took two generations for Sam to learn that Masujue was killed that Sunday night, and wasn't running away with an old friend at all but disappeared forever. The police closed the case after ten years of search, with no clues. Masujue's son had a son that found Sam two generations later, and that brought it to Sam's attention about what happened to Masujue. Sam knew then he had to do something to change events forever, and for better. Masujue's brother's grandson, Tamajue, became an inductee into programming. Tamajue and Sam both went back in time to find out what happened to Masujue.

"Chapter Fourteen: KAWHOCUMDIA"

Her wickedness controlled, and ruined him. As it did many others before him, he now realized that there would be many more to follow. In spite of the fact that he had never heard of, knew of, or seen anyone else with as absolute control in "devilish schemes" that she possessed. He, the professor, claimed to everyone, that she was as normal as anyone was. In addition, he added, if anyone knew, it would be him. This was, if for no other reason, his final failing, unless, he sought God's forgiveness.

Now, as the games she played with her oozing charm spilled out into the night air, he lay sleeping. Cushioned on a soft and billowy pad inside his sleeping bag, the thoughts of her dominated his dreams. Before he slept, he could see the stars out of the corner of his eye, keeping one eye closed waiting for sleep.

He had tried not to sleep for fear of the dreams but that only lasted until the days the exhaustion overwhelmed his mind, and body. It was then the illness set in. The Doctor had, six Doctorates in Psychology, which would have amazed anyone on the faculty of any given University. He had extensive lecture tours on his number one best seller for three years straight. He was the author of "Human Beings", and sub-titled, "how to live life to the fullest with more-pleasure that you can stand". His peers paled in comparison to his intellectual genius. Only this time he was covering something up. It was as if he was a different person, and this person had no say in the matter at all. Everyone could see that she had full control over him, and everything she asked for, he would give; if he did not or could not he would arrange for her to have whatever she asked for.

His education came from many of the best Universities in the world. She was the constant reminder to his friends she was the boss, now that she had him. Between the two of them, there were no good decisions made with good moral judgment, or any concept thereof. This was not comprehendible to what friends he had left. He was not just an avid reader with an excellent mind but had an incredible memory as well. His I.Q. at this day, and time, matched, and went well over the standard for genius. He ranked one of the highest scores in the world. He had thirty-two Masters Degrees in an assortment of fields. There were three in literature, and three in English Composition. He had six in Grammar and related word uses and memory of words. He had been a Professor at fifteen major colleges in Europe, and twelve in the United States. They were the top in the country for these fields. She had the power of all this education, and experience. She had it by the control she had over him.

Other than his many academic achievements, he also had many accomplishments in sports, theater, and the arts. He did many sculptures with the talents of da Vinci. He taught dance. It-is-said he had the talents of the Swedish Italian ballerina Marie Taglioni, and rival Fanny Elssler. He developed a modern ethereal style for romantic ballet. It was-thought he was the reincarnation of performer and instructor, Marius Petipa.

He accomplished, and was proficient with every instrument in the symphony, and orchestra. There were rave reviews about him being a protégée of Giuseppe Tartini. He undoubtedly gained respect and recognition from the most talented maestros in the world. Yet, he was not out to gain fame but fame followed him everywhere he went.

One evening, he contemplated the fiery red hair on her head where they invented a new color, or one might say, discovered. This was in his attempts to please her with every fiber of his uncontrollable feelings for her and yes, anything to please. Only by dying small sections at a time, did they succeed in finding the color they were looking for. When the sun had finished its business of the day and the glorious colors of its rainbow passage, had made the visceral feeling of what they were doing less important. Between the dull flash backs, and the lingering protracted spun out moments that were amid honest attempts to get the job done, there were glimpses of colors that never before seen by human beings. These were the things they thought and talked aloud as they would say them. They were both thrilled with their discovery. They were just talking to-be-heard, it was a frantic jubilation; there was absolutely a rare magical event that had taken place here. With his eyes glaring with anticipation, mingled with the coloring of her hair and blindly asking, why here, why this place? What an invention. How were they ever going to get the job done with so much excitement?

It took place in between positions she fought for to

hold her head. She thought it would scare, any man. She beamed with thoughts that it would triumph over him. Thoughts came from both of them about the inimitable beauty of the hair, and the woman. This was with both of them feeling the quintessence of the color.

His anguish of what she had done to him was over now but only because he was further away than she was capable of traveling. Now, according to her finances she had to stay put, confined and restricted her earlier funding was-squandered excessively. This was perceptible to all that knew her, and was her downward spiral. She had come to no good during this past year. He too, felt sorry for her in such dire circumstances. Even though his social standing and respect stripped from him now, a shunned man, it was the disappointment in his friends that he felt made him even more of a spectacle. This was what she made of him.

As the memory and fear began to reach a height that would have woke the dead, yet still, him being the one asleep, he was as close to death as he could possibly be. His heart throbbed thundering in his chest. He screamed and sprang to his feet in sheer terror. He had not touched anything or felt anything lift him but there he was on his feet, pulse racing in a panic. With blurred vision, and thoughts consumed with fear, he felt that misery was nearer than the thirty-eight he carried. He slept with it secured next to his head. Moreover, again he slept, and dreamed.

"Chapter Fifteen: KAWHOCUMDIA"

Loneliness was not in the forefront but just a moment away, and a continual, intermittent clang, as if hallucinations would follow the congruent, emotional digs in his mind. His thoughts were from her. There she lay with herself, berating him, with all of the disgusting things she could disgorge out at him in his lethargic moment of time. He too, had this unsanctioned loathing of himself. He would give himself the same digs for having allowed the depth of the involvement that they had with each other. In addition, the lack of control that he had with her, he was ashamed. He had become a weak, pitiful, empty shallow man. In addition, with all of his knowledge and experience he was helpless in time and space, he was lost in her feast. Even after being with her, he was empty, and starting anew with his famine and it was starting all over again. Never to be satisfied, with a lust so deep, except for a few minutes of extreme pleasure, to the depths of hell in a heartbeat he would go, every time no matter where they were.

He slipped back into his sleeping bag, and fell fast asleep. After the twinkling of the stars slipped past his face barely noticed but serene enough surroundings. He awoke screaming nine times this night, and there were more nightmarish nights to come.

The answer will be after sleep and after nightmares of what is. In addition, the witness, whomever they may be, will but not by nicely spoken words but by nightmarish words tell tales that is as deep, and as dark as the deeds themselves. Only the squeamish are to turn back now. Unless God of course, would have you to learn of such things only the dead know.

Maybe not knowing will be the danger, and then there is sin, and shame, and regret. In addition, maybe knowing will be the grace given to you by the one who has already been to the other side, yes truth, the one who knows the whole story.

Can being witness to something be enlightening? Yes! Is it too dangerous, too scary, or is it just too horrible to the imagination? Maybe it is too horrible to tell.

Quite sleep now, quite sleep. Sleep and sleep-on, for the child may already be grown. Whose woe, that do thoughts leap, out into the night, into the silence, where faint whistles blow, and cries from the coyote and the wolf. As if it were to say, I am here come sleep. Come sleep. I am here, says the coyote to the wolf. Why cry, why cry my dear?

Where was he, he then was awake, and where were the other two, Jimmy, and Danny? The ship surely would have called him if anything needed to be done, maybe duties that demanded his attention. Now, this amazing ship, what a miraculous vehicle, its abilities were hard to believe even after seeing what it can do. From the top to bottom, not a flaw anywhere the design was unfathomable. At times, you would wonder why the color changed, and then you were wondering, why not? Sam caught himself looking out the main portal searching for Jimmy, and Danny. Not convinced they were not out there.

He said to himself,

"stop, they wouldn't be out there."

His optimism kept him up and with some since of hope. The look on his face would have stopped anyone, and would have asked him,

"what's up?"

He stopped looking, and started searching the control panel and the whole cabin for clues for what could have happened to them. Since he was programmed for solutions, his worry was now gone.

He thought back on the dream he just had, and wondered what it meant. Sam went back to the recliner, strapped himself in, and closed his eyes. Sam slept but it was a dreamless sleep.

"Chapter Sixteen: KAWHOCUMDIA"

Sam awoke as the alarm in the ship went off. His arrival at the security check, and fuel station was on time. It was the moment he was fully awake he realized he had gone through this before. Not knowing why he was going through it again, he moved ahead in time as a security measure to watch everything and be able to protect him-self. This was not a dream. By knowing ahead a head of time, about each step that he took, he would be-able to avoid any disasters that might take place.

He knew he was in accordance with his schedule according to the flight plan. He looked out searching in all directions there was no one. He cloaked himself with all of the security procedures in the programming. Not only was he ahead in time watching the past move forward but he was there in the future capable of turning things around if they got out of hand. He then moved the second Sam ahead by two minutes, and stepped out to watch two future movements of the original Sam. Just then, he heard the air pressure inside, and out, in the time space that he was in, synchronize. The third Sam had already moved ahead further than that time space but he heard it too. All three of Sam's doubles were transmitting all information at the same time. The original Sam received it in sequence in the order that it happened. He heard the hatch door, and the ladder engage, twice within thirty seconds. He felt this was a good experience.

He could smell the outside air starting to come in through the door. It made him think of home, and gave him a clean fresh nostalgic feeling. As he looked back to watch him-self go through the same feeling he had just experi-enced, the Sam that was in the past now looked in the place that he already knew his double was in, made a funny face at himself, and stuck his tongue out. Then he thought about the cinnamon rolls he was thinking of earlier, and wanted to leave the ship to get something to eat. He was going to get some for his trip to the next fuel stop, and security check. He could eat some here, and take some with him. He knew there was food on board the ship but he really wanted to go look around. He might explore, maybe stretch his legs a bit, and do some flying. If he was going to be invisible anyway, what harm could he do, right?

At that instant, Sam got the message on the screen in his mind that read,

Warning, retract doubles, and all material immediate-ly; Warning immediate response necessary for survival; At-tack underway.

Sam read the message, and commanded the retraction

instantly. Entry of all doubles took a total of two point five seconds but Sam not being ready for what was to happen, felt the slamming of a door on his chest. The force was not that great but the surprise of the doubles entering his body at that high rate of speed was quite a shock. As soon as all parts of Sam were in place, another message came in to his viewer,

"Attack on your ship imminent, vacate this planet now!"

Sam made it back to the control panel, and yelled out the command,

"Retract from this station immediately, now Karole!"

Sam literally threw himself backwards into his seat and hit the button for the automatic straps. In addition, the ship was in high-speed retraction. Retraction is an emergency removal procedure only. Sam flexed himself in preparation for anything that might happen next, such as high-speed destruction. He called on any visual to bring up pictures of outside activity within one hundred and fifty miles, and could not see anything. Sam said to himself,

"uh oh."

The subtleness of the tones in both syllables was deafening. He yelled quietly to Karole in a speedy monotone voice,

"stand ready evasion tactic eleven, prepare for death restoration on all personnel including ship. Reach for any personnel outside the ship, and start a pod rescue immediately on my cue of now; now!"

Sam heard the faint cry of Karole saying in a loud unusual voice,

"aye sir."

Sam was sending signals in all directions hoping he was not making a fool of himself but choosing the fool over the consequences. He knew only a few seconds had gone by since he gave the command to evade any approaching substance or material. It would depend on the speed it was traveling, on the chances he had to evade, and maybe even survive. Nothing yet has been invented or discovered that can destroy programmed cells. The research will bear witness to this fact. Far reaches into the future have brought back nothing in the findings to prove otherwise. Yet, Sam started to pray.

"Our Father, who art in heaven,

Hallowed be thy name. Thy kingdom come,

Thy will be done, on earth as it is in heaven."

Sam's voice went silent; he was waiting, waiting for the impact. If nothing happened in the next minute, he was sure he would be saved, and safe, at least for the time being. He spoke to Karole,

"can you get me a status report on any objects larger than a baseball in the area?"

Before Karole had time to respond, he said to her,

"Thanks."

She answered him back with,

"you're welcome Captain. Are you sure you're alright?"

He sent her the response telepathically, and he said he was all right.

She told him there was nothing heading in their direction at all but they did have a narrow escape involving a collision with a burning ball of hydrogen, and some forms of solid and liquid rock. She left her telepathic mode, and said,

"something is identified as titanium extra resilient. Composite of pictures are coming. They will be up on your screen in a jiffy."

Sam replied with a question,

"how long is a jiffy Karole?"

She answered with a voice unfamiliar to Sam,

"not very long Captain."

Sam waited patiently.

"Chapter Seventeen: KAWHOCUMDIA"

Sam had a memory of the station with the fuel, and security check. It turned out to be more of a fun park for the Aukiauk Guard than anything. Anyway, while he was waiting for the pictures of the titanium fireball, he decided to scroll back through time to see if there were any clues about the hot extra resilient flying hunk of molten metal. He knew that it would only be another minute at the most for the pictures to come up but went ahead anyway.

"Karole, I'll take an extra upload on those pictures coming for me. This review may take more seconds than I have figured. Hold all my calls."

Sam closed his eyes, and saw himself as arrived at the security check right on time.

He said to himself,

"Wait-a-minute, let's fast forward to the going outside."

As soon as he had cloaked himself with all of the security procedures, the air pressure inside, and out, synchronized. He heard the hatch door, and the ladder engage.

He quietly said to himself,

"this is it; this is the place."

He felt this was a good experience.

He could smell the outside air starting to come in through the door. It made him think of home. He was feeling a clean fresh nostalgic, everything right sort of thought. Then as he thought of the cinnamon rolls, he wanted to get off the ship, and get something to eat. He was going to get some for his trip to the next fuel, and security check. He could eatsome here, and take some with him. There was food on board but he really wanted to get off the ship. Maybe he would explore, stretch his legs a bit, and do some flying. If he was going to be invisible anyway, what harm could that do?

To the outsider, Sam's mind would have been a scramble; he suddenly had the taste of lemons in his mouth.

Sam thought to himself,

"Why do I want lemons? Maybe I will have some lemon aid. Man, I must be homesick; lemons make me think of home."

He went down the ladder, and on to the dock. He noticed a funny looking substance and debris that covered it. He was unfamiliar with whatever it was. He crouched down to examine it, reaching out he touched his right hand forefinger to it. The slimy looking gooey stuff was also sticky. Sam removed his finger, and wiped it off in a dry spot. He then realized four strange looking men creatures that looked a little like man, were heading in his direction. He knew he had to analyze the situation quickly. He was already cloaked, and he shut down his breathing to maintain silence. He watched as the creatures headed in his direction.

One was dragging something behind his back. Part of it was over his right shoulder; Sam could not see what it was so he had to get a closer look. He made a flash jump to the top of the ships docking hanger. He was in flight in seconds. After hovering for a few moments, he knew he was still not visible to any of the creatures. When he magnified his vision, he could see a net the creature was dragging but there was only one dragging the net, and it was a large net. Large enough for a good sized man or bear. Sam's analyst showed it was extra strength material.

These men creatures looked like they had done this before. They marched as if in some type of military order or formation. If they spotted or heard him, it may mean con-frontation. In addition, that would mean a flight quickly back to the ship. The men creatures were dressed in black uniforms, heavy boots, and belts carrying an assortment of things unknown to Sam. He did not see a weapon, other than maybe the net. While he was making his way from the ship earlier, he was searching for a reference to the things, and people of the station. The Aukiauk Guard assigned to the fueling station as workers. They also took care of the security for entry into Veltrex Eta.

Sam whispered to himself,

"keep focusing, stay focused."

Sam was not letting himself get worried; he knew that he could create duplicates of himself to fight them off. On the other hand, create as many duplicates as he needed, four or five or more each one being equal to Sam in power, and strength. Sam could never have imagined these things.

Their boots were hitting the deck at the same time getting nearer, and nearer. He thought to himself,

"wait, wait."

Seconds go by that seemed magnified. They are approximately thirty feet away now. He eased his head around, to try, and find something they could be coming for. There was nothing, no clues. Sam could not imagine what they were after.

Sam still hovering prepared to make a quick flight to the ship. Then very sharply, one of the creatures pulled out of ranks, and headed to the bay door. It is the entrance to the docking bay. This was where Sam had brought his ship in to park. There are other ships but the creatures were taking the net far away to another door. The other creatures join the first one. Each one breaking ranked individually and follow-ing the other. When they reached the door, each one as they approached started helping with the net covering the door. Sam could see them clearly now, each wearing helmets with dark glass coverings over their eyes, on the other hand, where eyes were supposed to be. It almost made them look like bugs with huge eyes.

Sam is still in silent mode, and waiting. He now

knows that they are far enough away he can slip away from them. He made a motion to his left, and flies toward the exit leading to the station entrance. It is the main lobby to the exit to the outside world. Sam was almost home free from what could have been a situation where he did not want to be.

As Sam reached the outside, he realized there were beings flying everywhere. He could see them in an aeronautical free for all. He was not prepared he did not have a flight plan. They were like locust on a field of wheat.

"Watch out!"

After Sam spoke, he realized how easy it was to lose control in this environment. He flew down to a lower level, and thought to himself,

"this will be where the beginners are, maybe."

Another one zoomed in Sam's direction almost hitting him. Sam stopped in mid-air with a message coming in, the chaos around him continued.

"What's this I'm reading in my head?"

"These are the Aukiauk Guard; they live, and work on this station. It is just a security station; it really just looks like a planet. The Aukiauk here, can fly, and have a few of the powers that the programmed have.

Sam found himself wondering how God did all of this without revealing it to human beings until now. Now more information was coming to Sam about the Aukiauk.

The guards are with visual enhancement lenses, and breathing apparatuses. It is for security purposes. They will not harm you or even bother you. There is no alert to be on the lookout for you. You can go uncloaked if you wish. Warning, look out for the council they have power but nothing like you. Just beware they captured you once.

"Chapter Eighteen: KAWHOCUMDIA"

Sam realized now, that he had better pick up what he needed, and get back to the ship. He thought about his inexperience with these powers, which, he is still green. The voice, in message form, was giving him information. It continued:

"The council didn't want your escape publicized, for fear of embarrassment to the ones who captured you. It is not here that you need to keep your presence secret. There are other species here on the job helping with security. It was familiar for the Aukiauk to see strangers here. It is just a casual look, and that is all they do. It's enough of a check these days."

Sam headed back toward the entrance to the docking area, and looking straight ahead in flight. The three men that captured him were coming straight toward him. Their high rate of speed did not keep Sam from recognizing them. They were in the same clothes except for the hats. He felt safe knowing that he cloaked earlier. It was a false sense of security. He breezed right past two of them but the third one reached out with an extension on his arm, grabbed Sam by the throat. It cut off his ability to breath. He was choking almost instantly. He knew the force was damaging his windpipe. He started to analyze everything. The death grip from the third man started Sam thinking about the times he had come close to panicking. This time felt right, he did not feel panicky at all. Then without knowing what was going on, he felt a tingle in the back of his neck.

Sam stopped for a moment to reflect on his memory of this point in time, and said to himself.

"Yea, this was a weird feeling.

Then he continued with his review.

It flashed back to him as if he had never stopped. He said to himself,

"what in heck is happening now?"

There was a slight fizzle, a small snap, and a high-pitched snap that whistled behind him. He could hear the ruckus going on behind his back, as the third man released his grip. Sam began breathing again at once. He thought that in a few more seconds, it would have been renew the throat time. He looked back after the third man completely released his throat, and saw Danny, and Jimmy. The other two men were unconscious on the ground. They had tape over their mouths and tied up with rope. The third one seemed to be suspended, and unconscious. His hands and arms locked behind his back. Jimmy spoke where anyone who was listening could hear him, and said,

"I guess they want be bothering anyone for a while."

Jimmy saw the look on the Captain's face, and rushed to help him up. He had fallen to the ground after the man released his throat. When Sam was on his feet, he reached to Jimmy, and embraced him, and said,

"thanks man. I think I owe you one."

Jimmy embraced the Captain back, patting him on the shoulder he said,

"It's O.K. Captain, you can thank Zadator, and he's the one that had the idea. I will tell you about it telepathically, now on the way back to the ship, first. Danny, let's go man."

Danny still watching the three unconscious thugs, was glad they were ready to leave this planet, told Jimmy,

"yes sir, I'm ready, let's go."

They each had already turned on their visibility viewers to each other, Jimmy, and the Captain jump into flight catching up with Danny. They flew to the entrance together. Danny listened while Jimmy told Sam about what they called, size packing. This was where small holes were-made in the back of Sam's neck. Tubes are then place in the skin that is very small. They cannot feel them in any way. Jimmy and Danny whom are shrunk and placed in the capsules and were inserted in the tubes. Ejection achieved on the ready, when the alarm is-set-off by the nervous system. The capsule pops right out on time, and the occupants of the capsule eject. Moreover, they returned to their normal size.

As they reach the door of the ship, the Captain said,

"I've got reference to that I'll have to thank Zadator personally."

Sam reached in his pocket, and pulled out the pocket helm. He waved it in front of the door and it opened, all three went inside, there they were safe.

"Chapter Nineteen: KAWHOCUMDIA"

"Captain, Captain."

Karole called twice, and saw that the Captain's eyes

closed, so she said,

"the pictures of the titanium fire ball are ready to

bring up."

There was no answer from the Captain, so she put

herself on hold. She watched the Captain closely. He moved

his head in an upward movement, opened his eyes, and said,

"well, show me the pictures. Have you found any-

thing interesting?"

She just shook her head slightly to say no, and kept

on looking at the Captain. She said,

"you look so refreshed, what happened? I cannot believe how rested you look.

The Captain said to Karole,

"can you focus in on the fire ball, and look through the flames?"

"Good idea Captain."

Karole zoomed in closer, doing it without any signs of concern, and without any movement.

Captain Orrington said,

"very good. Now, do that one more time."

The Captain walked over to the screen, and circled around an area with his finger, he said,

"now bring up the best picture you've got on just that area."

Karole did it, and then walked up next to the Captain. He looked over at Karole, and asked her,

"now can you zoom in twice what you did before,

please?"

She said O.K. but I have to go.

Sam watched the screen zooming in, and as Karole moved away glanced her way and watched, she disappeared through a door in the front side. Then Sam saw the door disappear. Sam thought to himself,

"nice touch."

Sam was back, Danny was too. Jimmy started disappearing, and what looked like chasing after Karole.

The thunder of hooves from their horses, barking dogs, and the screaming tribesmen made a frightening sound, as you would imagine. Being innocent played no part in the treatment he received.

He was escaping this day, escaping the darkness in the lightless cell. We always think of lighted places, not the darkest of holes or the deepest of cells. This is where only the dredges of humanity have ever been, until now. They had kept him in this place mostly in darkness for the last eight years. Although he was in top physical condition, mentally he knew it was time for him to go, and time to escape this madness. His work in the mines where he toiled twenty-four hours a day, every day, with very little sleep would be for at least two more years of cruel hardships.

He listened to his instincts, the only thing he could trust. It took him years to get over the removal of part of his brain, which the tribesmen took. It was termed, brain plug, which was to get the secrets from the person having the brain plug removal. He was lucky to be alive.

It was a belief during these hard cruel times that by removing a brain plug from one person and placing it in an-other's brain, what was learned could be valuable. Each person would get the other's plug. Many men died, many were left mentally impaired for life. Then sometime death was their punishment for not taking care of themselves properly. The tribesmen and chiefs did not know what they had done for generations, and generations to come. Samuel, who was Zadator's son, had become a trusted prisoner, as trust goes in his position. The guards were there to watch him pick berries for the chief of the tribe, an extra duty. Each time he went to pick the berries, he would find a way to venture out beyond the sight of guards. At first, they would come running just as he thought they would but then, they realized he had only gone to pick the larger berries just beyond the main patch. At least that is what they thought. The tribal chief made mention of the bigger berries to his friends, about it being a great find. He also mentioned for him not to miss any of these wonderful delicacies. For picking the large berries, he got a reward, of full nights of sleep, sometimes, when the chief would choose. He would get safe guards to watch over him, and without any disturbances. This the chief promised but the nightmares continued.

This would be Samuel's first attempt to escape. No one would know it until it was too late. He would go his usual way, under guard. The same jog to the work site, where the berries were, and the equestrians that were guards with weapons, usually a bow, and arrow. They also had spears that had already killed many with their razor sharp points. This was their pride, and each having their own markings for each kill. They loved to show them off to the prisoners, especially Samuel. They would stick the spear in front of his face, and shake it making a lot of grunting noises. He saw the reasoning that it was to create fear by showing the point.

Upon arrival at the berry patch, he would ask the guards if they would like to taste his first pick, and naturally, they would respond positively. When Samuel said that he would bring them lots to eat, this made them feel as if they were getting an elitist treat.

He made his first trip to the edge of the berry patch, and brought back enough berries to keep the guards busy for quite a long period. Then he went for the second batch, and thought it would be a nice going away present. He brought them back another batch of the delicious berries, knowing they would make pigs of themselves. This would give him just enough time to make his escape. On the third trip back where he was out of sight, he sat the picking-sack down, and began to run.

Samuel tried to do away with all of the noises that a two-legged species made, when they turned tail to run. He was as quiet as a deer mouse. According to his calculations of steps per second and total steps he took, he had traveled about a mile and an eight when he heard the dogs.

It thrilled him when he realize how far he had actually reached before the sound of his pursuers entered his ears. When the sounds are behind your back, you use all of the strength you have, and all that you had developed. This was why he had conserved for the past two years. Now his time had come. If they could have seen him, they would have known they were outmatched but now the guards were not going to get that privilege. His run masterfully accomplished. Each step was a work of art, an athlete to behold. He reached for the animal inside of his alien muscle fiber. Not just down deep but beyond. This was a run to witness.

"Chapter Twenty: KAWHOCUMDIA"

Samuel's plan was to make it back to the place where he had first left the sounds of his parents. His built-in sonar would help him to find the actual spot where his kidnapping took place those many years ago.

His thoughts were on his parents, and the time he had slipped further, and further away from them. He was in search of whatever clues he could find to learn more about this great planet away from his own, far away. All had traveled so far to learn, to explore, and to take back with them, the knowledge they would accumulate to make their final judgment on human beings. This would be the knowledge for the judgment on this period.

His focus now would be on finding the place where his abduction took place. He would return there just for a starting place, and for his peace of mind. Here he found a place to camp, a place to organized, and to free his sprit.

Running hard now, he was running just as hard as he could. Not from the fear of his pursuers catching him but from knowing he would defeat them by beating them in this race. The tribesmen were not aware of his development of strength, and his unique powers. The connection he was feeling with his parent's was wonderful. He knew this escape would leave the tribesmen in total bewilderment, and confusion. He laughed aloud it was only for himself. He almost could not stop. The laughter echoed through the forest. His escape would make it hard for the guards to go back and face the others of their kind. The tribesmen would mock and ridicule them. This was their punishment for making their bragging statements, such as, they could keep him prisoner where he would never escape.

Samuel thought how it did not matter now. The sounds were slowly dying out behind him. Slowly he made his way. Even though he was, moving as fast as he possibly could, slowly, slowly but surely, their sounds were gone. They were gone. At last, he was free.

He thought about his recovery, and the temporary loss of memory he had. Many of his super skills did not come back for years. His ability to cloak himself did not come until someone told him about it much, much later in his future.

Samuel's first stop was at a riverbed. His wet hands were dirty, and weathered. He cupped them to take in the water his mouth so desperately needed, first a small amount, then a bit more. Then more, this was good, very, very good. He washed his face, the face that felt the cool water run down his cheeks, and neck. Then on to his shoulders, and chest, it was enough of a fresh splash to bring him to life with his new freedom. He wanted to fly. The excitement, now reeling into his brain as he realized what was happening inside, he knew he would regain everything. The repression Samuel had done to himself was in his mind for self-preservation, now it was over. He was free from fear.

He abruptly leaped with a newfound strength, and joy. His tears began to flow. He felt no restraints. This was nothing like what he had known for those long, long years. Here it was again, he felt freedom, and nothing but freedom could heal his wounds. Moreover, nothing but freedom lay in front of him.

He stopped crying while in flight but the tears gently slipped out of his eyes anyway, and then quickly disappeared as the wind on his face pushed them away into forgetfulness. It just made sense he would feel everything he had missed while he was a prisoner. Physically, and emotionally he was ready. He was in flight, he climbed, higher, and higher straight up he soared, like a bird in flight for the first time.

His wing was broken, and now healed. Higher, and higher, he went higher, and now he really knew freedom as if he had never known it before. He leveled out but did not know that part of his memory was gone, and the sense that something was wrong lingered but he still soared to claim his freedom. He tried to connect the dots but still, something was missing.

His eyes focused to find the tribesmen before one of the murders spotted him. At first he saw nothing, then his vision automatically adjusted to super power, and the very small specks that were like ants along came into focus. He saw the tribesmen that were guards looking to find something to eat. Samuel thought,

"Maybe they were looking for something, like me. It's too late for them."

He was too far for them to see him. He had no pity for them, not after what they had done. It came in small amounts but eventually he began to forgive them. They were actually very advanced for their period in time.

Leveling out more now high in the sky, turning around, heading for his destination, these were his thoughts,

"Not far now, I think I see it."

Of course, Samuel was using his super powered vision. He said it again,

"Yes, it's not too far now, just below those high trees. I'll pray when I get there."

Samuel still feels that something is missing, and that something is wrong.

"What is it that father used to do to reverse wrongs that were done to other people? I have to try, and remember what it is I am supposed to do to fix it. I will seek my mother's wisdom. I will be my father's son, home after a long stay at some school, or maybe travel in space, yea that is where I have been. The campsite will be old, and forest grown over it. It could have been anyplace, I could have been anyplace."

His account of the tribesmen taking him came to

Samuel as he flew.

When he awoke in a large cell, it turned out to be his home for the next eight years. It was a cage in a hole. His headache was a bigger problem than anything that Samuel could have had. The roar in his ears was like a herd of Buffalo running over the top of him. It was the same as if being buried underground in a shallow grave. It was constant, just the roar alone nearly drove him crazy. He could not stand the pain. He would grab the back of his head feeling the plug removal sore, not knowing what had happened to him. He did realize there had been some bleeding. Samuel thought,

"It must have come from a blow to his head". This would have been probable when they were taking him prisoner. He did not remember very much of the capture but he did remember the struggle. The time for the headache to start easing off was impossible to calculate. He remembered missing meals, and feeling sick, and that he knew it was from not having enough nutrition. There was no way for him to think straight because of the pain. It was just too unbearable.

"Chapter Twenty One: KAWHOCUMDIA"

After thinking about the pain caused by the removal of part of his brain, his eyes squeezed shut, and then opened again. What followed was a cold chill that went all the way down Samuel's back but worse, it went all the way to his soul. His memory went on when he finally started eating he was like a wild animal. The tribesmen saw how he ate, and wondered if they had made a mistake about the strange young man, maybe he was not a human being. They had no way of knowing he was really an alien, with no reference to speculate on, there was only superstition, and plain igno-rance. The difference between human beings, and the Zorvirax would have taken a medical exam. Just to look you could not tell the difference. Samuel had some mental failings that could not be noticed by the human tribesmen. He was still much faster than any primitive human being was. He did not get the change that had taken place inside his head it was so subtle.

After several months, Samuel got a visitor, a woman from the tribe. She fixed Samuel's hair. She knew the mark from the tribesmen that meant he was marked as a dead man. She could see the branded tattoo that was there to cover the scar. She fixed Samuel's hair with a tie cloth just above the mark. The tribesmen would change the women so that they never got-to-know-him, and more importantly, he never knew them.

The box he lived in was large enough to stretch out when he slept. His work on the day shift made him stronger, and stronger. His mining gave him plenty of exercise. He learned to hide his strength, and his power. In the beginning most of his power was clueless to Samuel too. He also learned not to disturb the guards or the tribesmen, and the chief would have been out of the question. Therefore, he was really a good prisoner. There were only a few chances missed to escape. The certainties of Samuel's chances were not exactly clear but if he would not then who? He barely remembered he had any power at first. For Samuel to use his power effectively he would have had to think to use it. He was very unaware of it most of the time he spent as a prisoner. Samuel would someday stumble upon a way to travel in time again, and this was the key to his changing history. The only reason his family could not do it was the decisions made by the unit, the committee.

"Chapter Twenty-Two: KAWHOCUMDIA"

It had been twenty years to the date since Samuel's capture. It was like any other morning. Samuel went for a jog, came back, and took a shower at the waterfall. He had his breakfast of wild blueberries, honey, and muffins, the muffins he learned to create after some of his power came back. The blueberries he picked from a patch not far from the camp. The honey came from an old oak tree, Samuel estimated to be at least fifteen hundred years old. His energy packed protein breakfast kept him going until lunch around one o'clock. He then ate his jerky, and a cup or two of juice he created from some herbs and fruit.

Before he came to the abode of mortals, he was a very good hunter. His time here wasn't wasted. He had learned to hide in the earth, as a hunted fox. As always, human beings did not seem to come around. This was part of the earth's forbidden but seemly, only to human beings.

Samuel had taken the time to look for the essential device that his parents would have left behind for him. If there was something for him they could have hidden, to help sustain his life, it would be the device to the ship or the portal to the ship. For years, he searched the trees, then under rocks. It turned out to be a food source where he found grub worms, and snakes but no luck on finding a device. Trying to find the fathom device began to slip away out of his mind. Once he thought he saw a raccoon with it in his mouth, so his chased him. The raccoon got away. Samuel finally got an idea to sector search the area for underground caverns, and washouts. He thought of starting digs to try, and find anything left behind by his parents.

Samuel really had learned to love the hills, and mountains to the north. It was without flight that he took most of his jaunts to get to the top of them. This was no easy task. Samuel had created a bag through his inventive powers, which carried his food. The strap of belt he made from a handmade rope that he bound together with a twine he created himself. He strapped it over his shoulder, and was off on another adventure.

He headed to his favorite perch, which was where he looked out over his whole Kingdom. There was nothing but animals, and birds to share it with Samuel. He was half a day getting to the top. With the jogging he did, the journey took less time.

Today he went pass a rattlesnake, a good fifteen feet off the trail. It gave Samuel no warning of being there. It was of little concern to him. Samuel progressed swiftly anxious to get to the top. This was his place he loved most dearly, his place he worshiped the creator. His speed was great today.

He felt efficient this morning, and enjoyed every breath.

Today's meal at the top he welcomed, his hunger filled by his pouch of his favorite foods, and his sadness would come because he was alone. His accomplishment will be the prize.

The Clovis people had been his keeper for such a long time; he learned that their skills were primitive, and barbaric, this he knew from the outset. He also knew the damage they could do to others. Even though there were other Clovis tribes more civilized, this tribe captured him. He would never drop his guard but he let them slip away out of his memory. He was far ahead of the tribesmen of the Clovis.

"Chapter Twenty-Three: KAWHOCUMDIA"

Kindly thought, the unusual part about Samuel and Peace in the beginning was her name. She did not have one when they met. Samuel gave her the name because that is what he was looking for in the beginning. This was after being a prisoner for so long. Then it seemed to be a daily thing, until one day he woke up, and realized he had had peace for a week, he looked around, and said to himself,

"Wow, I've finally found it. Peace, I have it. Wow."

Then, after two months of his perfectly settled life, came a whirlwind. It was a girl on a horse leading fifteen other horses. Samuel had cloaked himself that day while flying high above his camp, when dramatically, a cloud of dust appeared on the horizon. The worrisome part of the cloud was it was heading his way. His curiosity got the best of him, and he zoomed in on the little cloud by using his super vision. What he saw out in front of the cloud in question had to have been the most amazing thing Samuel thought he had ever seen. A woman on a horse-wearing animal skin, and having the most beautiful auburn hair with a light blondish tint streaked through it, like nothing he had ever seen. He watched, and waited while he hovered high in the sky out of sight. There were times when he could not see this aberrational malady, though the cloud of dust stayed visible rising ever so clearly above the pines.

Samuel waited high above the camp for fifteen or twenty minutes. After, when he first saw her, it was with his normal vision. She had made the point of entry at the clearing entrance. She brought her horses to a stop for a few seconds scanning the pasture. Samuel counted three seconds, and she was off again in a fast gallop. As she approached the camp closer, Samuel knew something was happening like never before. He swooped down to get there just as she arrived, and she did a dismount in one movement. She was ob-

viously an equestrian. As Samuel landed behind her, he uncloaked himself. He spoke to her by saying the greeting used
by many of the tribesmen,

" yat gooed."

She immediately turned to face Samuel, still holding
the ropes tied to each of the horses, she too spoke,

"yat gooed, nahae."

Samuel's suspicious appearance from behind made
the beautiful auburn blonde feel spiritually connected to him.
Her knowing who he was, and his leap of faith, made her
bond. She, all the while knowing something Samuel didn't
know yet. He felt he could communicate with her on a higher
level, and win her over. He was already analyzing her mind,
and there was an amazing amount of knowledge stored there.
She stared for a few seconds more, waiting for more of her
language to come from his mouth. Then, he decided to make
the telepathic connection with her. However, before Samuel
could say anything else, she spoke to him in English of the

future. This was a language Samuel had used most all of his life. She said,

"I must tell you, your father Zadator has sent me to you, he programmed me,
I am now like you, only I'm human."

Samuel stood before her, and waited until all of what she had said, immersed him. Then he asked, with the gentleness of understanding,

"what is your name?"

She spoke softly to Samuel,

"I was to be named by my husband in my tribe, now; I have left the tribe without a husband. That ends my chance at getting a husband out of my tribe. I am now yours to name as you wish, Samuel."

All of the years, and times Samuel spent alone came rushing over him. It was like the flood gates of the dam broke loose. He did not cry but she felt him inside her heart. He reached for her hand, and she likewise his. When they touched, he said,

"you will be Peace, your name is Peace. That is what I've waited for, and now I really have found Peace."

She smiled at Samuel, and said,

"this I accept. Peace it is then."

After Samuel and Peace had filled themselves with the love they were both longing for, they turned to look at the camp. Deserted for too many years; all of the things were no longer of any service. Unspoken commitments and an intermingling of each other in an embrace replaced frustration and the tears. Samuel spoke first,

"where do we start?"

Peace looked up at him as she felt his arms around her and said,

"I have something from your father, Zadator."

She pulled away from Samuel's arms, and took off a medallion she was wearing around her neck. The metal part was hanging low inside her primitive clothing that covered her top. It was not a large metal piece at all but palm size. She handed it to Samuel, and said to him,

"this is the device to the ship you've been looking for. Your father with his love sends this. He also told me to tell you, he is sorry. He said you would understand."

Samuel read her mind, and got the information she was sending him about all she had to tell of her journey.

"I actually found it over there but it was your father that gave me that information. It is a day, and a half ride on horseback to the river south of here. Three days back I left all of my horses corralled with a protective cocoon where they could drink. You were gone when I arrived; I believe you had gone to the top of your favorite place?"

Samuel answered,

"yes, go on."

"So, when I saw you were gone, I thought I would come back in a couple of days. Here I am. I took the liberty to get the device for you. I found it over there on that huge rock. It was on top."

Samuel looked up at the top of the rock, and back down at Peace. She said to him,

"you used to stay up there a lot."

Samuel answered with a smile,

"yes, I did."

Samuel asked Peace,

"how did you get up there?"

Peace replied with another smile,

"It was easy."

"Chapter Twenty-four: KAWHOCUMDIA"

Samuel replied to Peace,

"yes, if I remember right, I used to fly up there. You would have had to climb, at that time, are you still reading my mind?"

He leaned toward Peace, and asked her softly,

"could we just do conversation? I really like talking to you."

Peace did not answer but started walking toward the rock. When she got to the rock she seemed more sure of herself in Samuel's presence, and turned toward him, and said,

"sure, I really like talking to you too."

She too thinks there is something magical about the love they have finally found, and are sharing so openly. Samuel followed right behind her with a curiosity, and hunger to know more about her. The longer they are together the more he wanted to know. Peace slipped behind the rock before he got there. As he turned around the edge of the rock, he saw Peace scaling the monolith with ease. She got to the top and felt a breeze blowing her hair. Samuel could not stand it anymore. He leaped to the top of the rock himself, and landed in front of Peace. Facing her within inches, he kissed her with all the passion he had. The kiss lasted some time. It excited her so much she pulled away, and then back again, then stopped. She looked again at him with the loving kind look, and said,

"we have to wait."

She knew what he was thinking, and he knew what she meant. Samuel agreed with her immediately, after he turned his head off to his left, and said, "sure. We will have to wait."

There were a couple of coughs held in, and then he was silent. Peace pointed to the place where she found the device, and said,

"here, it was here."

Samuel asked her,

"where are my mother, and father?"

Peace answered after a slight hesitation,

"they are working on another time travel project. It seems that you father thinks that you can handle this without him. I think he feels as if I am there to help you, everything will be all right. I think he might be right. I'm feeling something human here I can't quite put my finger on, maybe you can help me figure it out?"

Samuel said to Peace,

"sure, we can figure anything out together. I think I know what it is because I've thought about it too, if I'm right?"

Peace then tells Samuel,

"there is supposed to be another guy named Sam involved, I don't know much about it.

She hesitated for a few seconds, and said,

"I know you don't know anything about it."

Her kindness shown to Samuel was her trying to understand everything about him, and all that he had gone through. She still had the inner love and desire for him.

Samuel put the device around his neck. He examined it thoroughly, and pressed several buttons, each making a beeping sound as they engaged. With Peace there with him he worried about what was about to happen. Peace had figured out what he was doing, and was waiting in anticipation. They glanced at each other. Peace started to move toward the edge of the rock. Samuel grabbed her arm, and said,

"wait, wait."

The urgency in his voice was clear. Peace stopped. Samuel spoke softly to Peace, "do not move yet, stay here. As much time as the team spent here, with my mother, and father they could have built a fortress in these rocks. The movable parts would have been tricky. We had better stay in the middle just in case."

Samuel expounds a little further,

"their thinking would have been, that I would come up here, and find the device, and use it from up here. They would have made it safe up here. Hold on, it may get unstable, shaky."

As soon as Samuel spoke, the ground began to move, it began to shake, the rocks began to roll out of their places. Some were falling, and rolling down the mountain. It lasted for a minute or more. It did scare both of them. Peace grabbed Samuel's free hand, and was holding it tightly. Samuel found out she had the grip of a very strong man. He said nothing to Peace about it but she read his mind. She said nothing to Samuel about it.

Unexpectedly as if the earth were going to feed, her

jaws opened wide enough to swallow, and consume anything close. The grinding started first. It had taken the place of the rumbling rockslide. The whole area was-filled with dust, then, as quickly as it started, it was over. It had stopped. Without warning, a blanket of lights was everywhere. They were coming from underground, and filling the sky. Peace and Samuel were excited, and filled with delight. They could see the entrance to the cave with the magic door. Without another second passing by, Samuel took Peace by the hand, and said,

"shall we?"

He was talking of leaping off the rock, and flying down to the entrance. They did the count of three, and down they went to the entrance. Both were moving in the same direction into the cave. Each was trying to figure out what was inside the huge cavern. Their thoughts were intertwined and each thinking the same thing, and each looking at the other for some sign of conformation. Peace smiled, and said, "it is O.K., I like this way of communication too."

She of course meant telepathy.

"Chapter Twenty-Five: KAWHOCUMDIA"

Samuel and Peace had no doubt, once inside the cave what was hiding there. The space ship Zadator and Belsha, Samuel's father, and mother, left for him, was hiding here all along. Through the years, it had reinvented itself over, and over in sections and grew three times larger. It also had created multiple innovations to the working of itself. Her work created flawlessly.

Samuel had gone through the regeneration process that his programming enabled him to do. All parts of the brain-plug damaged repaired through the remake in perfect working order. The human part, of the brain plug is the negative that made a difference. The part of Obit's brain in that section held vital information that now would belong to Samuel. The functionality or non-functionality would only be of concern to Samuel. He would eventually be able to classify or scrub that part of his understanding in what or if it needed attention. His clarification of all of the developments, and the actual experience would be his evaluation alone. Simply put he was unaided with it, unless, he thought it was necessary to bring someone in on what he thought they, should know about it, and it was to be on a need to know basis.

"Chapter Twenty-Six: KAWHOCUMDIA"

Obit showed no signs of being capable of having the capacity for rational thought, or inference or discrimination. He was a child of brain damage they thought. He usually sat around making noises with his tongue. He also had driveled down the corners of his mouth most of the time. The elders of the tribe would make fun of him, and laugh because he was different from the rest of the children. He did not speak to anyone until he was fifteen. It was an unusual time and way he spoke.

One of the older tribesmen rushed into the camp one night on horseback. He did not see the small boy standing alone in the dark. Obit was close enough to see the child but not close enough to pull the child to safety. He knew what he had to do, and with the fear that his voice might not work, he started to tremble. He had never used his voice in any manner, never. Obit knew if he waited a second, more the boy would have no chance.

He cried out,

"Nado, you must run."

It was such a yell and furthermore the child had never heard Obit's voice, so he ran in fear for his life. In addition, just in time. Obit saw the horse running by the boy; he had barely gotten out of the way. Obit knew Nado was close to death, and dropped his head with such relief but was still having trouble breathing. No one ever knew, except the little boy, and Obit. The tribesman on the horse never saw the child nor heard Obit he was too intoxicated.

Obit stayed an outcast. He never used his voice again until one day at the age of twenty-seven, the chief called him to his hut. His daughter had told the chief this unbelievable story. Obit was the father of her unborn child. Obit knew it was a lie he was still a virgin. He thought she disliked like him because there were no girls in the tribe that liked him. Because of this fact, Obit's family would have very little to do with him. They had tried many times to give him away when he was younger. No one would have him.

His family thought Obit would never be anything to anybody, just a burden on whoever got the job of taking care of him.

The chief's daughter had made the statement that Obit would make a good father, and since he was the son of a rich tribesman, he would be the perfect husband. She thought he was someone to be the father of her unborn baby, because no one knew who the real father was. The chief had never liked Obit's father, and he thought Obit was an idiot. Obit had one thing going for him; he was not a bad looking man. He did not look like the retarded son. Yet, the older women always asked about him. Only for them to find he was not a man mentally. None of the women his age wanted a little boy for their bed. He was not falling for them anyway. He did not speak but he was not an idiot.

The chief was standing in his hut when the guards outside let Obit go in. Obit knew something was very wrong when he walked into the hut. He saw the chief's daughter standing there with the stomach of a pregnant woman. He was no longer confused about life. He did not understand but for some reason everything became perfectly clear.

The chief laughed at Obit as he walked in the door of his hut, he said,

"you think you can get my daughter with child, and walk through my door free and clear?"

The chief reached to strike Obit but got the surprise of his life when he hit the floor of the hut. Obit did not bat an eye. No one saw where the punch came from or even saw Obit throw a punch. For a moment, Obit still does not speak but he reached to help the chief get up. The chief kicked at Obit's head missing, and hitting his daughter in the stomach. The kick was a powerful blow. It knocked her to the floor, and she screamed, and then yelled,

"you killed my baby! You killed my baby!"

She was crying with such loud screams and yells the guards came rushing in. The chief told them in an authoritative loud voice,

"he did it. Take him, he did it."

The chief's daughter was on the floor of the hut moaning, and possibly dying. Obit challenged the guards and the chief, with his fist clinched out in front of his chin and face, he said in a very loud booming voice,

"let go of my arms." This scared the guards, so they let go of his arms, and backed up to where the chief was standing. The guards had spears in their hands, and were poking at Obit with a motion for him to stay back. Their fear of him was too overwhelming. They did not realize the strength he had.

Over the past ten years, Obit started to realize something was changing in him. Something he did not understand, and was having visions or dreams of another life. He dreamed of himself as a small child. He was with a father of a highly intelligent race or species of people that were not like his. They looked the same but were different. Their strength was that of super power, magic, and they could fly. All of these things came after he took his father's place in the brain plug operation, the operation for stealing other tribe's secrets. This could be the accidental discovery by Obit, which would be his redeeming feature. It came as a shock at first. The headaches finally went away.

The first appearance of Zadator made Obit jump back, and slide backwards toward the wall of his hut. This Zadator was amazement to him. Zadator spoke to Obit, and asked,

"how are you doing my son?"

It was as real as real to Obit. Zadator told Obit,

"you will be learning many more things from me

now. However, you must listen very carefully to everything I

say. You must watch what I do. I am older, and much wiser.

You must learn, and grow. Someday you will know when it

is time for you to speak up for yourself, and be a man." Obit

listened, and never forgot what Zadator said.

"Chapter Twenty-Seven: KAWHOCUMDIA"

The afternoon of Samuel's capture, they brought him

to the village of the tribesmen where it was their brain plug

transplant event. There was talk of a replacement where a

son would stand in for the tribesman chosen. Obit would be

the one chosen for the brain plug operation. The people of

the village even talked about the possibility of it helping Ob-

it. That day Obit got a part of Samuel's brain, and Samuel

got a part of Obit's brain. Obit would turn out to be the only

one of his kind. He went beyond the evolution of man; the

formulas brought him to a higher intelligence, and a higher

super strength. His brain had more possibilities than even

Zadator. The chief and the guards in the hut did not know

what kind of chain reaction they set off that day. Obit knew

he could easily overtake them. He knew he could easily have

taken their lives. Something inside him chooses to turn swift-

ly, and run. He was going to run for his life. This knowledge

and power was a force rallying inside like a horse. He felt he

was the true athlete. He ran, and his distance away was be-

coming incredible. The wooded area around the chief's camp

was thick, and almost impossible to run through but he was

doing it. His knowledge was coming into view as he ran,

more, and more. Things that were impossible he was seeing

the answer to solve any problem. Something told him to take

flight. He could not believe what he was feeling. The intui-

tiveness overwhelmed him. He took the chance, and lifted

his foot to take flight. For a second he was off the ground

and weightless. His insecurity brought him back down, and

he said,

"wait a second."

The urge to push himself up again, and gain double

what he had just lost made him soar into flight. He looked down, and then quickly back up. He knew what to do next. It was already happening. He was flying, and it was amazing. He said it aloud,

"yes! I'm flying."

As he reached above the treetops, he could see visually a written message coming into his head. This language, he was reading it. His vision changed to seeing a grid, and focusing differently than his normal vision. He could see down into the trees and across the horizon where the picture was close-up, then far away. Perfectly, he was reasoning perfectly. Now it seemed that Obit understood what was happening. He was evolving and metamorphosing into all things where dreams and response to feeling drove his changes in life. Amazingly, it was his control now. Now he had tapped into, suddenly a brand-new source of information, confidence was building. All of the things that were in his head, Zadator, the dreams, and all of the information, Obit was responding to it. While he was in flight speed began to increase, and the capability was taking him to a new level. The message read; From the Information Center, reloading for all new updates, and assistance, any maintenance necessary for your safety, and your existence. We will bring you, as they create them, all formulas they bring to our attention. You will have all of the powers of Samuel, Zadator or any other programmed individual. Think about it complete it. Obit realizes his flying had just begun. His life had just begun.

"Chapter Twenty-Eight: KAWHOCUMDIA"

The sun was slowly setting in the west, with glowing orange, and red. The sky had a mixing of paint with a multi-colored confluence to make one blend but still in the mixing stages. Other patches were like globs of sunburst, slung to the canvas from a small veil. It made a big splash in the mix of orange, and red with azure blending in the background. The sun melting in the horizon as the clock ticked away. Obit had been flying back and forth free from distraction with no one to harm or bring him down. The campsite that Samuel and Peace just left days earlier was down below. It was just waiting for Obit to discover it.

His days in the air had been the best experience in his

life. The one hundred and fifty mile radius of travel was almost too much. His exhaustion was starting to show up in messages coming in on his visual screen. He was not quite ready to let go of his airtime. He really did not want to come down. His straight through, and no stopping seemed obsessive but he could not help himself. He loved it, response to wind, and had views galore.

The overall time had been thirty-six hours, and no breaks. The warning sign kept flashing. SLEEP DEPRAVATION WARNING. START SLEEP WITHIN ONE HOUR. It repeated itself over, and over. Obit knew the warnings he could not ignore. His time had come to land, and sleep.

The information came in that was giving him the location of the original campsite of Zadator, and his party. The location made easy to find with a grid. The closer he got to the location, the grid was-placed-nicely toward him. He spotted it from the air. As he flew over the mountain, Samuel's perch was at a slight elevation above everything else. Obit looked, and saw nothing left by Samuel to trace him to this spot.

Obit found he had the power to land as softly as a kitten. He landed and went to the rock that Samuel and Peace leaped from just days before. He started to scale to the top of the rock. With his keen sense he had recently acquired, he felt someone watching him from the woods. He moved around the rock with caution. He looked around before he got his footing in the first notch of the rock. He bounced, and was up, and in with one foot. He had the other foot ready to place in the next concave notched out step for the foot. This made the climbing easy for whoever tried it. He scaled it in seconds, and was on the top. He was ready for whoever was in the woods watching. He knew now there was someone out there. He still remembered the guards lunging at him with their spears, the sharpness of their points glistening with the threat of death in them.

As he searched the area on the top of the rock, he saw

a smaller rock with a piece of paper under it. He was using his super vision that could see through solid rock. He almost jumped at it. He got to the piece of paper, and started to read; Obit we are here, inside the cave. Your needs will be met. Wait for the cave to open. Peace.

Obit understood his message but what was lurking just beyond the camp in the darkness somewhere just out of sight? Obit needed shelter; somewhere no one could see him or get to him while he slept. Then, the sound of the cave started to open, loud grinding, and scraping noises. There was the creaking of metal on metal. The noise was so loud the sound had to have carried for miles. Obit had wondered the past few days about the men from the future, and what they had done bringing technology to this time. Getting this kind of power into the wrong hands could be a lot of trouble for earth, and its inhabitants.

Now the cave had totally opened up, and the bright light was spilling out everywhere. Obit decided to listen to the message, and meet the sender or senders. He gracefully descended from the huge rock that had become a watchtower. Obit picked up a fast walk as he touched ground. The walkway led into the cave filled with light. Everything around was well lit. Silently and quickly a figure appears. She did not fly in or drop in; she just appeared out of nowhere. She was in his way to the entrance of the cave, so he stopped. He thought to himself,

"who is this? I have no fear now. There is nothing that can stop me now."

He heard the first cry, and focused in with his super vision. Then she whimpered, trying to hold back the tears. It was no use, she started to wail, and the dam broke. Obit started to understand. He looked at her with compassion. He broke his stance. It was not a fight she wanted, he was sure of that. He dropped his guard. He stooped to catch the shadow from her head. He now saw it was the chief's daughter. She looked weary which would have been from the all day on horseback. It would have taken her at least a day's ride to here from her village. Obit asked her,

"what is your name?"

The crying continued. Obit could tell she was trying to stop her tears. He took a step forward. Then, there was a rustling of the brush just off to his left. Obit stopped but did not look toward the brush where he heard the noise. He was still concerned about the chief's daughter crying; still he focused on the noise in the brush. He made another step forward, and said,

"are you from my tribe?"

She had known all along whom he was. There was never any doubt that she recognized it was Obit. However, how did he get to this place, and how is it he is changed? She had never seen lights like this before. The crying stopped. Obit asked her again,

"what is your name? I know you are the chief's daughter but I have never heard you name. What is it?"

"I'm sorry,"

she said.

He looked away for a second to the direction of the noise, then back at her. He said to her this time,

"your name is I'm sorry?

She looked stunned. She thought to herself,

"he is really stupid."

"No,"

she said,

"I'm sorry I've gotten you in trouble with my father, and the whole village. I am Lalah, the chief's daughter. I am so sorry. Please forgive me. I was being my usual selfish self. No, I did not mean that I am always a selfish person. Really, I am not. My child deserves a much better man than her father. He's a mad man, or was."

Obit hears what she said about he was, but stands silently listening anyway. She continues,

"a brute, he's crazy. He beat me all of the time."

There was a long pause, and silence filled the air. She said,

"I killed him with a knife."

Obit made a face cringing yet still silent. She wants to get it all out, and goes on,

"my father forced me to sleep with him, he's a pig. I don't care if he is, was the chief, he didn't deserve to be the chief."

Obit asked,

"where are the guards that worked for your father?"

He was thinking about grabbing the girl, and flying into the cave. Even with the use of his power, he could not close the entrance to the cave quick enough.

"Chapter Twenty-Nine: KAWHOCUMDIA"

If only Obit had a few more days of experience, he would have known his control was time related, and with that, he could have done anything he wanted. He could have started the processing of the closing of the cave before he let anyone know about his plan. He could have scanned the area of the woods where the noise was coming from, and kept Lalah busy, then moved her with his own persuasion of whatever he chose. The truth usually worked in emergencies. At this point, he was not using mind reading, and did not know what she was thinking. He was not sure if she was in with her father, trying to capture him or not. He knew if it were tribesmen working for the chief, he would have to fight, and maybe over power, and kill them. He struggled with these kinds of thoughts but they were still coming to his mind. He then started the process of reading her mind as he questioned her. He asked her,

"how did you live through your father kicking you in the stomach? Is the baby alright?"

She answered Obit still bewildered, and on the verge of tears with,

"I don't know, I thought you would tell me. I am confused about all that back there. There were so many bright lights, like these. Are you sure you don't know what or who saved me?"

Obit then looked back at the huge rock, focusing in on the top. It was like a magical place to Obit now. He thought to himself,

"she really is a lucky woman.

Now he was listening for any sound that would give him clues if there were tribesmen in the area. He magnified his hearing with sonic sensory detection; also, it was for movement detection. Anything would be picked up, even the silent mover.

A voice from behind Lalah said softly but firmly,

"you both had better come inside."

It was Samuel; he had come from inside the cave.

Obit said to Lalah,

"it's O.K., he's a friend. I will explain later. Quickly, we must go inside. It is not safe out here. Quickly, please Lalah, inside quickly."

Lalah responded to Obit with,

"thank you."

It is a response of gratitude. She spoke, as she was moving with them through the entrance,

"I'm sorry, I'm so sorry."

Obit rushed her along. He gave her quick glances, and responding to her apology said,

"O.K..."

He repeated it several more times, as Lalah told him she was sorry.

Once inside the cave Samuel took a small device out of his uniform's pocket, and pushed a button. The cave entrance began to close. He told Obit telepathically that he would start filling in the blank spaces, and that, which, is part of his confusion. Whenever needed; all of the information that he needed to eliminate that, from now on, will come and still be updated. Obit's eyes gave it away that he had some trust issues. Without a word from Obit, Samuel looked at him, and said,

"trust me."

Obit nodded, and replied,

"O.K..."

He saw a woman standing at the entrance to the ship, and before he could react, Samuel told Obit telepathically,

"this is my future bride, Peace. Peace this is Obit.

Peace was ready for the introduction, and replied to

Obit telepathically,

"nice to meet you Obit."

Obit gestured with an open hand indicating Lalah, and said telepathically,

"this is Lalah; she is not programmed with anything as we are."

He then spoke aloud,

"Lalah, this is Peace, and Samuel."

Gesturing with his other open hand, he said,

"this is Lalah, the chief's daughter, I mean used to be chief, he is now deceased."

Obit looked at the ship as he approached the ladder. His information search started with the origin of the ship. Then a listing of things it can do started automatically. Obit said,

"exist on its own, that's one, collect, and send data to individuals that are secure programmed beings, that's two, understand, and commit to protocol of the chain of command, wow, search stop."

His interest went on but he was-still-focused on La-lah as she saw his mind working. She had started to catch on that there was something going on she did not quite under-stand. Lalah called to Peace, and Samuel,

"it is nice to meet you both, I'm sure you'll all ex-plain to me what it is that I'm missing here, for I feel it is a lot, I mean I don't understand all of this. I trust Obit. Well, you understand what I mean, I'm sure, right?"

She looked at Obit, then back at Samuel, and then Peace. Obit then said,

"right."

He pointed up the ladder, and said to Lalah,

We have to go inside here, up this ladder, Peace will go first, then Samuel, and then you will go, and I will follow, O.K.?"

Peace is the first to go, and turned to Lalah and told her not to worry, that she was as sure of the men as she was of herself. Samuel stopped at the bottom of the ladder, and told Lalah to go ahead of him, he said,

"I'll be right behind Obit, its O.K., you'll see."

Lalah headed up the ladder, and Obit followed behind her. He looked back at Samuel, and said,

"thank you."

Samuel followed the three up the ladder. The reason that Obit had gotten the wrong information about the departure, which was supposed to be a few days earlier. It was a security measure taken by Samuel. He stopped them at the closet as they walked in. He told them about the uniforms, and the dressing rooms. In addition, he mentioned there were showers, and baths, and they could get comfortable.

"Whatever you would like to do is O.K. with me. I will be your Captain, and you are my guest. I think I should set a course for Belshala, and we will be underway. As a matter of fact I'll take care of that right now."

He used his telepathic power to give the ship the

command, and it began.

"Chapter Thirty: KAWHOCUMDIA"

The rain kept coming down without stop for four days. Masujue said,

"I'm so miserable I could die."

Her symptoms were the same as the flu. To her, it was impossible to get sick. She said it aloud, as if someone was there to hear her,

"I'm never sick. I have never been sick a day in my life."

Her voice crackled with every word, and then she exploded, and said,

"Oh my God, I'm sick."

She rolled over in bed bellowing like a cow in the field wanting to eat, and nothing in sight.

The rain was still coming down like Virgil's Hamlet. It became a thunder, and lightning battleground. It fiercely rattled the walls like long forgotten roofing tin, clinging to the old rafters left behind forever, and was loudly protesting inside as well. The flashes were hitting the walls, and ceiling of her bedroom like the clash of a strobe light. You might have said it was less repetitious, and thank God. Her head was about to burst any minute. Little did she know of the surprises waiting for her just ahead in her future. She had just washed the sheets on her bed, and the smell was terrific. Only she was about to repeat the washing but for a very good reason. This was to be a history-making throw up. It was the first time in her life Masujue would have to puke.

"Oh my God, Urhuhaaak…"

It made the conventional splatter sound as it went all over the bed, all over the floor, and was a sickening site to look at for anyone. Now, she had to look at it. As she thought of the problem to clean it up it was ten minutes of washing her face. The rinsing her mouth out with mouthwash became easy because it kept her from doing that nasty thing again. Once she almost slipped back into regression when she said,

"I've got to call mother."

Faith was Masujue's mother, and Masujue called her all the time for no reason at all. She got her on the line, and said,

"Mother, I'm telling you I don't want to go back in that bedroom. It is awful. I have never seen anything like it in my entire life. What am I going to do?"

Faith told her,

"call somebody from a cleaning service. Call a maid service."

Masujue said to her mother,

"mother its O.K., I'll go back, and I'll clean it up, just

not right now."

The hesitation made it obvious she was sick. Masujue was still on the couch, and said,

"it won't be bad when I feel better. I am just afraid that if I try to do it now, I will do it again. You know, puke."

Faith asked,

"how many days have you been off from work now?"

"Mother just four!"

"And you are just now throwing up?"

"Yes mother."

Faith told Masujue,

"don't take anything, I'll be right there. I'll be on a plane, and I'll be right there."

"No!"

She was almost yelling it into the phone. Of course, at this point Masujue's yell was the quite squeak of a sub-dued church mouse.

"I'll be alright. Stop worrying. Good bye mother."

Faith is silent, then says,

"O.K...

She hung up the phone knowing her daughter was not going to care about the amenities at this point.

Masujue was on the couch looking out the window at the storm. She did not remember the rainy days of summer like this. She thought to herself,

"this is really beautiful. I wish I were not so miserable. I could really enjoy this." Masujue stretched her legs out just to get the aches out. She let out a breath of air between her lips. Her cheeks puffed out. She closed her eyes, and felt the sleep as it started to take over.

"I wish I could sleep, if only for a little while. Maybe, maybe I can. I'll try while I'm snuggled on the couch."

She sighed.

She was miserable but managed to get to sleep anyway.

Masujue woke, and the rains were still pouring down.

She got up, and went into the kitchen. She was feeling the nausea that being sick brought. Her hair was a mess. Her lip had splits that were hurting. She was feeling tightness in her chest, and her nose was starting to drain. She took some tissue, and blew her nose. Then she walked over to the refrigerator, and took out the orange juice bottle. She took a half of a nausea pill she carried for carsickness, swallowed it down with the orange juice. She held her head down with her arms draped across the island sink. She thought if she did this, it would help keep her from throwing up. She was down with her head between her arms, aching, trying to get up. She had no strength at all. Masujue said,

"It's going to be a long day.

This was to herself aloud in her gravel voice.

"Now is the time to leave the room, if your stomach is queasy, or you're feeling sick yourself."

Masujue said it as if there were someone in the kitchen with her but as far as she knew she was alone, alone, and suffering.

She pulled herself up. She went to the bathroom where she kept the cold medications. She looked at the day stuff, and figured this was what she was going to do.

"I'll take this, and hope that I don't die tomorrow, I hope I die today."

She laughed at herself at having the ability to-still-have a sense of humor with this rotten stuff going on in her.

She headed back to the kitchen, and found a man standing there looking at her as though he understood her pain. She screamed at him,

"what in the?"

She started to use the word hell, and stopped before it was out of her mouth. She finished,

"are you doing in my kitchen?"

She is then panic stricken, and turned and ran. She was sick but this could mean the difference between life, and death. She ran up the stairs, and tried to get to her gun, the gun she hated to buy. The one she had hated to carry in her purse. Now, it was so far away. She was crying when she got to the upstairs bedroom. The gun was in her purse. Then, the voice relaying the message came in her head,

"before you kill me, let me explain who I am, and what it is I'm doing here."

She grabbed the gun out of her purse, and pulled the lever back to cock the thirty-eight special. Her father had told her to get it. It was the best gun you could buy for a gun to carry. He helped her with the purchase, and the license.

Then without warning, the man appeared again in her hallway. In addition, the voice came in her head again,

"I'm sorry you have to go through this, my name is Zadator, and this is about your friend Sam. This is an emergency or I would not be here doing this. You must believe me. Sam needs you as soon as you can possibly get to his location. And by the way, I can fix that nasty infection you have."

This was too much for Masujue to handle, and she screamed,

"I'll shoot."

Zadator told her,

"no you won't I've taken the bullets out of the gun. In addition, I am not going to tell you I am taking a chance doing this, because I am not. I know how scary this is for you, and I understand but you will be asleep in a few seconds, and it will be because of the sedation I am giving you.

She looked at Zadator in the hallway, and said

"what?"

She was asleep almost immediately, and crumpled to the floor. Her gun was still in her hands where she was holding it ready to fire.

"Chapter Thirty-One: KAWHOCUMDIA"

As Zadator took the gun from her hand, he said,

"good girl."

He used his magic power, and lifted her from the

floor to the bed, and without even touching her. With Zata-

tor's power, he magically lifted her up and softly put her

down on the bed. Zadator then started to summon his team of

six men, and women of his species, the Zorvirax. They went

to work on Masujue as soon as they arrived. In a matter of

minutes, they had her back where she was in perfect health.

All of her symptoms were gone when she awoke. Zadator

sent the team back to the ship, cloaked, and hovering above

the building Masujue lived in. Zadator started the mind connection with Masujue as soon as the team was gone. Masujue got the information telepathically, and started understanding what Zadator had been trying to tell her. He explained again that Sam was asking for her, and was on assignment, which was what he needed now. Zadator had told her about the ship Sam was on, and where it was traveling to. She was amazed but willing to go to Sam. She was sure she wanted to get to know him better, if he wanted to contact her. She said,

"I'm sorry I left with my ex-boyfriend, this was where I started getting the flu symptoms."

Zadator telepathically told her,

"I'm here to change the future. Yours does not look to promising. Your ex-boyfriend was going to kill you. I have fixed it. I will fill you in later.

When Masujue woke, she started to think,

"why is this happening to me? She knew it must be real. I guess it will be O.K..."

Suddenly, she noticed something, and wondered why the rain had stopped. It had been going on for days. Moreover, the forecast was for at least another week.

"Strange."

"I'm going to pray for Sam right now."

Zadator was waiting as Masujue woke up. He told her they must hurry. She went to the closet to get some clothes out to pack.

"That won't be necessary, there are uniforms in the ship, and you will become part of the crew. Take only the things that will secure your home here and maybe a purse to carry your things, keys, etc."

Masujue grabbed her purse, and put in her keys, and toothbrush. She searched for her favorite toothpaste, which she had just started using. She found it in the far drawer in the bathroom.

She said to Zadator,

"this is really good stuff. I don't want to stop using

this ever."

He just replied,

"very good."

Zadator saw she was ready but asked her anyway,

"are you ready?"

Masujue replied,

"I'm as ready as I'll ever be. In fact, I feel great.
What did you do?"

Zadator just said,

"we healed you."

They both headed out the door of her apartment, and
to the roof where the ship was waiting.

Zadator pointed to just above the ladder, which
seemed to be leaning on the small building sitting on top of
the stairwell but the ladder was coming down from the ship.

Masujue said,

"neat, I trust you now, especially about my ex.

Zadator said to her,

"ladies first.

He made a hand motion to the ladder. Masujue started up the ladder. She made her way to the top. She looked in the ship; she could see the aliens looked as human as she did.

She thought to herself,

"they all look so nice."

She went through the entrance where the ladder turned into a stair that had a balustrade leading to the top. It was made of some type of material that was unfamiliar to Masujue. As Zadator reached the top, she asked,

"what is this made of?"

Zadator looked across the floor at the team working where they are busy with the ship, he said,

"it has been done since we landed; I think the ship created it from something here on earth called bamboo which is a giant tropical grass with hollow woody stems. Its origin is Malay or Malay bamboo. Nice isn't it?"

She asked, blurting it out,

"why did it stop raining?"

Zadator thought this was a cute question coming from this woman of Sam's. He thought to himself that he liked Masujue. Zadator paused,

"the weather, it's unpredictable."

Masujue responded,

"O.K., I thought maybe you had something to do with it.

Zadator replied,

"no, I take credit where credit is due, sometimes. But it would have been a nice thing to do."

Masujue waited for Zadator to move, and then he said to Masujue,

"you can clean up, and rest or join me at the helm. I will show you where you sleep, and you can rest. Whatever you think you need to do first. We will have a discussion later about what we are doing, and what you would like to do. You can either join us or simply observe. The choice will be yours.

Do not be afraid to ask me any questions that you would like to ask. Now, I will be at the helm if you need me for anything. I am Sam's guide, in another since but I will be your guide on the ship. You are my guest, and I will see that your needs are met."

Zadator moved away, and headed to the helm. The one sitting at the helm moved out when Zadator arrived, and Zadator took his place. They started to converse as he sat down. They all seem to be busy as bees.

Masujue sighed, and walked toward the dressing room.

"Chapter Thirty-Two: KAWHOCUMDIA"

When the ship landed at Belshala the entry had a cloud hanging over it, and visibility was nearly nil. The clouds in the higher elevations were also as thick as pea soup. Jimmy and Danny had been anxious upon arriving, and were watching the monitors and portals closely. What they saw was the most unbelievable sight. They could never have imagined what was coming into their view. Had it not been for their programming, they would never have been able to understand what they saw.

The sky flowed over with the advancements of billions of years. There were inconceivable, incomprehensible, human looking beings that were actually airborne. They were not with air machines of a type; just on their own in flight, in the air, and flying with the greatest of ease. They were not the geniuses of the programming like Zadator and his team, or any of the others that had programming for thousands of years but the regular people, the species of this planet. The explanation was they leaked the formula on purpose because of the rumors and sightings of these flying Zorvirax super powered beings. Zadator and some of his followers thought it was as an advancement of the species, to be able to fly, an advancement of all time. The majority of the species did not realize some of their people had already been around inventing other super powers for much longer than anyone in their time could ever have believed.

Jimmy and Danny were spell bound. They watched until they were staring. Then they watched some more. No one was coming close to the ship as it entered in near the fly zone of the Zorvirax. The ship seemed to be pulling away from the crowd of people in the sky. They had their own air space, and the craft had its fly zone. The ship was unseen by anyone because it was cloaked.

The city was not a city, as we know it. Its disguise was of a covert nature. Concealment of buildings and places of gatherings would have been hard to spot with just the naked eye. Maybe there were hidden windows or some way they could cloak everything.

Sam was beginning to wake, and Jimmy was the one to bring up mention of his head injury. He asked as Danny looked on, and he began,

"how is the analysis of the head injury Captain? We noticed your sleep as being of solid undisturbed rhythm. I hope you do not mind me asking. We were just concerned about it."

Sam stood up, and stretched. Before he was through with it, he started talking by saying,

"you young men don't need as much recoup time as

us older men but thanks for your concern, I'm doing quite well. I am fine. I'm really better than that I'm great."

Jimmy looked at Danny with a glance looking away at what the ship was doing. He pointed out to Sam what the people of Belshala were doing, and asked him,

"what do you think of this?"

He made a gesture of beckoning to him, wanting Sam to come to the spot with Jimmy and Danny. He walked over to their position, and said,

"yea, I experienced something like this at the fuel, and security station, it was something else."

They had gotten a front row seat, and were not going to miss a single movement these characters were making.

They saw the pad, which was marked on the grid of their screen. The screen was in a shade of orange, which was an alert color. Danny was the one to make note of it when he said,

"cool, that's cool. I am O.K. with it. We can handle

it. Right sirs?"

Jimmy responded with the nod of his head, and said,

"right."

Sam caught touchdown as the light went on and said,

"touchdown landing is complete."

Touchdown was never felt. It is just too smooth.

Jimmy with his enthusiasm almost ran down the ladder. He wanted to explore the whole planet from top to bottom. Danny was right behind him. He was always a little more cautious and slower even before his programming. He said to Jimmy,

"man, you'd better be careful of what you're running toward."

Danny then thought of what he himself was running from. He said it to himself with the idea that Jimmy would listen, and understand,

"she's a crazy old lady, my grandmother; you know I love her but, _____."

He paused, then said,

"she's the only mama I've ever known_____."

He paused again,

"I wonder what my real mama would think about me now. Life is sure strange."

He made a leap past the last three rungs on the ladder. He hit the ground running. Sam flew to the ground without even touching the ladder, and was right behind Danny. Jimmy turned and called out,

"wait, I was going to lead off."

He took off in a fast pace to catch up. The other two were already ahead in good speed. Jimmy saw a small vehicle parked a hundred yards away. He turned in its direction in a faster sprint. Sam and Danny saw what Jimmy was up to, and stopped. They yelled out to Jimmy,

"drive back over here, since you're going for it."

Danny was unarmed but in uniform. His voice sounded that of a thirty-five or forty-year-old man. He was not the size of a grown man. Naturally, his voice threw the listener off. When anyone saw the frame of the teen-aged boy, it was eerie. However, he fit perfectly into his uniform, and his appearance was that of a young uniformed military man.

"Chapter Thirty-Three: KAWHOCUMDIA"

Jimmy picked up what he thought was the device to keep the ship in touch with any party or parties off the ship. He was unfamiliar with what he picked up. The device he was looking for was in the other zipper pocket. As soon as he got to the vehicle, he realized what he had done. His search mode went into effect immediately trying to find out what he had put in his pocket. He found it in the exchequer of information that seemed to be stored somewhere in his mind. The formulas are a part of the retrieval process. They were different from this type of information. The speed that things get to mind with this system of formulas was an amazing event.

Jimmy said to himself aloud,

"this whole thing is more than amazing."

Moreover, the weapon in question could destroy a huge compound half the size of a city, a city the size of Belshala.

"That's all I needed."

He headed the vehicle in the direction back to pick up Danny, and the Captain. Jimmy knew Zadator was not at home yet but Sam being here meant that Zadator would be on his way. On the other hand, maybe he would just make an appearance telepathically. Jimmy's admiration for all of the participants in the programming was overwhelmingly on the positive side. His newly found friend, the personality of their ship, had brought to the forefront a newly found insight and appreciation for what their mission was. Jimmy saw a light coming from above, and windows that let that light in. Obviously, they were to conceal, just like the ones coming into the city.

Jimmy picked up Sam, and Danny. Danny made the remark that neither Jimmy nor Sam had ever heard used before,

"sweet. We can have some fun in this baby."

Jimmy said to Danny,

"we will go for a short spin, just to get a picture of the size of this place."

Jimmy turned the vehicle around, and headed in the direction of the house. It seemed to be another four hundred yards past the hanger. There was a huge doorway separating the tunnel from the hanger. There are windows in the tunnel just like the ones in the hanger. The lighting is perfect. It is like fluorescence yet better. Lighted extremely well, everything is extremely well on the lighting.

Jimmy got to the hanger's exit, and noticed a closed office space. There were no lights inside, and no one was there to check them in. All three notice the temperature was perfect. Jimmy said, "it must be seventy-two or three in here, temp's great."

From out of nowhere a voice said,

"enter, areas cleared."

It was an automated voice recorded with clearance warnings. The cameras were a part of the security, and connected to a voice almost sounding incapable of having any value of security at all.

Jimmy accelerated the vehicle to a normal speed. The tunnel ride was short but sweet. It only took a few minutes to go the four hundred yards. There was no dust in the air or any visible sign of dust anywhere in the tunnel. Jimmy said to himself under his breath,

"this is very pristine, cleaner than my room after my mom cleaned up."

The tunnel had an exit at the end. From the outside, it had an entrance carved out of the side of a mountain. As soon as they exited, the door closed behind them, and disappeared without a trace. The unusual event did not concern the three at all. Their programming always gave them enough information. Jimmy said to Sam, and Danny,

"security measures taken by the team with Zadator."

Jimmy looked at Danny, and made the statement,

"some vacation, huh?"

Danny replied right back,

"right."

Danny speaks up again,

"second Timothy 4:5.

Jimmy handled it by saying,

"you use that one a lot do you?"

Danny then asked Jimmy,

"can you find the door to the house?"

Jimmy pulled the vehicle closer. The house was no longer fully in view, only part of it was still visible. Danny said it a little quieter than he generally spoke,

"and there are optical illusions everywhere."

Danny then asked,

"what happened to the rest of the house? It was here a minute ago."

Jimmy hesitated a second or two, and said,

"this must be part of the cloaking they do, it unsettles people."

His ambiguity noticed. In their world of certainty, it brought their Americana unity in focus. Their possessing the power did not make them forget what they have back at home. Danny stated,

"one for all, and all for one. I read The Three Musketeers."

Jimmy looked at Danny and Sam with a half-smile, Sam smiled, and shook his head thinking the three of them were a lot alike.

Danny noticed the large parking lot out in front of the house. There was not a front door. It seemed odd but this was not the U.S. 1960.

Jimmy turned to Danny, and Sam, and said,

"let's try out back."

Sam said,

"go for it."

Jimmy sped around to what he thought should be the back door, and that was no good either. He looked at Sam, and Danny asking,

"any suggestions?"

Jimmy looked at Danny first. Danny asked Jimmy,

"can you fly?"

"Chapter Thirty-Four: KAWHOCUMDIA"

The thing with Jimmy, and Danny now was the change in maturity, each being his own man made a combination of wise decisions, and laughable situation. Jimmy almost wisecracking back at both Danny, and the Captain said,

"well of course."

Danny then turned, and said to Jimmy,

"why don't you try flying up to the roof then? Maybe everybody here can fly, and it is up there, you know, the door.

Jimmy agreed.

"It is possible, it could be up there."

Sam said to both,

"just one of you go, the other one stay here, and guard the vehicle, I'll have a look around down here.

Jimmy said,

"you're right, I'll go.

Jimmy didn't know that Danny was wanting to go all along, he sat, and pondered about what he was about to do. Giving it some thought might keep him from making a mistake. Not a second before Sam started to tell him to get going he made the move, to get out of the vehicle. As he stepped out he looked once at Danny, and Sam, leaped into the air, and was in flight. While in flight, he made a surveillance trip around the top of the house. There were windows but he felt like he was window peeking. He knew that he had the job, and ignored his feelings to turn away, and he continued his surveillance.

Jimmy connected with the Captain and Danny at the same time, telepathically, he said, "there's no one at the windows, and there is no door up here. So, what do we have left?"

Immediately, Sam said back to them both,

"we had better get back to the ship, unless you've found something Jimmy?"

Jimmy replied,

"no sir, nothing here."

Jimmy started back down to the vehicle where Danny stood guard. He was rounding the front when just out of curiosity he used his super power to look through the building, and to get a glimpse at the vehicle and Danny. First, he saw the Captain moving toward Danny, and then he saw the group of men in trench coats, sneaking around behind Sam. He whispered to the both of them telepathically,

"sneak attack six o'clock, five maybe six men trench coats possibly armed."

It was too late; they already had their weapons drawn before Samuel could get a visual on them. The Captain,

Danny, and Jimmy had already had a confrontation with the trench coat men. Sam called out to Jimmy to stay up above them, and not to attack. Danny confirmed Sam's order with,

"stay put man."

Jimmy said telepathically as he hovered,

"aye sirs."

Sam gave the command to Danny,

"armor insulate with cocoon, and stand defensive guard, don't attack."

As Sam finished his sentence, he spun three revolutions, upon completion, doing four back flips midair, and landed behind the trench coat men. He said when he landed,

"gentlemen, I believe you were looking for me."

The six men spun around hitting each other with their weapons. As they made it around to look toward where the sound came from, Sam forced at them a blast of air, knocking them to the ground on their backs. Sam reached up with his hand making a swift swishing noise, and created a cocoon for sleep. The six men could not move or keep from falling asleep instantly. Sam said to the two young men watching,

"that ought to keep them busy a while. Let's get back to the ship."

Jimmy flew down to land by Danny and they were waiting for the Captain; Sam made one leap from where he stood behind the six men, and landed in front of Danny, and Jimmy. The three jumped into the vehicle, and sped away back to the entrance of the tunnel. Danny was still seeing what just happened visually in his head, and said,

"good God, what was that about?"

Sam immediately spoke up, and said,

"I'm not sure but I think they are still after me. From all of the information that I have, they cannot really hurt me in the sense of do-me-in. It's still a safe bet where I come from, to beware."

He looked at Jimmy, and Danny, and that was the

end of it.

They got to the tunnel, the huge door was open, the house had returned to its regular size. All of it had reappeared. There was still no one around in sight. Jimmy stood up in the vehicle, and looked back, and said,

"once, and for all, I'm going to see if there is anything in that house that we need to know about."

After he scanned the whole area with all sensors on, he said to Sam,

"Captain, I think we had better hurry as quickly as we can, and get back to the ship."

Sam told Danny,

"step on it."

Danny responded,

"yes sir."

The Captain called out, ship, get ready for take-off, raise her up, get the door opened ready for escape. All three heard the ship reply, "aye sir, ready, and waiting, doors opened. As soon as you're safe inside, we're out of here."

Jimmy asked the Captain,

"are we going to stop it for Zadator?

Sam said,

"no, not now, it's too late. We only have a few minutes, five to be exact. We will be gone when it goes secure. I checked."

The ship's door was wide open but no ladder down. All three jumped simultaneously as the vehicle stopped, first Sam, then Jimmy, then Danny went inside, and the door shut behind them. They were safe. Danny and Jimmy rushed to the helm while Sam stood back, and said,

"go get her men."

Each seeking comfort from the other said in unison,

"we're moving up."

Sam called out,

"let's go, let's go, let's go."

The seconds ticked by, and Jimmy asked,

"what about the men in the cocoon, they're trapped?"

Sam said it telepathically,

"watch, and you'll see them coming through the door right about now, still in the cocoon, yep, there they are. Now to the holding cell, and I've even let them sleep through the whole thing."

Sam gently sat them down on the cell's floor, still in the cocoon. The door slammed shut, tight. He said,

"you guys hang on; we're in for a rough ride out of here.

Jimmy and Danny said,

"no problem sir."

The monitor showed the explosion as it went off. It got bigger as if it were following the ship.

Danny asked,

"how much explosive was in that baby?"

Jimmy looked at Dan, and said,

"too much?"

The ship started to shake, and vibrate from the force of the explosion. The ships warnings were silent. She was moving the shields in the rear to flexible, the setting to keep the force from destroying it on impact. She called out,

"Captain, shields are in place."

Sam quietly said,

"very good."

He then asked everyone,

"are we all strapped in?"

Danny felt the air squeeze out between his lips, and his cheeks puffed out just a little.

"Chapter Thirty-Five: KAWHOCUMDIA"

We found ourselves in a cocktail lounge much later than the time of these events. These pages contain what we found. In addition, this is how it went according to the information we gathered. The owner of the lounge said,

"wait a minute, you mean, you are one of them?"

The conversation had only been going for a few minutes before the brother of the server acted like he just realized, or so he said who Don was. Already knowing something was up, Don replied,

"well, yes."

It was with a slight smile to show whoever, mainly

this guy Baxter, that Don still had it as far as being an enter-
tainer, and still eating it up with his public. Besides, he had a
drink in his hand, and that was license to thrill. Heck, anybody knows that. The brother went on,

"you mean to tell me you are one of the Tre'gics?"

Don answered the brother again,

"never heard of um, what the-hey man, I told you
yes."

Again, he came back at Don with more pushing him
close to insult,

"you're old enough to be my grandfather."

Don replied with an easy out,

"yea, that's right."

"Ah, how did you, how did you stay as young looking as you have? I mean, if you don't mind me asking?"

Since Don had made it this far, he was pretty sure he
wasn't going to throw up, so he said,

"no, I don't mind. What I do mind is you looking at

me like you are fixing to eat 'Mrs. what's her name's choco-late cream pie'. Now, would you calm down? I'll buy you a drink if you think that'll help?"

The brother of the cocktail server just stared with no sign of him comprehending at all.

"That's a question. Sir, are we alright here?"

Don was amused, and a bit ticked off at the same time. The brother came back to making sense, and said,

"I'm sorry."

Don quickly came back,

"it's O.K., just calm down.

The young brother tried to patch it up with,

"O.K., I didn't realize. It is just that I am going out of my mind trying to find you. I mean, they said you were dead."

Don's stone poker face now becomes unbelievably unconcerned with just a hint of do not give a big hoot. Then, with all the suddenness of a car crash he very politely said, "wait, wait, wait a minute. Who said I was dead?"

Everybody knows that "a whole lot of people," is as ambiguous as "they," and, yes that's what he said, except he started his sentence with,

"Ah, a whole lot of people. There was something in the paper just the other day about you being on a, a Chinese Junk in Hong Kong, and three men slitting your throat. I mean it was horrible. I had never even met you, and I nearly cried. Don't look at me that way; I'm not a cold person."

"I'm glad to hear that.

What kind of person are you? And, what are you doing in a place like this?"

Don's show pony started to turn into something different now, and wanted his diamond back, so this is what he offered up,

"What do you mean a place like this? I own this place. I've had it for a year now."

Then all of a sudden he turned into the girly man

again, his eyes opened very wide, and his lips did this disappearing act. He squeaked out the short speedy line of,

"am I in trouble?

It made Don think he was not the moneyman he had just tried to be but Don replied anyway,

"well, don't look now but isn't this the place I heard had a shooting two weeks ago?"

Don trying very hard not to say anymore or use the word dive, stopped dead in his conversation, and his talkative new friend said,

"yes, but look that was the first shooting since I've been the owner here.

Don couldn't help himself, and asked,

"have they got the guy in jail?"

The cocktail server's brother replied,

"I sure hope so."

The conversation had dwindled down now, to pass me the saltshaker would you? In addition, Don almost had to drag that out of himself, and then he mysteriously said,

"I've got to go to the little boy's room."

As Don was moving toward the men's room, he was trying to keep from thinking,

"I just don't know what to tell the guy. I am not interested in playing a gig in this place anytime. In addition, I know he is not looking for my story. That is just not his thing. I really don't want to know what this guy is up to, nothing to be said and nothing more, period."

As Don made it to the men's room, what he found in there would have been anybody's nightmare. No easy way to say it but a corpse, or it was what he thought at first. Now his ditch was a bundle-up. Now, his ditch was not supposed to meet him in the men's room, and this was going to take him longer to get back to the table. Getting rid of the annoying person that owned the place was not going to be easy. To put this mildly, Don could not stand the person. The expletive was not audible but it still rang loudly in his brain, loud, and clear. Enough said about that.

Earlier Don heard Baxter say when he was talking to the woman bartender that he was talking about hiring this person that was a draw in other clubs around town. In addition, he said to her they had standing room only within minutes of opening. Then he even pointed out that he thought that it was the person at their number three table. Don said, that the owner could not remember his name, and asked the woman,

"what's his name? I can't remember, what's his name?"

The server said,

"Don, its Don H, E, N,"

She tried to spell it out but could not finish, and said,

"oh crap, I always get him, and Don Henley's names mixed up. Now I can't remember the last part of his name, oh shoot."

The woman server had not worked this club except

for a few days, and really did not know much about rock entertainers but her memory of country singers was all about Don Williams. Baxter told her,

"forget it. He's not that good anyway."

Don said to himself,

"I can't leave this man lying here on the floor like this. I do not think he is alive, and there is so much blood. Wait. What is this? He is still breathing. Good God almighty."

"Chapter Thirty-Six: KAWHOCUMDIA"

Don ran out of the door, and headed straight back to the table where he left the club owner. He was not there, and Don said it to himself walking up to the table,

"oh crap!

He remembered hearing it come out of his mouth but later said it did not.

On his way back but before he got to his table, a woman passed him in the hallway as he was leaving the men's room, and she asked,

"what is the matter sir? Can I help you?"

Don knew how he must have looked to the woman,

and automatically stopped, he said,

"yes ma'am."

Just as calmly as he had ever been on or off stage, he kept his cool. He asked,

"would you call the police? There is an almost dead-guy in the men's room. And, tell them to send an ambulance now, please."

The woman suddenly got it that this was an emergency, and let out an,

"oh my God, of course!"

Don still kept his composure, and asked,

"where did your boss go?"

Don was almost frantic, he began to shake, and tremble inside. She yelled back at him as she headed back toward to the front bar,

"he's not my boss, he's my brother.

The woman whom Don did not recognize turned out to be the woman bartender. She had ditched her apron, and tray she always carried, and was going to the women's room

herself. He was relentless about telling me she nearly made

him gag. He had thought about asking her out.

Don called out to all of the people in the room,

"is there a Doctor in the house?"

There were a lot of them turned to look but no one

said a word. He said it was as if he was performing there.

When he told me about it he mentioned that it was like tell-

ing a joke that bombed, he finished with,

"you could have heard a pen drop."

The server was running to the phone that was behind

the bar. She was fast on her feet. Don was feeling like dead

wood while she made the call. He knew he would have to tell

the police what he saw when he walked into the men's room.

He sat down, and finished his drink, Scotch, with a touch of

water to bring out the flavor of the Scotch. All of the experts

say that is the way to drink it. He said it was his favorite

drink. His hands were shaking; he was like a nervous girl. I do not remember Don ever being that nervous about much of anything.

He had not had a drink since the divorce but he knew it was time for him to let go, in addition, relax. Don had started the policy to quit drinking while performing. Eventually, he would have a drink though, and usually get a sniff from the crowd, and it would get out of hand. As if it were anybody's business as long as he did the show with professionalism.

Some person would come up as if to ask him for a request and it was not a request he had in mind. He would tell him to turn it down just to see if he could tick Don off. If he had a bit too much to drink, he would crank up the guitar as loud as he could possibly stand it. Moreover, it stunk, and his show was blown. He always would profess not to drink, and drive. We are not to judge.

Don knew the police were excited as they came rushing through the door. They went straight to the server and she pointed him out. He stood up hoping they were not suspicious of him. They always had that look; everybody is a suspect at a crime scene. When they headed toward him, he said heading toward them,

"he's in the men's room."

They were automatically on their radio, back to whomever it was they talked to about backup. Don did not want to use his super vision but could not stand the temptation. There were more cars full of police officers on their way.

Heading toward the men's room, he told the two officers he was with,

"he's alive, or he was when I left him."

They looked at Don, and were saying something garbled that could not be understood for the noise on the radio. When the female officer looked at him, and smiled, he was almost shocked into an endearment thinking she must like him but then, she asked him, "have you been drinking sir?"

He responded very soberly,

"yes, one Scotch and water, my limit."

They kept walking toward the men's room. The male officer got to the door first. He put up his hand with his fingers touching the door, and his right foot with the toe of his shoe lightly pushing with his fingers. Don could tell he was in superior strength mode, and knew what he was doing; he was just that type for a cop. Don knew he was going to do it before he did it, he told the female officer with a quite deliberate voice,

"Cat, call backup out front and tell them not to come in here without one of us calling first. If anything happens, let me put it this way, do not call out for a while."

She did not understand his reasoning but had always trusted him; she ran it back sharply, and quietly,

"you got it."

He eased the door open, and peeked in. He had his

weapon, and part of his arm through the opening of the door. He also had the position where no one else could see in but looked back at Don, and his partner. What he said next was the biggest shocker Don had ever had in his life. Surely, he was kidding but Don did not know. It was as if he thought Don would go through all of this trouble to pull a silly stunt. The cop looked at Don with this look, as if he didn't believe him, and said,

"tough break, you know Cat I think this guy wants a date with you."

She gave him an empty sinking look of distain, now she was upset. Don did not know if it was he or the cop.

Then the male police officer said,

"there is nobody, I mean anybody."

He pushed open the door with his fingers. The wall that was extending out had a small section hidden but mirrors were making it visible behind the wall, except for the floor. As they entered into the men's room, Don heard three shots fired, and he was down on the floor. The person he had seen earlier with blood all over him was in a sitting position with a small revolver in his hand, still smoking. This was not exactly what Don was hoping for when they walked in. However, there the gunman was just waiting for someone to happen through the door, or maybe, he was waiting for the person who did this to him.

The man stood up, which seemed to be very difficult for him to do at this point. He made it to his feet. It looked to Don like the male officer was dead, and the female police officer was almost but still breathing. It did not look like to Don the man with the gun could see very well, and he had lost a lot of blood. Don was wrong thinking the man was nearly dead; The man looked at Don, and said,

"I think I'm going to die."

There was a long silence, and Don waited to speak. The man said to Don again,

"I think I'm going to die, and I know what you know

about the people of Belshala, and Veltrax Eta.

There was another pause of silence. Don became uneasy by what the gunman said, he wanted to get up, and take the gun away from him, and hit him with it or something. He did not do that. He said,

"what did you say?"

The man then said,

"can you help me?"

Don was still shocked that the man knew anything about him, here he was bleeding badly somewhere on his body, and did not know where exactly. He said to the man,

"put the gun down."

He said it as sweetly as he could in his nice-man-daddy's voice. They both then heard the female officer trying to revive herself, breath out, and groan. Don told him,

"I'll help you.

Why did you shoot us?"

The man still standing very limply said,

"because, I thought you were with the ones who tried to kill me. If you do not help me soon, I will be dead anyway. Please, tell me, what did I do to them? The officers before looked different, and there were men in trench coats, and hats. I thought they were all police officers, I trusted them. Then they tried to kill me. Why did they do that?"

Don was frantically trying to understand, and to get the man to put the gun down, he said compassionately as possible,

"I don't know. Come here but first put the gun down. What's your name?"

He saw that Don was reaching out, and said,

"I'm putting down the gun, and my name is Monday, O.K.? I am right next to you. Can you see me? You look like you are hurt bad. You are going to be alright aren't you?"

Don answered,

"yes, I think so.

Sit down Monday. Come on, this floor is clean, it's

almost brand new."

Don looked bad but actually was in good shape. He always looked somewhat bad. He said he was just lucky that way. He had been concentrating on the wound, and it had been steadily healing. After his self-analysis, he realized he had suffered a gunshot wound to his diaphragm, and liver. He had to bring the bleeding quickly to a halt. He started a process that fed the bullet entry, and torn tissue of the diaphragm, and liver with a chemical created by a formula. It elevated the heart rate, and accelerated the healing process. This is a process thousands of times faster than normal. It is tetibreaicula.

The man sat down near Don. He told him,

"unless this is done right, you could die. Did you know that?"

The shooter said,

"yes."

"Chapter Thirty-Seven: KAWHOCUMDIA"

Don started not to say anything but said to the shooter,

"how did you know?"

The shooter felt safe with just those few words from
Don, he said,

"I've talked with several Shamans. They each
claimed to have special power to heal. They said it was from
the travelers that are from far off places in the sky.

Don recognized the truth when he heard it, and believed the shooter. He spoke again to the dying man,

"when we're done, you have to promise to take me to

these people, so that I can meet them. We must talk."

The shooter answered,

"we will do it."

Don asked,

"where are you wounded?"

"I think it's near my throat, and in my chest. Several knife entries, six I think. I'm not sure."

Don told him,

"take my hand, and place it on the wounded area that hurts the most."

The shooter told Don after a few seconds of placing the hand of the healer on his wound,

"O.K., it's done, now what?"

Don gently told the wounded man,

"that's it; just give me a second or two."

Don's long drawn face seemed to have the answers to all of history's mysteries. The shooter could not believe he had shot the only man in his world that could save him. In addition, possibly pass on the powers of the Universe.

Don asked,

"how is it feeling?"

The injured man was coming out of shock, confused about his state, and said,

"I don't know. I am not feeling anything now. It was hurting like a really bad injury a minute ago."

Don told the shooter with fervor,

"do not wait on it. Expect it to be finished, and it will heal faster. Your mind will not play tricks on you anymore. You will become one with us, and for as long as you live, you will be a healer, and a power keeper.

The formulas will start coming to you within minutes from now. It will be a process while you are awake, and while you sleep. Try, and get some good rest. It will do you good.

I think the ambulance is here, and the paramedics are coming down the hall. Do not worry about the police officers or me we will be all right.

You must go. I have opened a place in the wall. Slipping through will be easy for you. You will see. Just put your foot through first, and then step on through with the rest of your body. It goes into a hallway that leads to an exit door. There is no one there to see you.

Now, go. I will find you later. Go."

Don raised his voice slightly to emphasize his sincerity, and the shooter slipped through the crack in the wall.

Don said to himself but said it aloud,

"if I had shantung, we could have covered my hand, and the wound, and had a real Chinese shake out.

I wonder what the rest of the people are doing right now. It would be funny if they were sending me an invitation to, an old sixty's bash. Yeah, right now at this very moment, an old sixty's rock festival. What an event that would be."

He reached out to where the officers were lying on the floor. They were both facing up. He could not reach what he wanted. He said to himself,

"no, I think I'll stand up now."

He got up, then knelt down beside the blonde female officer, and touched her temple. She opened her eyes, and asked,

"what happened?"

Don spoke calmly to her,

"you were shot, just lay still, the paramedics are coming now."

She barely could speak but said,

"O.K., we'll be O.K..."

Don stood up, and took a step over the blonde officer, and the male officer was not breathing. Don touched his neck on the brain stem. Within seconds he was breathing, and asking,

"is my partner O.K.?"

Don spoke firmly to the male officer,

"sure, just stay calm,

He looked at the female officer, and said,

"say something to your partner here; he's in a panic worried about you."

She said,

"I'm alright man, give us a break, and relax a second."

Don got up again to open the door of the men's room for the paramedics. The bustle gave Don the diversion he needed to slip away. Down the hallway he went. He knew they were going to be fine.

Don's blurry-eyed vision left out of his head. He spoke,

"so that's in my future? What you just showed me is in my future? And, your name is Samuel? In addition, your father's name is Zadator. From what planet did you say? Hold on; hold on, I am asking too many questions too fast. What just happened?"

Samuel told him,

"it is O.K... This is only the beginning, believe me

Don, it is only the beginning."

"Chapter Thirty-Eight: KAWHOCUMDIA"

Embedded in the blonde officer was the feeling that a higher power saved her life. She was not sure who this person Don was, other than what she had already heard. She did know she was going to find out.

The paramedics had rushed in, and got the credit for coming to the rescue of the police department but Cat knew that this man Don was the one performing the mysterious miracles.

Don had left the scene without the two police officers he saved, Cat, and Jack, telling him thank you. They felt the mystery man, Don, deserved all of the credit but were compelled not to say anything. His finding the body was never questioned whether he was innocent or guilty. Since it is the business of the police to investigate all of the facts, it never coming up was strange. Did Don do the cover up? If he said it, it must be.

No one knew that Don had let the shooter get away. It seemed that this would have helped the police clear up who did it. At least it would have cleared up who shot Don, and the two officers. With this man, the whole investigation would have been transparent. Still, no one would have known where the men with the hats, and trench coats came from.

A man that no one knew about would go on to some-day save thousands of lives and it would take the whole team to figure who the men in trench coats were. Yet, no one went any further than the shooter escaped. Don knowing about the event did not keep them from having to experience the horror. When Samuel told him, Don had not yet been pro-grammed. These things are facts about the events in the men's room that day. Only Don, and the programmed with the power would ever know, except for the shooter, and he became one with them.

Cat went on and on about Don to Jack, and wanted him to find Don. She wanted to know him, even if it was to know about just a small piece of him. In addition, even if it were only for a short while. Cat was assuming that Don would be delighted to have her company. She had been through a few relationships with men that never worked out. In her mind, it was never her fault. She was the one that had always broken it off because of something that the men had done, the final deal breaker.

The wounds on Cat were healing very fast. She was only in the hospital for a couple of days. The doctors seemed to be pleased with her progress. They had no idea there was another power working in the mix. Jack also was healing very quickly. His stay lengthened for a few more tests, which the doctors told him, it was only a routine test.

The doctors at this hospital had found something about Jack that was unfamiliar. It was a rare blood disorder or at least that is what they considered it to be. They were not sure what it actually was yet. Jack was not pleased with the hospital or the doctors. There would have to be another full blood work-up, which would mean more of Jack's blood drawn, and from the arm he already had a wound in. It caused him severe pain at different times, and nobody liked to have his or her blood drawn anyway. Jack really hated it.

They did know his disorder was causing a growth, made up of some soft and cushiony tissue. This the doctors had never seen before. There was a covering not of flesh, and blood. It was not like the organs of human beings but similar to the appendix. There were some of the doctors from three years ago that had already removed Jack's appendix and they were baffled.

The hospital also did not know of the switch that was about to be made. The switch was going to be Jack. The council had already assigned their henchmen to take the double they created to take the place of someone in the organization; it had to be set up before the doctors could find out what was wrong with Jack's blood.

The fourth day Jack was ready to go home. However, he decided that whatever the doctors thought was necessary, he would be happy to stay on a bit longer. He knew that there was going to be a new partner assigned to him. Jack having the blonde boom-shell riding with him was past tense. Cat was going to have a new partner too. Jack knew he would really miss her. He knew this kind of life was what she wanted but hated the thought of her life being put in danger. It was the job. She had always wanted to be a cop, and worked very hard at being a good one. There was not another police officer he would rather be with than Cat.

Cat walked into Jack's room, and as soon as she hit the door, she said,

"sure isn't going to be the same, life that is."

Cat loved to bug Jack with things she knew irritated him. Like incorrect grammar, she just did not do it too often. She knew he would have fought her about it. Jack really enjoyed being the one to correct it. Could be, he was not really that qualified. He just wanted to be. When he saw who it was, he said,

"the street girls are going to be so sweet to me, you know, beauty queens stop the machines. That keeps them from coming for me. You know what I mean?"

Jack started to say something else but Cat interrupted,

"you don't have to explain to me, I know it was just a joke.

Jack recoiled, and said,

"Cat, that's not funny, I've been injured here. I am in the hospital.

She answered him saying,

"O.K. Jack, I was wrong, you're funny.

She started to tell him a story, days gone past, and

said,

"remember that time when the girls walked up to the car, we had pulled up behind them. They were walking down the sidewalk on the strip in a row. We quietly pulled up behind them, and when they realized the car was there, they all bent down to see who it was, and when they saw me, said, Hi Jack. When they came up to the window on your side, they all were squatting down, and they looked us over again, and said in unison,

"oh, you two."

It was with that thick down home red neck drawl they put on, remember that?"

"Chapter Thirty-Nine: KAWHOCUMDIA"

Jack was having some difficulty keeping up the happy partner face, when he said,

"you dumb butt, yes I remember that. You will miss me you wait and see."

Cat was also having trouble keeping up the happy face, and couldn't wait to get out the door but still managed to stay, and said,

"you are so sweet; I didn't know you were in love with me.

Jack was really getting into the best partners connection now, and he threw in, "and the sweet ride we had."

He was taking ever advantage of it now; it was about his best friend of anyone he knew. Then, without thinking, Cat said,

"shoot, you don't have a prayer without me."

She stopped in her tracks, and came back quickly,

"I'm sorry Jack; I didn't mean to say that."

The silence was so thick you could have cut it with a knife, not to try to steal an old saying. Cat was sorry she said it but was only kidding, and in a kidding everything fair. Jack knew it. Then, they both turned their heads away, and the tears started to well up.

Cat said to Jack as she turned to walk away,

"call me, and let me know who you get..."

"Yea, you call me too!"

Cat was already out the door when the big old tears hit. She could not stand it anymore, and was glad she was out of the door. Just a few more steps and she would be down the hall. Some person in a white jacket asked her,

"are you alright."

She just nodded, and said,

"thank you."

He came back again with,

"are you sure?"

She replied again with a slightly different approach,

"no, I'm not sure but I'm out of here, so thanks again.

When she got to the elevator, she thought she heard
Jack say softly,

"goodbye Cat, I love you."

She thought to herself,

"this is unreal, I'm not hearing this."

Then, without further believable things happening for
her to regain her senses, she heard, Jack sobbing, real wail-
ing. Cat said recoiling into herself,

"shoot.

Then, she heard Jack,

"shoot, Cat, this is really messed up. I love you."

Cat was in the elevator headed down to the lobby, and looking around wondering how this was happening, her thoughts on leaving her partner, and changing to a new one. Still trying to figure out how this could be happening said,

"shoot, shoot, shoot."

Recoiled, and ready to strike out at anything that said anything to her, she waited on her ride down the elevator. She thought again about the changing of partners,

"it will be like the changing to a new job, that's all."

She was having all of the emotions, and feelings that a new job brings on. There are good, and bad jobs. Then, she thought in her exasperation,

"he has never even kissed me, he never even asked me out on a date. Why am I having this set-to over Jack? Jack if I thought you could hear me right now, I would tell you what-for. No, I wouldn't."

Jack's voice came back loud enough, and clearly was

a question, and more questions.

"What for, what do you mean? No you wouldn't?"
What the, is going on?"

Cat looked around expecting to find Jack but with an
eerie suspicion, she would look around and find nothing,
which is what she found, nothing. She was getting a bit too
worried, and said in a sweet soft voice,

"Jack? Are you close by me?"

Cat still using the sweetest voice she could muster up
said,

"I can't see you."

Jack did not handle it and spoke up.

"Cat, Where are you? I thought you were like outside
the door or something."

Cat's reaction was like a slap that backed her up
against the wall. There is a fifteen-second silence. Both had
the same cop reaction that put them on guard.

"Jack."

Cat calling him now, and Jack calling her,

"Cat."

She pleaded with him,

"Jack if this is one of your practical jokes, it's not funny."

Jack returned the confusing banter that turned out not to be what he thought,

Cat, I am not practical joking. What is going on?

Cat tries to rescue Jack to help keep him sane, she said,

"Jack, just breathe easily, we'll do this better with each other just like on duty, and do it together, and calm. Are you still in the room you were just in a while ago? The same room where I just left you, are you still there?"

Jack slowly spoke the word more assiduously than calm,

"yes."

Cat said it calmly,

"Jack, I'm on my way back up there. Just stay put.

Hurriedly, she said with the courts authority,

"stay put Jack."

Jack, now worried about Cat, said it with an inquisitive tone in his voice,

"O.K..."

Cat rushed back up the floor where she had left Jack. Although she could not tell because her heart was beating out of her chest, and her mind was racing with fear of losing Jack, it only took her less than two minutes. She vigilantly kept her calm, not wanting to alarm any one that might see her. She was incensed without showing it.

When she got to the room, Jack was sitting up in his bed. He told her as she moved closer to the bed,

"the doctors came in, and told me they were having me moved to another hospital. They said it was because the hospital not having the right equipment to do the test they wanted to do."

Cat did not want to give it away but thought his voice sounded strange and unfamiliar, nodded, and said,

"O.K..."

Jack or this perfect look alike repeated nearly everything he said before with,

"they needed some kind of special advanced equipment that only this one particular hospital keeps around. The ambulance is waiting to take us over there now."

Cat noticed Jack's veracity was gone, he said nothing about them reading each other's minds or about the love that they were sharing just a few minutes earlier. What Cat thought was a replacement for Jack said,

"well Cat, I guess I'll see you when I see you huh? O.K.?"

"Sure Jack. See you when I see you."

She was not going to let on that the deception did not fool her, for now. The real Jack's life may depend on it and her life too.

The fake Jack knew he was about to leave the room. He said,

"Good bye sweet girl."

Cat looked at the guise on this familiar face, and said,

"Bye Jack."

A word from the author;

Countless times, we reach a point in time reading a book when we have unanswered questions that we would like to ask the author, what you meant. On the other hand, perhaps the reader would just like to quiz them to see for ourselves what is going on with them that they would write such things. I know I have. I have taken time at this point so that I can tell you from the creative perspective that this fiction is completely from the inventive part of me that I really don't fully understand which is what makes this writing gig so much fun for me. I think that when an event happens in the story that I fabricate, another event just naturally follows. Makes sense to me to keep the story in order of some kind that you would have to keep it real in some rationality. I hope that you enjoy this read as much if not more than for me this write. If that is, what happens to the reader it will all have been worth it from the successful point of view of writ-

ing anything.

The Author

"Chapter Forty: KAWHOCUMDIA"

Cat knew this was not Jack they were about to roll out the door, not on this hospital gurney. It may have been a perfect version of Jack but not Jack. The hospital orderlies in their stiff and starched uniforms wheeled the impostor out the door. That is when she left the room in a hurry as soon as they were out of sight. She was out the door, and down the hall to the elevator. She pushed the lobby button repeatedly with her inpatients waving red flags everywhere. Luckily, the elevator door opened. She was inside, and headed down in seconds.

She got to the lobby, and then outside the front door

of the lobby. Stopped, she waited ten minutes. She thought about calling the Captain but fears that now they could have some monitoring going on in what she thought, she waited ten minutes more. It was possible that Jack could be sedated, and unable to communicate. Still there was nothing going on.

What if this is telepathy, some sort of malady from the damage with the shooting, and our wounds? These things were going on in Cat's mind. Maybe, he would try to contact her when he wakes up. More of the same kind of fears kept creeping into her head. She said to herself,

"quiet down now, calm down. He's alright, just calm down."

Cat stepped into the street, and hailed a cab. As she was about to get into the cab, Jack called her name,

"Cat, Cat can you hear me. I am so sleepy, man, I do not know how much longer I will be awake. Cat listen!"

Cat answered Jack saying,

"yes Jack, I hear you go on."

She asked the cab driver if he could wait a minute, and he told her he had to start the meter. Cat told the cab driver it was O.K., and said,

"fine."

She said to Jack stepping back away from the cab,

"I'm listening Jack, what happened? Can you hear me?"

"Yes, I can hear you but I'm really sleepy. Do you know I love you, Cat do you know?"

Cat cut him off laughing. She said to him still feeling the anger, and frustration from the events over the last few minutes,

"oh shoot Jack tell me what happened."

She got out her cell phone, and put it up to her ear. The cab driver would probably not think anything about it but Cat did not want him to think she was talking to herself. She heard Jack's response,

"O.K., I will.

He paused, then said,

"Cat."

He paused again.

"I was whisked away to some remote place, I've never even been."

He paused,

"and, I never even heard of this place. They blind folded me, and I still have the."

He paused again.

"Anyway, they gave me something to make the ride easier, that's what the doctor said to me as they were loading me onto the gurney. Now I cannot remember the name of the place. I know I heard it a few minutes ago. I don't know where I'm at."

He paused again, this time he repeated the same thing he had just said, only sounding a tad drunk,

"they gave me something to make me sleep to make the ride easier. Go to the twelfth street over-pass. When you get to the top look out at the tallest building to your right, it is the basement of that building, I remember now; they were talking on our trip over here, Suite two-sixteen. That is where they have taken me. I do not know the name of the place Cat. I am going out now. Cat come and find me. Cat.

Jack listen, I think we are reading each other's minds, I do not know how but I am going, Jack, Jack.

Silence fell from Jack, and Cat asked,

"Jack are you still hearing me, can you hear me Jack?"

"Jack, its O.K. I will find, oh crap, it is O.K., and I will find you.

She was sure Jack was out, gone or incapacitated in some way. She took the cell phone from her ear lingering in the same position she was in when she had Jack on the phone.

Cat got in the cab. She gave the driver her address, which was her fake-out address. It was two blocks away from her real address. She goes through to an apartment complex that has a walkway to the backside with another gate that leads straight out to her gate. It kept the creeps off her trail.

Cat told the driver,

"never mind about the address I gave you, take me to the twelfth street overpass, and go up over it."

The driver sighs with a growl, not from anything that Cat had done or said but from the pressures of everyday life, he said,

"O.K...

He is now relieved he knows where to take her.

With the workout from this morning, and the events that have just taken place, she felt the exhaustion in her body, and mind.

She thought again about Don H.,

"I don't think he is the ultimate, or the, uh, oh shoot, what's the word?"

She laughed at herself. It created a puff of air emitted from the bottom of her lungs. This made the upper part of her body flinch upward, and air escaped as a laugh. It was a snicker effect. If anyone heard it with their back turned, they would think the laughter was about them. The cabbie looked back at her through his rearview mirror, and puffs of air came out of his nose. He was in convulsions as he laughed at the way Cat was laughing. If he had been drinking water or a soda pop, it would have been coming out of his nose in squirts.

Cat thought to herself trying to contain her laughter, and looked away from the cab driver,

"I think I'll call the manager of that lounge in the morning, and ask about him. Maybe they have heard from him. Maybe they know where he is or something about him."

Suddenly, Cat got a vision of someone outside of her apartment. She strained visually, and thought,

"it's, Don. He's pacing back and forth in front of my

front door."

Her next question to herself was,

"where is that coming from and what is happening?"

"Chapter Forty-One: KAWHOCUMDIA"

She almost missed the front edge of the seat trying to
see out the front window of the cab. She was still seeing Don
in the vision in her head, pacing up and down at her front
door. She fixed her eyes with all of the power she could muster, trying to see the vision. She just wanted to peek at him.
She thought he was the most gorgeous man she had ever
seen. She asked aloud, trying to communicate with Don,

"are you here in my head?"

He said to her striving to be as straight forward as he
could,

"yes, and I'm right outside your door. Can't you

see?"

Cat plunged backward against the back seat of the cab making a loud sound. The driver of the cab looked back in his mirror, he asked,

"are you alright?"

Cat heard the cabbie, and quickly replied,

"sure, I'm fine; I see the building I'm looking for. Can you take me to the rear entrance? Oh, do you know if it has a parking floor in the basement?"

He said,

"oh no, no it doesn't, no it doesn't have a basement parking space."

She thought of Don and seeing him at her place, in front of the door, she took out her cell phone to try to hide what she was doing. If she did become too carried-away with too much talking, it would look like she was talking to some body.

"Will you stop pacing out in front of my house; the

neighbors will call the police?"

The reality of the power this man had just leaped out at her, she said to Don,

"its frightening knowing what you are capable of man."

She thought to herself,

"what if he can't be trusted?"

She does not have time to think about what she just did in front of her cab driver. She only thinks about the question in her mind,

"what if it isn't Don?"

She thought soberly,

"what if it is Don?"

She cringed. Thinking softly, trying to do it quietly so anyone who could read your thoughts, as if that was going to help her, she said to herself,

"if he can hear me, then I can tell him it's O.K. to listen to me. Then, I can communicate with him, just as I did with Jack. Now I wonder if Jack can hear me too. If he's conscious, I don't want to make Jack jealous when he's just become my ex-partner."

Her thoughts collided with each other. She, torn between the different choices she had available now at this time in her life.

"I wonder if Jack can hear me."

She had the thought,

"it is not a dream, or is it? Maybe all of life is a dream."

She said it again,

"maybe all of life is a dream, and the rest of it is reality, the calming of the storm the eye of the hurricane, why am I twiddling away?"

Then, she heard,

"Cat. Listen to me. I am not Don that is my stage name. I know you've been looking for me but you'll have to wait till I'm ready for you, don't worry, I'll find your partner."

She looked all around, and said,

"what did you say?"

She did not give him enough time to answer, and she said it again,

"what did you say? Don, what did you say collaborate?

She could not get another sound from Don in her head, so she watched out the window waiting to arrive at the building. She was hoping that Jack would be all right, and that she could rescue him. She said wantonly,

"Don, I hope this will turn out alright."

"Chapter Forty-Two: KAWHOCUMDIA"

"After I saw him, I was saddened. He looked like a whipped puppy that did not know what he had done. He said that he was not guilty, I do not know. He was guilty of many things. It looked like he had gotten away with bad things for over twenty-five years. I knew he was always pulling stupid stunts.

He was the world's biggest liar. He was the world's biggest gambler. He thought making moonshine whiskey was any working person's way of catching up on the bills.

His daddy before him did it, and so on and so on. Back at least six generations they all had made some at one time or another. I knew the time was going to come when he was going to have to pay, and that is just what happened. I just did not know when. There had been so much time that had elapsed; I had lost hope that he was going to get the help he so desperately needed."

This was what Don told me, and this is the story of how it all came about. I knew him to be a good kid, and then Viet Nam happened. If this change had not come about, well, let us just say thank God it did. He started telling me the part about coming back to Florida and this is what he said,

"I got back to Florida just in the nick of time to tell my wife what had happened. In addition, just telling the part about Daddy at the jail would not have been a problem. You realize things, as they happen, not before. She did not like what she heard. I think she thought I was crazy, and making it up. I do not know why she thought I would make something this wild up, and expect anyone to believe it. I just do not know.

I was traveling about sixty-five miles an hour on the open road, not an interstate but an older hi-way. The wind was blowing in my face, and the slapping of my hair was keeping time to the music on the radio. I will never forget it was "Oh Carol," by Chuck Berry. I was really enjoying Chuck he does it. I had not heard him play and sing in quite a while. The Chuck Berry sound is one of the best I think I have ever heard. My mouth was dry from blowing the harmonica, and I needed to stop, and take a break.

I really needed a break. The stress from thinking about Daddy, and the murder trial was really getting too much for me to handle. Since I had not gotten to go I felt guilty for not standing behind him. I did not even think about the pressure that could have caused. I thought about the victim, and her family all of the time. I always felt the love from the hometown people that supported school kids in all of their activities. I can imagine that would not be what would happen if I came strolling into town without a police escort, and the several hundred bodyguards to replace the police officer that tried to help protect me. This could only be my imagination. Besides most of the people, I knew moved out of town a long time ago.

That was a spooky thought, I just revisited my past, and I heard someone yell out at me. It used to happen all of the time. I think most of the people I was around were insane. I know they had some severe psychological problems. Those are the things that I think can-be-passed-on by the people in your environment. If you cannot find a way to ignore it, you have to escape it. You have to tell yourself that you are not going to be a part of it. You are just going to rise above it, think your way out, and do better than they did. I could not do it. However, Jesus Christ our Lord and Savior could and he helped me through. I believe that he was there for me all along. He knew how it was going to be, and he pulled me through. On more than one occasion, I had the challenge of either to run or to find the right words, or to fight. I suppose most of the time the words were not right but they helped me to keep from fighting. That must have been a blessing in itself. I was a small frame thin young man until I was older, much older.

My car was the six-cylinder Malibu, sixty-five in tip top condition, light blue but a somewhat darker light blue than you would usually think light blue would be. I should look up the color. I used to know it but I cannot think of it right now. A beautiful car, and was what everybody always said. I agreed. It was beautiful. I must have been about a half of a mile from the minute market, combo gas station-grocery store. I looked in the rear view mirror. The throngs of Hades itself must have been just around the bend or up the road somewhere. Even though 'I was saved' when I was a young boy, my sins were without redemption, for I had not asked for forgiveness in a long, long time. It was probably a fact that if I had died in a car accident that my soul could not have been saved. In addition, I was a serious sinner.

I could not believe what was happening. The whole back of the car was or seemed to be at the time, on fire. Totally engulfed in flames, it was as if it just exploded with the fury of Hades. Again, I could not believe it, fire burning every part of everything in sight. Me included, only one thing, I was not feeling the pain, there was heat, and it was really getting hot in there. However, it could not have been the heat of what I had imagined real flames would feel like. This was not a real fire.

What was it was the next question? Why was this happening to me? Was this a flash back from the acid that was slipped into my drink at a party? Was it an act of God?

Then it came to me with a thought so quick I moved as if a rattlesnake had just jumped out in front of me on a trail where I used to go fishing. My arms snatched the steering wheel of the car to the left. The tires squealed, and as I hit the gravel driveway, the car went into a slide. Therefore, I turned the wheel back the other way. Still holding the car in control, I hit the brakes a little harder, and brought the car to a sliding stop. There was dust everywhere. As I realized there were no flames, I also had stopped.

I was in shock. Everything was surreal. My brain had not registered yet what had just happened. It could not, it had all happened too fast for anyone to understand in an instant.

What was real was that I was at a minute market out on the road where no one knew who I was, and I had just slid into someone's driveway like a wild crazy man. Like the cool young man, I had always thought myself to be, I first got out of the car, and I closed the car door with a slight push. Then, I headed toward the door of the minute market.

What had happened to me in that instant was the redeeming feature of the lifesaving miracles of God.

It came to me. This sign could be to save my life from something up the road ahead.

I knew I needed something cold to drink. Therefore, that was my target. A bottle of pop, or some people call it soda pop, maybe some juice, or something to keep my mind off what had just transpired. The pop box was the old style, with the ice-cold water that kept the glass drink bottles ice cold. When you took out the bottle, it dripped with velvet smooth cold water. There was a bar towel draped over the side of the drink box. This is what by most people used that came in the store to wipe off their drink bottle. There was the choice of Coke, Pepsi, strawberry, orange, root beer, and several other drinks that were in these glass bottles. Moreover, just maybe if you hung around long enough, someone would use it to dry their hands after reaching into the drink box.

I pulled mine out of the box, and sort of rolled it around on the towel until it was dry enough to open. That first drink is always the best, so I always drink it the longest. You have to make sure you do not overdo it or you will get one of those headaches that come from drinking something too cold too fast.

As I finished my first drink, I saw the young heavy-set-girl-looking-at me-from-the-counter! As I continue to look her way, her eyes start to glisten, and had a cute appeal to them. She was not cute, just her eyes. She said,

"hot day."

Don told me that the reason he was on his-way-back to Florida was he had to visit his dad, who was in jail. He did not forget it for one second. His dad accused of murder; his part was telling the boys, which were just kids, that they were to rob, and kill the woman, she later, found dead in her house. The boys arrested, gave him up to the District Attorney, so they were getting a lighter sentence.

As horrible as it sounds, this was not what Don was telling this story for; it was just part of it.

"Chapter Forty-Three: KAWHOCUMDIA"

The girls of his dreams had been in plenty of realities of Don's in his life. The girls always were-treated with respect; no matter whom or what they were. He goes on to tell the story by acknowledging her comment with a gesture of flipping his own nose with his fore finger which by the way was done to him at a birthday party that was held at a Mexican restaurant,

"I replied with just a yes, and nodded with the movement of my head to emphasize my acknowledgment that I agreed with her assessment.

She asked me,

"have you been traveling long?"

I thought now I am about ready to cut and run but I said it as nicely as I could,

"all the way from Tulsa."

"Good God man, how many hours have you been up?"

I said,

"I sleep when I get home."

She stopped in mid-air with the vulgarity when she said,

"son of a,"

The pig snort came after she stopped in mid-air, and I wished I had walked out, and left her a twenty, just to have gotten out of there. However, I thought to myself,

"I'm truly grateful for that mid-air freeze."

She then said something I have heard at least a thousand times,

"do you know how dangerous that is?"

I answered her jokingly,

"no, how dangerous is it?"

Never mind was my next thought, I was sure she was about to tell me all of the dangers when driving without enough sleep. In addition, all of the drug, and alcohol lectures I had probably already heard. I called out to her quickly,

"how much do I owe you?"

she said it with all of the bitchen down home girl she had inside of her,

"A buck and a half,"

I pulled out a five-dollar bill, and gave it to her. I told her to keep the change, and she replied sweetly,

"thanks man."

I thought her sincerity was genuine because of the look she gave me, as if it was a surprise that I was that decent human being. She knew I was not the rich sucker I was playing, you know, just a feeling you get, nobody was that stupid, and definitively not her. I asked her as I was leaving,

"which way do I go to get to Orlando from here?"

She whispered, almost humiliatingly,

"catch the signs a half a mile down the road, you can't miss it."

I pointed in both directions as if I were lost; she pointed to my left, and said,

"south, my direction headed home."

I stood there for a few more seconds guzzling down some more of the second coke I had purchased. After I had finished the drink, I put the bottle in the crate that was sitting by the door. I said my thank you, and was gone, out the door. I could see now that the girl did not need my kindness be-cause she was as tough as a boot. I bet to myself though, that there was a heart of gold inside of her, beating with love, and compassion for every soul on earth. I knew better than to treat anyone nor anything other than polite. Respect is the first word my mother taught me which I will never forget as long as I breathe the air into my lungs. As I went out the door, I tried to catch the screen door but it slammed anyway. I turned back around, opened the door, and told the girl,

"my mother would never have let me get away with that, I'm sorry."

She said,

"it's O.K., it didn't hurt anything, and I'm not the scared type."

She could have been a Pittsburgh import acting as if she was a southerner with a southern drawl, so I said very politely,

"thanks, you're a doll, have a good one."

Moreover, I went away into the evening.

I had decided the fire in the Malibu was a sign from God. The close relationship to fire, and burning in Hades was to close for me. I tried every way to figure out what it could have been. The only thing I could come up with was that if I ignored it, and it was my last warning or something, then I would be a goner for sure. Besides, what did I have to lose if God loved me that much, that he gave me an extra sign, wow. I believe, I believe. Yes, I believe. Whatever it was that made that happen, I must thank God no matter what. Any time you get the ba-gee-bers scared out of you, just thank God for what you have.

The tires did not look flat, and everything was the same as when I left it, so, I climbed back into the vehicle. I was still wondering who saw me. I am sure now, my exit will be less exciting than my entrance. I am always, well usually sometimes the calm one. At least now, I have cooled down some but I still have that fire in my back seat in my mind. I cannot get it out. I got in the car, looked at the back seat to see if there were any signs of fire. There was none anywhere.

The driveway was just a gravely, dusty driveway. Therefore, I took off with no signs of dust as I was leaving, easy, and everything's cool. The time I spent at the minute market left me facing dusk. The drive home will be cooler at night anyway but not as good to me as the daylight. I loved the sunshine better than the night.

I had been on the road for only about twenty-five minutes when off to my right, I saw an owl flying, heading for my headlights. He did not look at me or turn his body to escape my coming his way at all. The speed I was traveling was too fast for me to slow down before impact; none at all. It was all over in just a second. Here I was again, facing something, something I did not want to face. My headlights must have blinded the owl. Maybe he wanted to get to that spot before I did. On the other hand, maybe it was something he saw in the road. Maybe he was trying to pick up a bug-buddy of his or something. I did not want to think he committed suicide but from where I was sitting, he made a plunge just as he saw me coming.

"Chapter Forty-Four: KAWHOCUMDIA"

"The owl came from a tree along the side of the road. The angle of his flight was a downward direction. When he hit the corner of the car, I knew he was dead. I cringed inside my gut. I stopped the car, and backed up. I had to see for myself if I had killed him. I knew it. There he was lying on the shoulder of the road. Still, and lifeless he was, and not a feather moving.

My heart sank for the poor owl. They had always been sacred to me. They were the strange birds of the forest that made a funny humorous sound. I loved the owl. Now, my life would go on but I had killed something I had always sworn to protect. Never would I hunt or kill the owl. Not kill the symbol of wisdom; never, ever kill an owl.

I had a newspaper in the back seat. I pulled it out to

wrap the owl in something for its burial. I would do it when I got home. As I opened the paper, I saw the clip telling about an alien sighting just miles from my mom's place in Georgia. I thought that is strange. I am getting all kinds of feelings from this information. With all of the things that had happened today, it just felt somewhat weird.

The article went on to say that, the space craft was hovering over this man's barn, and just disappeared. They showed a picture of the barn, which had no spacecraft, but the barn was identical to the barn at my mom's place. My mom did not have a man at her place. My question was who was this man? The barn looked like it had a fresh paint job. Now, why would a spacecraft be hovering over mom's barn? The paper went on to say, there were no signs of any landing. There was nothing else, not a clue of anything ever happening. The newspaperman interviewed my mom, and she said it was somewhat creepy. She felt like after it disappeared it was or might be still up there. She said, and they quoted her to say,

"you just couldn't see the dang thing.

This rang true for me at the time because my mom was forever suspicious.

I grabbed the owl as quick as I possibly could. This was without affecting anything in my brain that would lead me to believe that I was doing something that would be disrespectful. I know somehow the owl, and I am brothers. It is just a feeling I have had since I was a boy. Common sense would have told me not to get involved with what was going on at my mothers. I spent the rest of the night driving home without stopping. It was early morning when I arrived. My wife did not say good morning give me a kiss or even acknowledge that I was here. I had dropped her and the kids off there before I took off to go visit my dad.

I was making a pot of coffee when she asked me,

"how is your father?"

I said,

"do not call him that, he's doing well, and he's going to prison. They've got him for murder, remember?"

She soothingly said trying to calm me,

"O.K., I'm sorry, how's he doing for where he's at?"

I realized I was being rude, so, I said,

"I'm sorry too, I've been driving all night, and I've got so many things to tell you, I don't know where to start."

She apparently had seen the owl, and asked the question that preceded her laughter,

"where did you get the dead owl?"

There were screams of laughter coming out of her mouth, and I asked,

"what is so funny? Are you insane?"

She said,

"no,"

however, she could not hold down the shaking of her head, as she was saying no for the one hundredth time. I guess she thought something was funny about it.

I asked her while she tried to stop her idiot frenzy,

"are the kids up yet? How did you know about the owl?"

We were talking at each other, and mixing our sentences, and answers, and I said,

"O.K., do you want to hear about the owl?"

She never answered me about the kids. I tried to get in as much of the story as I could in a few seconds or maybe it was a few minutes, I do not know. I stopped in the middle of my story, and asked her,

"are you still laughing at the owl?"

Before she could answer, I said,

"it's not funny."

She said,

"no, no. I cannot. It is just too funny right now, maybe later.

I couldn't help myself, and said,

"you are a jerk if you're laughing at the poor dead

owl."

Her laughter suppressed she tried not to make too much fun of me. I did not get it, and still do not.

She got up to go to the bathroom. As she was leaving she said,

"my father wants to talk to you. He will be here in a few minutes, so do not go anywhere. You and your mission of mercy with your father, he is guilty. I know you see that. He is guilty, and I am sorry. What can I do? I do not want to be around him. I don't want the kids to be around him."

I spoke softly when I did, and mostly I spoke to keep her from saying any more,

"would you stop it? I feel the same way you do, you know that."

She stopped and turned facing me, and said,

"why are you following me into the bathroom?

I came back, and said,

"I was just trying to talk.

She finished our time, and conversation with,

"O.K., stop we'll talk later. I have to get ready to go in to work. I am working in Stacy's place today. It's a double, can you handle it?"

"Sure. What time will you be in tomorrow?"

She had on her poker face, and said,

"six-thirty, A.M..."

I said just trying to keep her talking, wanting her near me,

"that's not a double; it's a triple or, what the heck is going on?"

She said it back to me as calmly and sweetly as if it were true,

"I don't, or I can't tell you what I'm working on, you know that, it's kind of an undercover thing, and we might be on a stakeout for this evening, it's a long way from here.

I just let it slip off my back like water off a ducks back, I said,

O.K., stakeout, I see. It is O.K.; I will see you when I see you.

She mildly and sublimely said,

"thanks, you're a good daddy. You know how to feed the kids when they get up. You people can go to the park to-day, you know, something nice, whatever you want to do.

I moved away from the bathroom door as if nothing was wrong but I knew. She had been acting strange for quite some time now. If I had made a move for a kiss or anything worthy of calling it affection, she would have with-drawn as she had been doing. I just started to figure she wanted it that way, so I left it alone, my mistake.

I went back to the car, and got the owl out to bury him. I put the small package wrapped in the newspaper on top of the car. I felt something breeze past my neck, and the hairs were starting to stand up. Something had just happened, electrical energy pulling my sensors. What that was, were my thoughts, thinking they were mine alone.

I looked up in the sky for some site of something but there was nothing there as far as I could see. I thought of my mom, and the events that were happening at her place. It did make the news.

I was just thinking of something a very famous man used to say. I said it all of the time. Not to mock or make a funny at a time like this I will not say it.

I looked around again to see if I could see anything around. There was not a thing in sight. I went to the garage, and found the shovel. I went to the backyard, and buried the wise old owl. I laid him gently in the small hole I had dug for him. I also told him good-bye, and called him old boy as I did it, and that was it.

My wife kissed the kids good-bye while they were still in bed asleep, and whispered that daddy would fix them breakfast, and take care of them today. She would see them tomorrow. Her job made me sick to my stomach worrying about what could happen to her. I tried not to let on about it.

She wanted to do this more than anything she had ever done in her life. I did not know what else to do but to go along. She made me proud she wanted to be a police officer in the beginning. What happened, I do not know? Too many things happened, I guess. The one time you want to be a hero, you turn out to be a stupid fool. Not trusting her was never a problem it was the other cops. Mainly it was the male population that I had a problem with, trust."

That was the last time Don gave me any information. The rest of the story came from the others. I am still hanging in there for Don, and all of his missions, we all wish him well. No one is going to believe this story but I am going to tell it anyway, unless someone tries to stop me; then I am just going to work harder.

"Chapter Forty-Five: KAWHOCUMDIA"

Don had to leave, and was gone in an instant. It had something to do with some future madness that had taken place that he wanted to be a part of, and I knew it would be the last time I saw him for a long, long time. The remainder of the story came from reliable sources. This is what they said he had to say.

"I packed the car with a few things, loaded the two kids in the car, and left for Georgia. Even though I thought about it, my good byes to my in-laws did not happen. I really wanted my wife to tell them I was going to my mother's place. I would have to tell her first of course. I thought it would be best if I did not tell my mother-in-law what was going on. The deception was there, it was just what I thought was good for everybody. I was not going to let anybody stop me from going.

Something was already happening to me that I did not quite understand. Not understand in the way that I thought most people say they understand. To me that meant they have just skimmed the surface and only know a small amount of whatever. I think I just wiped out on what I'm trying to say, maybe it'll come to me."

This is where Don and the others telling the story gets a bit clumsy. His programming came later but he did not know that it was coming yet. Not to give it all away, he actually had powers beyond his years in wisdom, and mental abilities not known to human beings. However, what he was going through during this time was even depressing to me, the confusion about his wife, and his family with his mom, his dad. We all still love, and respect him as one of the great-est, yet what he had to go through is not comprehendible. Only God could have brought him back from the depths of depravity. The two that told me this part have history docu-mentation to prove all of it or I could not have been able to tell this part of the story. He went on with,

"I took the back road out of town, which was just a side street two blocks from the main street. It led us out of town without being visible to anyone we knew usually. I al-ways would take that way out to work; anyway, I knew the street very well. It was comfortable, and I knew no one would see us leave.

My wife would be waiting for a call from me to the station, just for me to let her know how things went with the kids at the park. The kids did not really want to go to the park, and I promised I would not tell their mother we did not go. I told them we would tell her the truth that we stayed home all day watching each other try to stack the wood that she had bought. The wood was to build an A-frame dog-house. If we got that built, then we were going to get the dog. He was only to sleep out when the weather permitted.

When the men that brought the lumber were unloading it, they tried to unload it by sliding it off the truck. The truck had a hydraulic lift on the bed of the truck. It was a big truck, and they were confused about what they were doing. The one person Dave had cut the bands that kept the wood together. When they lifted the front of the truck bed, the wood slid off, and fell into a pile on the lawn. If I had known what they were doing, I could have told them it would not work. I would have told them to load it off by hand, and save the returned lumber to the yard. The truck was on an incline to one side, and that is the reason it slid off in a pile. The poor men, they did not know what to do. I told them the next time to watch their angle on the truck. They said they would, and

"yes sir, we'll watch the angle next time."

I thought,

"poor wood."

I hoped there wasn't any damage but didn't say any-

thing.

My wife did not know that she had ordered five times

the amount of wood that we needed to build the one dog-

house. That was O.K. too; she was trying to do something

good for us as a family. I could tell her about that in the next

conversation we had.

We got on the interstate hi-way headed north but first

we had to go a hundred miles east. That is when I made the

call.

She was in the middle of her investigation, and said

her usual,

"are you sure, is it going to be O.K. with your mom?"

I told her with a short,

"yea, it will be O.K...

Then she said,

O.K., O.K., I will see you people when you get back. Tell the kids I love them for me.

I told her I would, and that was that. I knew I would get no sympathy from any direction, and I dropped what I was thinking, and moved on.

It was getting too dark for us to see much as we went down the hi-way. We talked, and I told them their mother said she loved them, and would see them when they got back. They were to have some fun at their grandma's house. Then we talked some more, and played the game where we guessed where each car was going that was coming down the hi-way. In addition, when we came to a cluster of cars we would try to say each one as fast as we could. This was so that we would not miss one, and lose ten points. We laughed every time the clusters came. I usually lost points. We would each do twenty cars at a time. The person whose turn it was next had to pick up where the other left off. We eventually got tired of the game, and started sitting quietly in our seats.

The kids were good for a long time, and then they drifted off to sleep. My kids were the best kids in the whole world. This was coming from a man who only had two, and would have liked to have a dozen, or maybe more. That is just what I wished I could have, not what I am actually going to have.

I just do not understand what is happening to me. I did not sleep all day today, and I am not sleepy. This has been going on since I left Oklahoma. Maybe, my need to sleep will come after I am settled, and I find out what happened at mom's place. I just do not get it.

"Chapter Forty-Six: KAWHOCUMDIA"

Suddenly, I saw more words in the article than was in the newspaper. More than I saw today and there it is the picture. It was, clear as day. How is this possible? I have never seen things in color. These are not visions; it is like memories of what I saw today on the paper. Only, this stuff is much clearer. Now I can read the whole article. Wow, what a story, what is going on with me?

The only thing now for me to do is to check with mom to see if it is true. I am not moving fast enough. I am sure that short cut is coming up soon. I will go through Ocala that made me start to think of my Aunt again, I hope she is in heaven.

There it is, the turn to Ocala, and I can follow the road almost all of the way home, I mean to my mother's house. It is O.K., calling our parent's place home, even though it is not really our home. Then I saw the sign. We were coming into Georgia. Therefore, I asked the kids,

"hey, do you guys want to see the Georgia Florida line?"

There was nothing but silence. They are both sound asleep.

I drove for another hour, and as I was thinking about my mom, and all of the brothers and sisters I have, I saw some lights moving just ahead of me in the sky. I thought about 'Albert Einstein', and what he said, "Imagination is more important than knowledge." I knew my mine was not playing tricks on me. They were small to compare them to the whole sky but moving in formation. Moreover, yes they were moving just ahead of me as if they were leading me home. The lights, or crafts, or whatever they were seem to be staying just ahead of me all right. I could see them above the trees, and traveling in a V formation.

I got a cold chill, and I was scared for my kids. My heart started to pound. The only thing I could think of to do was to pull over to the side of the road. It was a test to see if they would keep going or stop as I did. This may not have been such a good idea. They stopped too.

Now, I was beginning to get scared. Are they after me? What would I do if they came after me? I did not know what I would do. Who would?

The fear of it all, and the confusion going on in my head, I thought,

"I've got to protect the kids. What am I going to do?"

I got out of the car, and walked around to the back. Since the road was deserted, I decided that maybe I could get away with it, so I unzipped my pants, and pulled myself out, turned back toward the lights, and began to relieve myself. It really felt good, and I started to chuckle, and laugh almost uncontrollably. Here I was facing these aliens in space ships, or something up there, and I am taking a wiz in front of them. What is funny is I had the consideration to turn my back to them after I started. I am a funny man. I did not know if they would have the decency to stop looking or not. It was just a thought.

As soon as I finished, I got back in the car, and started the engine. If they started up again, I would keep going until I got to my mom's or until they stopped me. Not knowing what they were capable of, I had to prepare myself for whatever came. So, I headed down the road to my mom's place.

As I am driving, I kept a close watch on the lights that could have been alien space ships. I guess it is good at a time like this, that I have some semblance of a sense of humor. This, if it was in any of the funny books I could possibly read, was not funny, and it was not funny then.

They kept a steady course. I did not know what they were doing or what they intended to do but they stayed right in front of me doing the same speed that I am doing in my car. I am doing fifty miles an hour easily.

The whole trip there must have been only two or three cars pass me going the other way. I was tempted to flag one of them down but changed my mind as I thought how stupid it would be to say,

"excuse me sir, I think I'm being led by an alien space craft just ahead of me, see those light up there."

My wife had already made me feel bad enough with what she had done already. I knew the divorce was on her mind.

The kids were as quite as they could be. Sleeping through the whole thing, I am glad they did not wake up to witness it, and gotten scared. Although, it may have been only me, I do not know. They could have helped me figure out what to do, and could have done it without getting scared.

They are both exceptional kids. Did I say that already? Well, I should have. Jeux is a perfect ten that was ten years old, and Law, an eight year old that is a regular boy. They both had many questions but they both already had many answers too.

The private tutor was my wife's idea. I think the kids are benefiting better than many of the kids in private, and public school. The tutor reported this to us after their tests this quarter. My wife and I are sure we have smart kids.

We arrived at my mom's house just in time for early breakfast. She came running out to the car to greet the kids, me too. She was almost screaming.

"Oh my God, I can't believe you all are really here. Let me get a look at you two.

She looked at me, and said,

"you're looking good son, what's that girl been feeding you? Looks like you are as healthy as a horse to me. Have you been working out, and running that jogging trail next to your house? I guess you've heard about the visitors, huh?"

I just quietly answered her,

"yes momma, I did but only by accident."

She replied strangely,

"really? Tell me about it."

 I told her about the owl.

"I picked up a paper to wrap a dead bird in it, and found it."

She stopped me saying,

"you can tell me about the bird later. It is some story. Is it for real? Never mind, you don't have to verify it to me, I believe you."

I was glad to be visiting with my mom, and told her, and she said,

"boy, it's a good thing you said that."

"Chapter Forty-Seven: KAWHOCUMDIA"

Don's mom said it light heartedly but Don knew the underlying implication because of events that had happened earlier in his life. He knew not to take his mom by the light-hearted way she would say something. The seriousness made him pay attention to her.

Don was reporting to his mom with lots of the information that kept him out of trouble with her. She did not get it all though, not yet.

She grabbed both kids as they got out of the car, and hugged them as if they were never going to get away from her again. She really loved Don's kids; I think she really loved all kids. No matter who or what, any child or young person that ever did anything, she would always have an excuse for them. On the other hand, if there was a reason behind the offence, it did not matter about the validity of their offence. I think she thought it would work out better for kids, if you tried to understand them with more love, and less punishment. She did keep a close watch on Don's activities, and kept him in church until he was old enough to go on his own.

He was sorry he spent the better part of his teenage years running the streets, instead of going with my mom to church to worship.

His kids seemed to love their grandma with the same affection they had for their mother. That was a good thing to me. Peace and harmony is what we have always wanted Peace, and harmony.

As usual, the breakfast was heavy, and full of butter. There were scrambled eggs, cooked in butter, hash browns, cooked in butter. Grits topped with a dab of butter, and toast covered with butter, and strawberry jelly or what some people call jam. The bacon was thick, and a descent size. Not like a lot of the thin kind that always fried up stuck together.

It taste good but does not look as good as thick slices of beautifully prepared breakfast bacon.

Don had a bowl of cereal with a banana, and milk. Two percent, I think he was losing some weight.

His mom was finishing her breakfast of scrambled eggs, and grits, when she asked Don the question,

"have you met Sam? He has had a problem with his memory like you. You do still have a little bit of a problem, don't you?"

Don was wondering where she was going with this but answered quietly,

"yes, well sort of. Who is Sam mom?"

She replied right back,

"you'll see. He has entrusted his security with me, and wanted to meet you. Believe me; I got some information the other day that will knock your socks off. Anyway, Sam will explain it all to you."

Don does not say anything. He did remember all of

the things that had been happening, and wondered what was next. He said to her,

"mom, do you know where this guy Sam has run off to? When will I meet him?"

His mom told Don,

"as soon as he gets back then you can meet him."

Don countered,

"where did he go?"

His mom came back quickly,

"I don't know you'll just have to wait and find out when he gets back. I think he said something about going for a spin or just cruising or something like that. He is about your age I think. Well, and it is difficult to explain. I suppose I am going to have to do whatever it was that he was explaining to me. I get it but you know me. I will have to see it to believe it but that is just me. It'll probably be different with you guys."

Don's mom closes with one of those looks-to-die-for.

She was so cool like that, as though she knew everything about your life that had ever happened in it. Don was hanging on with a great deal of anticipation; this could be an explanation. He thought to himself,

"I wish that guy would get here. I think there must be some kind of connection. Maybe it is too far out, maybe not. It is just too weird; I just cannot put my finger on it. In that moment there was a knock at the door, and in the same second Don's mom Elaine said,

"come in Sam."

Sam spoke with a soft and courteous voice,

"good morning."

He headed straight toward Don. He put his hand out to shake Don's hand. Elaine said,

"Sam, Don. Don, Sam. You two shake, and let us get this thing on the road; I know Don is going to love it. I do not know what you did to my head last night Sam but the headache is much better. I have not felt this good in twenty-five years.

"Chapter Forty-Eight: KAWHOCUMDIA"

As Sam and Don shook hands, the magic began. Sam let Don in on the huge secret, that, being the programming. Sam was from the past, and having visited the future, sent Don's head into a spin. Don was a crack shot with any weapon that he had in his hands while in the military but he never saw this coming. Even his suspicions pale in comparison to what just actually happened. He said,

"I'll have to sit down now mom."

Elaine knew God's hand was in control of Don's future now. She also remembered the quote from Aristotle in Nicomachean Ethics about the past or history, "This only is denied even to God: the power to undo the past." She said it in a pleasing motherly way,

"it'll be alright son, just sit down. When I touched him last night for the first time, I thought your father had come back but in a different body. For a few seconds I felt I was in love again. No really."

Sam takes on some strong resistance but only for a moment. Elaine smiled silently but also was pleased.

Don spoke softly where he was confused about what just happened,

"mom!"

Before he could ask her to explain, Sam said,

"let me explain."

Even though the magic had already begun, he reached out, and touched Don's temples, first with the middle, and ring fingers from each hand, and only for a fraction of a second. Now, Don was in the process for programming.

Don stood up, and said,

"if you'll excuse me now, I think I'll go upstairs, and

lie down for a while."

He walked over to his mom, and kissed her on the cheek. He said to her,

"see you in a little while."

She responded with confidence,

"O.K. sweetheart, you rest well."

Sam spoke up to reassure Don,

"rest well, I'll see you later. It was nice to meet you.

Sam knew Don was going to be out for quite some time. He had already been working on him in different ways. The flames in the back seat of Don's Malibu, was the only way Sam was sure Don would pull off of the road. Sam knew Don's future, and had to make a move that was drastic. There would have been a fatal accident, and Don's chances of ever seeing his kids again would only have been in heaven. In addition, maybe the few visits he would have gotten to make back to earth. Sam knew with Don's memory, he would have to have special attention.

Don's kids had gone in on Grandma's bed to take a nap after their bite of breakfast, and were already asleep. Don went in to join them but decided to go to the spare room. When he looked at Jeux, and Law, it felt good and changed his mind again. It was the first time in a long time he had lain down on his mother's bed. He felt like he was at home. He fell asleep in just a few seconds.

Sam and Elaine were just like old friends visiting after a long time away with no contact. Sam was telling Elaine about his family's Law practice, and his computer business. He was also assuring her of Don's safety, and the advances he was going to be aware of with the programming. Sam led Don home with his spacecraft. The extra lights were fakes to make his presents seem bigger to Don.

Elaine was just about to make her mind up too. The offer was made to her last night by Sam as he was about to leave. He realized what a great mind she had, and considered her a good candidate. Sam said to Elaine, "let's let Don rest for now but what about you? Are you ready for what I asked you about last night?"

Elaine said,

"yes."

Sam was ready for her answer, which he already knew. He said,

"great, I'm sure we'll work out really well. Have you tied up your loose ends yet?"

Elaine was ready, she said,

"yes, I think so. You did say we would be back from time to time. And, that nobody could know where I was going. I am going to love it, let us do it, now, right now. Oh. I hope I wasn't too pushy."

Sam said to Elaine,

"no, great, let's do it."

They headed out the door with Sam leading going to the ship. It was still hovering just above the barn. As they walked down the pathway, Elaine said to Sam, "how do you like my barn Sam?"

He looked at Elaine, and responded confidently,

"it's a great barn Elaine; I like it, Great barn."

"Chapter Forty-Nine: KAWHOCUMDIA"

As the climb into space revealed the barn, Elaine saw
how small it kept getting the further away from it they got.
She wondered how she was going to tell her son. She spoke
her thoughts to Sam,

"I don't know how I'm going to tell Don that I'm going to do it. Your touch will inform him of the programming,
and get that started but I'm just not sure if he'll want me to
be a part of it too."

With her voice slightly trembling as she spoke, Sam
understood why Elaine felt the way she did. Don's past, and
all of his problems with memory, and let us just say some of
the decisions that may have looked like poor judgment came

from a life of making excuses for his mistakes. Elaine helped him through his adolescence with the greatness of their understanding, and teaching but still it was no picnic. He learned from them to be an independent thinker, and more a leader than a follower did. Sam told her,

"don't worry, he'll be there for you, I'm sure of it. And Elaine, I'll be there for you too."

Sam did not waste any time convincing her but used telepathy to communicate his thoughts and feelings. Elaine's childlike references such as, in for a penny, in for a pound let Sam feel more of a child than his normal self. He said to Elaine,

"good, I'll tell Don you're in programming after this short spin we're on. Nice view up here isn't it?"

Elaine was so proud of Sam, and herself too, she beamed it very politely,

"yes it is Sam."

Sam showed Elaine where to get comfortable. He

gave her an injection to keep her sustained through her pro-gramming. He could not believe he was getting them both to come with him. Elaine was set now; Sam turned the ship around, and headed back to earth. With Sam's ship, they are quite a distance out above earth but just a few short minutes in time.

He got back to the hovering spot over Elaine's barn, and opened the hatch. He left Elaine where she would be safe, and protected by the ship, and the sensors that guard Sam and his crew. He took the device that secured the ship where it is unable to leave without him. He knew there was no one there that could steal the ship but thought it was a good habit for him to get into. Besides, he could introduce Don to the device, the ship's ultimate control except for Sam.

Sam walked into the house through the kitchen back door. It was just as if he were at home. Don was sitting at the kitchen table having a cup of coffee. Sam spoke to Don, and asked,

"did you have a good rest?"

Don still just a bit groggy, said to Sam,

"oh yea, it's just I'm a bit confused about you, and the touch you gave me though. Can you explain to me some more, before I give up on what I used to know as sanity?"

Don does not know how to explain his frustration, other than to tell Sam of all the things that have been happening to him. Don got to the question about his good rest,

"yes, I had a great sleep. Better, I think than in a long, long time. But, I think I should tell you about what has been happening to me."

Sam said,

"understandable."

He paused, and Don asked,

"do you get me Sam?"

Sam paused slightly,

"yes I do, don't worry about it, I've got to tell you

this. I have been monitoring you for a while now. Let me say also, it is normal for you to be confused at first. Besides, I am new at this too, and I am probably not getting it all out just right, yet.

Sam hesitated, and said,

"give me a chance, and I'll get it right once it's all laid out for you.

Don not feeling too sure of anything now said,

"oh, I'm sure you will. After what I've been going through, the next thing you'll want me to do is sign up with you."

He looked across the short space between them. He stammered almost into his old fears again as he said,

"wait a minute; is that, what's going on here?"

Don trusting Sam any more at this time is starting to worry him, and it is about his kids, and their grandmother. The mixture of all the things blended together with the good, and the bad staring Don right in the face. Sam said it as plainly as he could,

"I need to know if you can commit to a few weeks at a time away from home. We can be in constant contact with anyone we want at any time. I am sure by now that you are already aware that you will be able to read minds, and contact them through mental telepathy.

Don speedily replied,

"no, no I didn't, well I sort of thought, I'm sorry, this is all happening to fast.

Sam speedily feeds him more information without Don having to make a decision about anything yet. Don's eyes are blinking at a rapid uncontrollable speed trying to keep them from bulging out of their sockets, he said to Sam,

"yes, I think now I got something about that while I was resting. Could you excuse me just a minute; I think I'll check on the kids?"

He started to speed out of the kitchen, turned back, and asked, "oh, by the way, where's mom? I guess she's doing fine?"

Sam spoke to Don confidently,

"absolutely she couldn't be better."

He reached in his pocket, and pulled out the device. He then pitched it to Don, and said,

"check this out for a pocket device. It secures the ship where it will not leave me behind. Check out the screen, and bring up the cameras. You might spot her on one of the front views."

Don stepped out of the kitchen after catching the device. The instructions came up on the screen with a menu, and were self-explanatory.

He thought about the kids, and being so far away while he was on these trips with Sam. He called back to Sam from out of the kitchen doorway politely asking,

"would you excuse me Sam?"

He replied,

"sure, I'm not going anywhere."

Don thought to himself,

"maybe I could get permission for them to come with me sometimes, who knows, this might turn out to be one of the best things that could possibly happen to me, and my family."

He got to the bedroom where the kids still lay sleeping. He leaned over Law, and kissed him on the forehead. Then Jeux got a kiss, only she woke sleepy eyed. She said,

"what are we doing daddy?"

He leaned over, kissed her on the forehead, and said,

"nothing baby, go back to sleep."

"Chapter Fifty: KAWHOCUMDIA"

Juex said to Don,

"O.K., I'll see you in the morning daddy."

She went immediately back to sleep with no problem.
Don thought about his mate back at home, and the possibilities of calling, and catching her at home. He did not know if
she was at home but picked up the phone in the upstairs
hallway. He dialed the number for the police department
where his wife worked. There was one ring, and someone
answered. Don recognized the voice, and said,

"hi Mack. What's up?"

Mack recognizing Don replied quickly,

"Dude, where have you been? Your wife is going to

kill you. She's been worried sick man."

Don not knowing what was going on, was a little leery, and asked,

"what? I thought everything was all right.

There was a silence on the other end of the phone line, then laughter beyond sane. Mack said,

"hold on man. You did not really believe me. It is cool.

Don said in a voice not really trying to be furious, and trying to be funny, said,

"Mack, I am so mad at you, yes! I did! Could you get my wife for me please?"

There is more laughter in the background as well as what was still coming out of Mack. He kept saying,

"I got you man. I got you. I got you man. I got you."

Then he stopped the laughter, and said,

"let's get serious just a minute now. Are you playing at the club tonight? I sure could use some good guitar tonight."

Don came back with,

"no Mack, I'm not, and probably won't be for a while but I'll be back baby.

Mack said to Don,

"good man, good man. I will see you when I see you dude. Oh yea, she is not here. I will tell her you called. You want for me to tell her the usual?"

Don knows Mack, and what he will tell her, he said,

"yea, that's good, tell her the usual. See you later Mack. We love you too. Be sure, and tell her, you know, I love her.

Mack tried to hurry the good bye, and said,

"yea, I know. Bye.

Don caught him before he hung up, and said,

"Mack wait!"

Mack replied,

"yea, what?"

Don really opened up to Mack this time with,

"did you want to be a cop or did you just become one?"

Mack hesitated a couple of seconds before he said,

"yea, let's see, no. I just became one. I needed a job, came in, filled out an application, and waw la, I am a cop. Well, you know a little more complex than that, with training, and riding with other cops. But, same ole same ole."

The silence is deafening, so Don made a cute comment,

"that's your story, and you're sticking to it, huh Mack?"

Mack, being the agreeable kind person, said,

"yea, that's it."

In addition, he laughed boldly, partially not getting or even caring what Don had just said. Mack was just a carefree kind of a person. Don said,

"see you Mack."

Mack heard the tough guy tone in Don's voice, and said using a lisp,

"don't use that attitude with me tough guy."

They both laughed, Mack's was a shade bit louder than Don's was. They both said good-bye at the same time, and hung up the phones.

Don came back downstairs to the kitchen. There was no one there. He thought about the device that Sam had given him earlier. He reached into his pocket, and retrieved the unique small wonder. He examined it superficially, and put it back in his pocket. It then vibrated, and made a small, barely audible beeping sound. He reached back in his pocket, and pulled out the device again. A voice came from the device that Don recognized as Sam's, he said,

"are you ready for the full tour of the ship?"

Up until now, Don had not thought it was possible for all of this to be true. He was between an almost maybe, and an "I don't believe it because it ain't true." Then, the-reality-set-in, somewhere between the refrigerator, and the kitchen sink. Here he was at his mom's house and some person with this power over her, and everyone he met. Then he touched me on my temples, and what is going on? I have never let anyone control me like that.

He spoke back into the device in his hand,

"yea why not? Let's shoot the works."

Don's interest was building as he laid out the words. Sam gave him his direction to take,

"O.K., start heading out to the barn, go inside, and climb up to the loft. There is an exit to the roof on the cat-walk; you will see it when you get inside. Climb up there, and come on out on the roof. I will be waiting inside the ship with Elaine, unless of course you want me to come and es-cort you. I will if you want me to."

Don replied,

"no, I'm fine. I know where the catwalk is located, and I will be there in a minute. Let me get a cup of coffee first.

Don went over to the coffee pot but there was no coffee. He noticed it was a big coffee pot. His mother had gotten it new since he had last been home. He held back his thoughts, and walked out the back door to the barn. Don could see there was nothing over the barn but decided to check it out. He opened the front barn door, nothing. He looked to the roof, and with the power starting to work on him, he felt a sense of self-worth that he had never felt before. He did not understand what was happening yet. With his enhanced perception, he now realized he was going to do this no matter what. It was bigger than he was. He felt it in his soul.

He made his way up to the loft, and over the catwalk. Don went out the roof door, and waiting at the top was Sam, he said to Don,

"I see you made it. The ship is cloaked so you can't see it yet."

Don looked to the sky for some a sign of a space

ship. He was thinking it must be high if they were not able to

get a visual. Then, there it was. As he saw the ladder starting

down in a straight position, it reached the top of the roof.

Then it went out at an angle, Sam said,

"follow me."

Sam made it a point to be as polite as he could with

Don, as he would with anybody. Don did not say anything.

He was amazed. As he got to the top of the ladder, he

could not see the outside of the ship with it cloaked but was

starting to see the inside, and the beauty of it all. His mind

was blown. He said,

"good God almighty. Where did this thing come

from? I know it is not one of ours, is it? What the, my, this

can't be."

There was a few seconds of silence, he tried to finish

his sentence but closed his mouth, and just started shaking

his head as if it was just too unbelievable. His mind did not even comprehend where he was at that very moment. He was amazed, and really digging all of it. Then he saw the controls at the helm. Sam told Don,

"first, I'm the Captain. This is my ship. We will all be a part.

There are things that you must know in order for you to understand what we are. Are you with me?"

Slowly Don said,

"yea, I think so."

Sam corrected Don,

"no, you either are or you're not. You must know, you cannot think so, and that is O.K. for now. I will still give you time to think this through. So, do not worry, if you need more time you will get it. Now, I must tell you before I ask you to commit to joining us that Elaine has already joined.

"Chapter Fifty-One: KAWHOCUMDIA"

Is that a problem? I did not think it would be or I would not have taken her on first. With what my understanding is now of deductions, and the calculations that I am capable of, I know I have made the right decision. We are not so much in a hurry as we are in a waiting period, although, we can get underway as soon as you make your decision. Your children will go home with a ride in a space ship. I have a safe sleep mode that will keep them occupied during the whole trip, and is only a very short amount of time.

How are you feeling right now? O.K., I hope."

Don almost announces his state with,

"I'm starting to come around. It is very overwhelming you know.

Sam compassionately sympathizes with Don,

"yes sir, I know."

Don responded with the question,

"did you just call me sir?"

"that's right, I called you sir. Isn't that what I'm supposed to call you, if you're to be the Captain?"

Don was puzzled, and questioned the future possibilities,

"I get it, you're thinking of the future with me as
Captain of a ship, right?"

Sam spoke as Don's thought came,

"yes, you're right. However, we all share respect, and
responsibility for the position of Captain. You will understand later if you do not now. Let me explain more about
what will be happening to you. There is a brief period where
you will go through programming. This is what your mom is
going through right now as we speak. Each person goes

through indoctrination, there is a history of where the Zorvirax people live, and the powers they possess, and where these powers come from. Moreover, one of the most phenomenal things is the age of the people, and their planet. It will all be covered in the programming."

Don moved his head in an up and down motion listening as Sam talked on,

"we have a mission to change the worlds we live in, and help our fellow man understand a better way to live with each other. Big job, I know. You will get information on time travel, mind reading, cloaking, human beings, and alien. There has never been a time on earth like now, as far as we know. The future is ours to learn ahead of time. You will have the ability to fly. There are many more powers you will have. For the good of all they are to be utilized by you and by all of us. You will become a leader, and the skills that you are most interested in, and apt at will become your thing. Cool?"

Don still moving his head showed he understood but was as anyone would, still waiting for the seeing is the be-lieving conformation. He said,

"cool."

Sam asked,

"I would say you seem to be thinking it's impossible, is that a fair calculation?"

Don tiring of the wondering about it all said,

"no, I'm not saying it's impossible. I am saying it is hard to believe it is possible. You know what I mean, right?"

Sam replied quickly,

"yes I do, and to let you know a little bit of who I am, I went jogging one day,"

Sam goes on to tell the story of his capture, and the trip to the planet Veltrax Eta, Zadator, and his experience. The escape and finding the ship he now possesses. He tells Don,

"you and your mom are coming in just in time for the

coming together of the family, and some new elements that will be interesting to all of us. Now, you see, I am from the past but because of the process that stopped the degeneration of the human cell, I will look your age but I am your senior by quite a few years. Are you still with me?"

Don answered,

"yes sir."

Sam simply said,

"good. Let's get underway."

Don wanted to be no problem to Sam, and responded with interest.

"Yes sir. What do I do first?"

Sam created a look on his face, and tilted his head to one side indicating less pressure, and said,

"it's very simple. Just take a seat, which would be the one next to your mom. She is already asleep, and in the programming process. This shot I am about to give you is to sustain you nutritionally, and something to help you relax before you go to sleep. Do not worry everything is going to be fine. Trust me, you'll see."

As Don lay down, Sam helped him with the strapping in for take-off. Don could not see his mom because of the position he was in reclining in his seat but he said to her in a low soft voice,

"I love you mom."

Six days past, and Elaine had finished her programming, and was taking part of the ship's activities. Interested in what is going on more than actually having a full time job. There are things that can come up in an instant but with everybody's attention on watching everything, there is no stone unturned. As other things went on, jobs were going on, each a. s. a. p...

"Chapter Fifty-Two: KAWHOCUMDIA"

Don only had a few more minutes of programming left, and Sam was waiting to tell him some interesting things. These were things now coming from Zadator, and Sam must relay it to the rest of the crew.

The meeting of the minds must be in an inviolable place. For their meeting there had to be a feast, and expedition. Therefore, the coming together had to be a campaign where they had several related operations aimed with geographical and temporal constraints but with the capacity to relieve those constraints. Therefore, again, it will-be-carried-out with cloaking devices on and in a place where no man had ever been on earth. Back in time to the place that came to be-known as Huang He or Yellow River in what is now China. The length of the river is 3,395 miles. That should be enough territory for them to explore, and give them enough time to get to know each other in a different way. They will travel back after the creation of man by twenty thousand years. This will get them to a period when the river existed. The visual will-be-done from inside their ship and after enough time for things to settle down, they will explore the region. Don woke up, and Sam said,

"did you get that last part about the meeting?"

Don replied with a different tone in his voice, very collected, and together,

"yes sir."

Then, Sam spoke to all when he said,

"I'm afraid I have some bad news, and some good news. Don will not be able to go with us. The good news is his mission is here on earth.

We will still have you in communication Don but you

will be alone for the time we are gone. A special talent will be yours to evolve into something uniquely different from the rest of us. It will come to you as you go on with your life, and mission. It has to do with your talents alone, so good luck."

Everybody prepared for reentry and landing, there was a bustle onboard the ship. They all gave Don a team high-five as each individually passed by to say good-bye. Jimmy and Danny told him,

"we will see you later. We are looking forward to working with you."

Danny leaned in to get close to his face as said,

"keep the faith man."

Don returned the gesture of fellowship, he said,

"you too."

Don does not believe the acceptance, and love he felt from all of the crew. Everybody took his or her position. Time was slipping away. Elaine was the last to come by. She said,

"I'm proud of you Don."
This makes me a very happy mother. I will see you when we get back. Take care of yourself."

Elaine kissed Don on the cheek, turned, and went to some of the crew. She started the involvement with them of taking care of the ship. What Don was going to miss was at least three months of exploration, adventure, and more work. Moreover, more fun than a person could ask for. He thought to himself,

"I'm going to have a nice little work load."

He leaned back in his recliner, and closed his eyes but not to sleep. He started envisioning the things that he had never seen before or was ever able to see before. His mind was free, receptive, alert, and ready for the new life.

Don did not know where the ship was landing. Sam came to Don and told him to stay cloaked until he was out of sight from everyone. Sam went on to assist Don with more security,

"if you need me call immediately, telepathically. You have the power that is beyond imagination now, so go with your instincts, and feel the power. Remember your mission is a secret. Even though it may seem difficult, it is life, and death. You must not fail. I know you will not. See you when we get back."

Search mode had already started in Don's mind. The process was only a few seconds on any given entry. He knew now what his mission was, and how he was to do it.

The door of the ship opened, and the ladder started down. Don cloaking himself turned to wave, and remembered he was invisible. He turned back toward the door, and headed down the ladder. What he found when he found the underlying cause was a shocker, and a showstopper. He stood in silence and watched what he could not believe was about to happen. He knew what he had to do. The man sitting at the window with the rifle in his hand was about to get the surprise of his life.

"Chapter Fifty-Three: KAWHOCUMDIA"

The fear was popping out of his pores in the form of sweat. The small drops of vile evil liquid; observed only by the invisible man. This invisible man was now waiting to make a mockery of the shooter's planned deed. His trick would be to make the sharpshooter think he missed his target. It would not be his years that let him down but the impending doom of what he was about to do, and the unseen witness of this demonic deed; no, not his years but the reality manipulation by the one man who can save the President with just the push, one small push of the gunman's barrel.

All of the building up to this moment for the real gunman had been balancing on his ability to frame an innocent man. With the help of the others, it looked like they were going to get away with it. They were to assassinate the President, no one would be the wiser, and that would be an unbelievable thing to pull off but why not? It was all set up. The patsy was in line. The gun that was to do the killing, it was his. The finger prints on the gun, left at the scene. He was a prime candidate, and suspect to the police. Everything was going perfect, except for one small thing, Don. He had his finger on the barrel of the gunman's rifle and cloaked. Don could read his mind, and will know at the exact moment when the gun will go off. Just a nudge with his forefinger to throw the trajectory off, the would-be deadly metal coming from the crazy man's weapon, Don heard his thoughts, felt the finger start to squeeze, and the pin of the gun start to engage. He pushed with upward English on the barrel it fired, and missed. The gunman was shocked. He was panic-stricken. He reached for the bolt of the rifle. He knew he must throw back the bolt, and push back forward. He trembled and filled with fear. The reaction was quick, and decisive, just as any pro would have done, imperceptibly, his fear increasing now making him crazier than even the craziest of fiends. The panic had also hit the motorcade. There were Secret Service men all over the President's car. The President now pushed down in the back seat with a pile of people on top of him. The endless amount of men came along and they were climbing in to give more protection. The President's wife was hugging the men that had jumped in front of her to protect her husband, and there were now men surrounding her. It was madness all around.

The crowds that had gathered to see their President and the First Lady were now terrorized, and most were screaming to the top of their lungs. Some form of panic-stricken word or words, like, stop, help, stop you murders, help them, somebody help them, just screams that were as if they themselves were being attacked, and stabbed or shot to death. The crying from young women, and young men running toward the car screaming,

"no, no, no, no you can't kill him! I will not let you! No, no, no, no!"

One young man yelled out,

"somebody get me a gun, I can shoot back, and I am a marine!"

He ran crazily across the lawn yelling,

"somebody get me a gun! Please somebody get me a gun!"

Don had already looked down at the motorcade, and knew what was happening. The gunman put another round in the chamber. It was locked-and-loaded ready to fire. He aimed, and instead of spinning off as many rounds as he could in such a short time, he took his time. It did not matter, Don was there, and ready for him on whatever decision the crazy man made. Don heard him inside his head saying,

"one more shot, and it's all over, right in the middle of the back, of the one on top, straight down to the President."

The assassin's brain had a voice; it was the man's own memory of how he sounded in real life when he spoke. Don heard it exactly how it sounded. The man was in fear of his own life. He said,

"then I'll grab my bag and run. Steady, steady."

Don knew exactly when to push it slightly up, and over. The gunman squeezed the trigger, the pin engaged, and Don was on top of the kill. It did not happen. The gunman screamed,

"what? Oh, my God what is wrong! No, oh my God what is wrong!"

He panicked, and in his hurry going out the door, he ran into Don. He did not see him but Don's six foot, one hundred and eighty-five pounds of solid muscle, and bones knocked him down with the hard-hitting force. He did not even try to figure out what knocked him down. He jumped up with the gun, and started to wrap it in the bag, breaking it down as he left the room. Just like a pro, only he left the

shell casings behind. He started to go back, and looked at his

watch, and knew he didn't' have enough time. He ran out the

back door.

Don still cloaked, went out right behind the gunman.

He used his instinct to take advantage of the ability to fly.

This was something he had only dreamed of but never

thought about it happening while this horror took place. Now

he knew the man could never get away no matter what he

tried. Don could observe, and follow wherever he went. He

could read his mind getting all of the information he needed.

Even if it took him weeks, he would get this man, all who

were involved would be brought in by Don. No matter what

it took.

"Chapter Fifty-Four: KAWHOCUMDIA"

Don was flying high but still cloaked, and watching the gunman on the run. He knew what the gunman was thinking, and Don read it loud and clear,

"at least I didn't get caught. Man that was something missing like that."

Don watched the man run for quite a while. He must have been at least five or six blocks away, and he turned left, and started to walk. Just at the turn, he could see there was no one around, and he put the gun down a drain, which had a stick jammed under the edge so that there would be easy entry. Don took a mental picture, and put it in storage for retrieval later. He scanned the area to make sure no one saw the gunman put the rifle in the manhole. Don still had the sounds that were coming from where he had just left. The sirens were blaring, and the shouts, and screams that were dying out gave Don this feeling of being in two places at the same time. The human part of him shuttered from the site of this man he was following. Don was observing very carefully not to forget any detail to aid in the capture of this criminal.

The walk went on further, and Don flew just above but descending every so often, to make a close visual of the man. Don did this for his own satisfaction to know that he was really just a man and a human being kind of man, not some creature changing form. Don now knowing this could take a while settled back to fifteen feet, and landed.

Don still cloaked, walked behind the man he was following, and watching. As he followed he read his mind getting first names, and part of addresses. Still listening, and getting locations finding out things where people spent their time. Don did not know how high the connections went with this man and whoever was responsible for this attempt on the President's life. He knew he was willing to stick it out for as long as it took to get them all. He thought to himself,

"it almost doesn't seem fair to these bad guys, they don't have a chance."

With Don's super powers there was nothing he could not do.

Sam and the rest of the crew by now have reached the Huang He River, and within a few minutes, its change and new formation would begin. The other ships have arrived too. They are all hoping to get visuals overall formation.

The first earthquake began, and the first underground spring opened up. The crew with Zadator had already visited the future, and saw the devastation around the Huang He. Their idea to make depths in different locations along the river to stop the flooding, and save millions of lives here will soon be a reality. In addition, there is a possibility of even saving hundreds of thousands more at other locations.

The three ships started with blasts that created the underground caverns, which created the lakes. Elevations were-figured-and-mapped, and then the calculations brought forth a beginning of the river that made it a paradise. The vegetation around the river was lush, and green. The surrounding forest developed into a habitat for all of the species of China to live, and thrive. This was through the evolution process helped along by the team and over the years was created.

Each year there was another reunion, and several tributaries added to make even more lush land that developed into an amazing asset for China, and its growth, and prosperity. There were farmlands with agriculture that became more highly developed than in any part of the world.

As Don followed the gunman, he got a message from Sam and the crew, that if he needed help they would see him soon. Sam said, "we have got a good start on the project. We will all be involved in one way or another for the next twenty years.

Be careful, we know the danger you are in. You can handle it."

That was the last thing Don ever heard from Sam, his mom, Jimmy, and Danny. The rest of Sam's ship made it out through the pod, and landed safely on a planet called Yevbalcavna... A Russian astronaut named it because of a signal he kept getting from the pod. It was self-sustaining but was still developing and needed at least five more years before it turned itself into a full-blown ship.

The Russians did not know how he was getting the signal from Yevbalcavna but claimed it was from the Russian advancements in technology. He did not know how far behind they were from the people of Belshala.

The Zorvirax were not amused. Of course, it was only a few, such as Zadator, and his wife Belsha, finally Samuel, Zadator's son. Peace knew but she was human, and from the past. Her position as an ambassador for the Zorvirax would never happen; she was all-human, even though she went through programming. Faiocak the father of Peace, had escaped the treachery of primitive life, and left earth with Samuel, and Peace. It was because of the hidden-ship left by Zadator and Belsha that enabled this to come about.

Samuel and Peace took off for a place that later was named Khrami River Valley, which was located in central Georgia. Their location near Russia, and claim for independence from Russia made it a danger zone for the Georgian people. Samuel had gotten the idea from his father, Zadator, that he could find a leader in their history that could be programmed, and possibly solve the problems with Russia. Maybe it was possible with a new kind of persuasion.

Don thought that his gunman had no way out but to go and face the music. He had failed to do his job. What would the ones who wanted this done, do to him? Was this where he was going? Was there an alternate plan? Maybe he was going to escape the city.

It was up to Don to secure this man from anyone that might attempt to assassinate him for his failure. Don jumped back into flight to check what was up ahead. He saw a black Chevy Impala that was speeding around a corner with four large men with ski masks. The three of them were carrying sawed-off-shot-guns. He realized these men were going to kill the crazed gunman he was following. He read one of the gunman's minds that was in the car just for conformation. It was a positive read. They were going to kill him.

"Chapter Fifty-Five: KAWHOCUMDIA"

Don knew he had only moments to gather information from the gunmen coming to kill the man he was following. He tuned in on their conversation, and their thoughts. The men did not have an accent from this area. It sounded like men from the docks up north. He used his powerful eyes to take a mental picture of each man in the car. Then, he broke into the FBI database; it is only a thought away for Don. He had the formula even to reach a phone number through telepathy. In addition, again it is just a thought that makes it work. He ran a photo I.D. check on each one of the men, and got a hit.

The whole group; wanted for murder. They each had

at least fifty or more counts of murder on their records. They each escaped prison, and death, by natural disasters causing their prison walls to collapse with no guards to stop them. There was someone waiting for them to pick them up just outside the prison grounds. Don thought to himself,

"what do you think of that?"

He saw the car getting closer. It was only two blocks away now.

Don flew back down to the gunman he had been following, landed in front of him, and uncloaked himself. Don knew how much speed his movement could produce. So, he rushed up to the man he had been following, and told him,

"I'm here to save your life, if you don't do what I tell you, four gunmen are going to kill you."

The man asked Don,

"who are you?"

Before the man got the words out of his mouth Don was answering, and telling him at the same time,

"I'm Don, and there is no time to explain, you're just going to have to trust me on this one!"

Without another second passing by the car with the gunmen rounded the corner. The man saw the gunmen hanging out of their windows with sawed-off-shot-guns. Before the man could ask Don what to do, he said to Don,

"get me out of here, O.K.?"

Don did not waste any time, he yelled out,

"hang on."

Don spun him around with super speed causing the man to yell, grabbing him in a Heimlich, cloaked himself, and the man, and leaped into flight, airborne. It was just in time. The gunmen opened fire on the place Don and the other man were just standing. Seconds went by, and the gunmen that had come to kill this man and anyone that got in their way realized now there is no one there anymore. This disappearance baffled them of course.

The driver of the assassin's car slammed on his

brakes, and brought the car to a skidding stop. They all four get out of the car at the same time with their guns pointing in all directions. They were looking for their target that they were just firing on seconds ago. By this time Don and the-would-be Presidential-assassin were high above them, and cloaked where they were invisible to the four confused gun-men.

The men were shaking their heads asking each other what the blank was going on. In addition, where in the blank did they go? Everybody knows what, 'what the blank' means but that is what these thugs were saying. I am sure when Don told me this he was not trying to clean up what they said it was just the truth. Remember, these were crazed lunatics out to kill again and it just did not sound like what they might say.

The man on the passenger side up front yelled out a command at the others, while he tried to figure it all out.

"Get back in the car, all of you."

They stood there looking at him, silently. The man seemingly, the leader screamed it again,

"get back in the car, now!

He had been standing with his gun pointing to the sky but dropped it, and aimed at the other three. They each looked at the other, and got back in the car.

Don saw the leader looking up toward him, and the little man he was carrying in a hover position. Don started to move away slowly, and something snapped on the man's shirt, its button. The pressure from Don's arm holding him pulled the shirt in different directions. Pop, the button was off, and falling. Down it fell, and hit the gunman standing below them in the forehead. The gunman looked down at the sidewalk, and saw the button. He still has not figured it out but picked the button up off the sidewalk. Looking at it and back up in the air above him, he started to scream to the other men.

"Get out of the car, they're in the sky above us, shoot

them! They're up above us, shoot them!"

He screams mercilessly,

"shoot him! Kill him! Kill him!

He stumbled on his words just a bit, and changed
what he said,

"kill them, kill them, kill them!"

Don did not wait a fraction of a second. He invoked
high speed get-away, and he could see the gunman shooting
up, straight up. He got a look at the license plate, and made a
mental note to run it through the FBI's database; the report
back said, stolen. It belonged to some teacher two hundred
miles away.

Don looked out over the horizon, and the beautiful
skyline, and where the city ended, and the wooded landscape
began. He said to his passenger,

"it's time to set down, don't try anything, I'd hate to
hurt you, or worse."

The little man cried out,

"O.K.! I will not, believe me, I will not! You have me convinced after flying me up here, in the sky! Do you know what I mean?"

Don landed with the little man, not saying anything to him. He then fell to his knees, and just started shaking his head in disbelief. He said,

"what is happening to me?"

He was still just shaking his head back and forth when Don looked at him, and said,

"yea, I get that a lot.

I am making that up. Still, it felt good to say it."

"Chapter Fifty-Six: KAWHOCUMDIA"

Doubt was creeping into the gunman's mind as he thought about the possibilities of dying at the hands of Don. He had decided that the only reason Don saved him, was to kill him himself. He asked Don,

"why are you keeping me out here, you know, in the woods like this?"

Don knew what he was getting at but responded inquisitively anyway,

"what do you mean?"

The gunman's voice trembled now with fear,

"look, I'm not too stupid; I know what you're planning to do to me!"

Don answered very childlike toying with the killer,

"you do? What's that?"

Now begging with tears in his eyes, the man pleaded with Don,

"don't kill me mister. I have a wife, and two kids. I know you have super powers but do not kill me, please!

Don still toyed with the gunman he had captured,

"who would marry you?

Don felt what he had just said was too much, and too cruel a jab no matter what the gunman had done, he said angrily,

"and have babies with you. Do you think that if she knew what you were trying to do, she would not leave you in a heartbeat, and you would never see those kids again? You tried to shoot the President and the First Lady. Not to mention the other people that was in that area. In addition, the children, a stray bullet could have killed any number of them in the crowd. What kind of monster does that?"

"O.K. mister, I know how bad it was, and I'm sorry."

There was a silence. The man spoke softly,

"I got roped into it."

The man was barely audible, and Don yelled out,

"what?"

Now, the man trying not to offend Don spoke louder,

"I got roped into it, and that's all I'm going to say. It was a stupid thing to try. I'm never going to brag about anything again."

Another silence fell between the two of them; Don continued to look at the man as he stared into the dirt in front of him. He was still on his knees, and went on,

"that's how it got started. It was a stupid thing. I am never going to get away with it anyway. They are going to catch me. You know, the fed's. Alternatively, the big shots are going to have me killed. They are the ones who are having it done. The big shots in..."

He hesitated.

"I can't tell you which ones. I do not really know anyway. But they are the ones."

More silence, then, Don started his story.

"In my whole life, I've never wanted to kill anyone. Oh yea, I forgot. There was this one time. It all started when a person that came to visit a friend of mine, he lived down the street from me. I was at the friend's house, and the person drove up in this beauty of a nineteen-forty Ford, it was a clean, customized, painted white, cherry. I have not thought about that term or used it in a long, long time.

Anyway, I met him in the driveway of the friend. His weight was nearly double mine. I remember because he kept bragging about his weight. He had been to reform school, and they worked him almost to death, that is what he said while he was bragging about his fabulous body. I really did not think he was a very good-looking person but I guess his girlfriend did. Maybe she liked him because he looked muscled up.

My neighbor friend and this person talked for quite a while. Therefore, with me hanging around, and listening to them the person grew to know what I looked like. From then on, when he would see me walking through town, or somewhere on my way home, he would stop, and give me a ride to the house. He was a vicious hot-rodder, and was always showing off by squealing his wheels. I think without saying too much about him, he really was a smart mouth person. It was as if he could not pop off enough.

This was the person I almost wanted to kill and it was only for a fraction of a second maybe a few fractions more than a few. That does not really count. Anyway, it was a good reason. He nearly beat me to death over a girl. He was dating a cute dark headed girl. I will not mention any names. You would not know her name anyway. To make a long story short, I got banged up pretty bad by this guy because she kissed me in the mouth."

The man asked Don,

"why are you telling me all of this?"

Don just simply replied,

"I don't know, I thought it was an interesting story. Now shut up about me going to kill you. I am not going to kill you ever, unless you force me to. You aren't going to force me are you? Stop worrying, I will not. You are safe with me. Do not make me kill you, just a joke.

The man replied,

"some help you are just remember I have kids."

Don had many ways of putting someone to sleep through pressure points. But being the nice guy he was he asked the gunman,

"what's your name?"

He replied,

"Ra el."

Don said,

"good night Ra el."

With Don's new power, he waved his hand over Ra

el's sleeping body, and created a protective security barrier that would alert Don if anyone came within one hundred feet.

Don leaped into the air, and was in flight. He would still have enough good light to do some investigating. He had some names, and it looked like a night of tricky surveillance. He scanned the area that the car came from, and found its exact location. He immediately headed there continually scanning. As the night began to fall, he used his night vision along with checking the section of the map that was color-coded. His night vision color-coded the streets to the precise location of the house. He landed behind a well-hidden stand of bushes. Don used his super sensors to detect that nothing was out of line in this neighborhood. There was nothing to connect the four gunmen and the car. He did notice that this was a very nice section of town for a teacher. He ran a check in the FBI's database again, and found nothing on the Allen C that the car was-taken-from. Don said to himself, "they have probably already ditched the car by now and on a plane back to wherever they came from."

He then scanned his memory for something that could help him find the car. Don knew he could do this without too much of a problem. He got a hit; a memory heat sensory formula that could detect the memory of the exact temperature of the car from today's scene. Moreover, that would be exactly when they were shooting at Don, and the gunman he had with him hanging around in the sky today.

Don found the connection, and jumped into the air, and was in flight. Now, he was up over the city, and it only took seconds. He started scanning the area immediately with his power sensory eyes. The alert screen showed a section waiting for recognition. Encased in a red blinking square, waiting for lock, and ready to pinpoint a location would be his target. He scanned the whole city. Nothing came into the viewfinder yet. He flew toward the airport, nothing happened there. Then it came to him, they would not have flown out on a commercial air flight. It would have been too dangerous for them to leave town after the big bad miss. With security tightened to the maximum it would have been a private plane but not a jet; it would have been something less noticeable. Like a small Cessna, this would have done the trick.

Then, he said it to himself in a whisper,

"scan the small airports quickly Don."

It only took him a couple of seconds, and he found it. The car came into the viewfinder, and the address popped up on the info section of the screen. He flew at nearly maximum speed, and in seconds, he was at the airport parking lot. He saw the car sitting alone at the back of the lot. He checked for airport personnel, and only one older night watchman, a security officer of many years, Don could tell. He peeked into his mind, and got the information he needed. The security guard had one weapon on his hip. Don saw that the guy was a bit too sleepy. He was sitting in a chair with his cap over his eyes, and his head was nodding down every few seconds.

Flight to the car only took a second or two. He hovered over the car looking for clues. He set a barrier around the car to sound proof it, and isolate it for an overall scan for fingerprints, and gunpowder residue. All of the things that the police and the FBI would be doing, this time, Don with super powers helping with the crime scene. Every type of registry under the Zorvirax Sun and Planet Earth Sun was all through Don's new power. He thought to himself,

"I may just top the charts tonight on this one."

It is his people now that he kept thinking about, and wondering if they were all safe, and how much fun they were having, he then though about Cat.

Again, he thought to himself but aloud,

"I see we've got the job done, this should pack 'em in tomorrow. They will not know who did all of this in such a short time, and there will be no names for credit on the paper work. I wonder who will do the honors, and take the credit for it all. This is undercover just to get it in the works. It's important, huh guys?"

"Chapter Fifty-Seven: KAWHOCUMDIA"

Don knew he had to move Ra el by sunrise or the traffic just from out of nowhere alone could find him, and that would not be good. No one would have been able to figure out the cocoon much less Ra el being in it. He had also given some thought on how to handle getting Ra el to the FBI alive. The plan was for Don to join the FBI, and then turn him in. Don thought that maybe he could watch over him to keep him safe. It did not mean Ra el was safe even while in protective custody. He just wanted to give him the best shot he could get. He thought,

"if I could beef up security around him while I was there, he would be safe when I had to leave. Maybe I can come up with something. I do have super power now."

He sped away at high speed to get back to the wooded area where he left Ra el. As soon as he arrived, he
checked to see if Ra el was stirring inside the container. Don
quickly removed the protective cocoon, and let Ra el out. He
turned off the alarm system, and created a backpack for the
container. He strapped it on Ra el's back. He grabbed him
from the back, and under the arm pits and they were in flight
in a second. They were only in the air for a minute or less,
and Don set down in an alley behind the Federal building.
He released Ra el, and told him,

"when you see me the next time, I'll be an FBI agent,
so don't run from me, you will not get away. Understand?"

Ra el responded positively to Don,

"yes boss, I understand! Would you hurry and come
back and get me?"

Don answered quickly to satisfy Ra el,

"yes, I'll hurry. And speaking of that, time's a wasting, got to go."

Don slipped away, and out of sight. As soon as no one was able to see him, then Ra el hurried out of the alley. He did not want to be a suspect in any crime that had been committed in the last few minutes. He knew there was always crime going on in this city.

Ra el disappeared down the street. He did not know that Don had planted a tracker inside of him, and Don was not worried in the least bit about finding him again.

Don tried not to draw suspicion to them so he walked to the FBI building. When he got to the steps, he realized how huge the building was. He thought about the awesome power the building represented, and the many lives that the people that work here had saved. He found out after a quick search that scanned for the information that the number was low compared to the figure he thought it would be, and was that much more determined to sign up. More so now than ever Don thought about keeping the secret of his power to himself.

Don stopped when he reached the top of the steps. What chance will he have to make the things happen he wanted completed on this mission? He reached for the time travel formula to make the process start. Stepping back in time to start the history he needed to create his present, then from this present to the future if necessary. The changes that he created made it possible for him to get into the FBI. The connections were made and Don now knew they were endless, and powerful. His own personal experience enhanced, he was thrilled with the outcome of the things that had happened in his life. What he made up, are now the things that have happened. After the mission is finished, they are up for reevaluation. Now they are real, and identified as such. Because of their deaths, connection with the real people is impossible. In addition, some with disabilities that kept them from functioning because of brain damage or memory loss: invented back before their accidents. He also needed a psychiatrist to examine him for any psychological problem he may have had or have. His new evaluation will begin in two weeks. They can accept him under these conditions. It is all set up, and for the sake of Ra el, Don hoped he could keep him hidden.

He went through the first two weeks without a hitch. Everyone in the unit liked him except for Dunk. The name came from the first case he worked. It seemed a female they named Cheyenne that had a record a mile long led him on a chase through the woods into a septic tank left open on purpose. Cheyenne made it out of the woods, and got away. Dunk got his new name when his partner had to fish him out of the nasty mess. Hence, Dunk.

Dunk was not a person you would want as a partner. He was cranky, vulgar and made everybody he could, mad, just to prove he could. He just did not care what anybody thought. Some said he was older than God was, and nobody knew how long he had been with the Bureau. They said it was since its beginning, nobody seemed too really know. Only time will tell if he ever comes around to liking Don but according to Don he was grumpy, grumpy, and grumpy. He said he was not going to let up on him until something turned up on Don or something would happen that would make them bond.

Monday rolled around, and he was-officially-established as an official FBI agent. He would work assigned cases alone. Some of the time it was required that two agents work together. You were lucky if you got a car when you worked alone-or-with-a-partner. Don told his boss Lance that he had a person that was the shooter in the assassination attempt. Lance snapped back at Don about doing the paper work on it. Don answered Lance,

"no sir, I didn't do that paper work for the third time, no sir I didn't."

Lance replied,

"oh, O.K., make sure...."

Don told Lance more,

"boss I've told you I'm hiding him to protect him from being killed. There are bad people after him. They tried to kill him once already."

Lance again stuttered and tried to cover his bad memory,

"that's right, O.K., that's right, go get him, and bring him in for me, please."

Don answered back,

"thanks boss."

There were too many things going on in the department for Don to feel bad about Lance not being able to keep up. They were always behind in every case. It was craziness.

As he was on his way out to go pick up Ra el, Don had a future flash that made him change his mind on what he was about to do about Ra el. When he got to his car in the parking lot, he reached in the open window, stuck the key in the ignition. He went to the open area, cloaked himself, and jumped into flight. He erased the whole thing. His ability to control the past, present and future made it easy to make up his mind on what to do.

He landed back in front of Ra el just as he was answering, and asking him,

"yes boss, I understand? Would you hurry and come back and get me?"

This time Don told Ra el,

"you know what, I've got a better idea, hang on!"

Don took hold of Ra el, and with one leap, they were in flight.

There are times when a man thinks that what he is doing is the right thing to do. There are circumstances when other men see that man, and know he is doing the right thing, and the only thing that these other men can think of to do is to try to stop that man.

"Chapter Fifty-Eight: KAWHOCUMDIA"

Through the revelations that time travel gave Don, he knew that his moves with Ra el were bringing his life closer, and closer to an end. Three shots in the head would have killed Ra el without a doubt. That was Don's conclusion after making a check on the future for Ra el's sake. No doubt, Don could have saved him in another way but why go through something when you had other choices. With the telepathic conference he had with Zadator, Don discerned that his suggestion was not just a suggestion. Thus, a check on the future was necessary.

Don had hidden the facts from Ra el but was watching him just as if he were in the healing process from the wounds he would have received. Even though Zadator's connection was through telepathy, Don knew it was very real as real could get. Now he was feeling the excitement of having the power to make these changes, and knew why Zadator had shown him these things. Cat too, would be getting mental messages now. She was in, and would become a part of his future life.

Don was flying at almost full speed, and had cloaked himself, and Ra el. Ra el had already closed his eyes. Don started the mental telepathy with Ra el but not knowing this, he asked Don,

"where are we going?"

Don answered,

"for now it's Georgia, ever been there?"

Ra el's opinion showed when he recoiled with his answer.

"No! Why would I want to go to Georgia?"

Don still spoke back to Ra el through telepathy, and Ra el still did not notice, "no reason. I guess I just thought I would ask. You will like it. It is a beautiful state. Just be careful of the people though, they are real crazy mean if you do not know them. They are a bit clannish.

Ra el showed the fear by raising his pitch,

"do you mean the____?"

Don still getting a kick out of ribbing Ra el said,

"no, they're just clannish. Have you ever tried raw oysters on the half shell?"

Ra el's response came repulsed, and he said,

"No!"

Don went on still poking at Ra el,

"um good."

Don picked up their speed but not too fast or he might lose Ra el. He asked Ra el,

"you O.K.?"

Ra el yelled back at him thinking Don could not hear with all of the wind noise, "yea!"

First he got a chuckle to himself but then Don's eyes started scanning the countryside for things of interest, and to find a place to set down to get Ra el to a rest stop. He would find them a place for Ra el to use the bathroom. He saw an old rest stop along the hi-way, and peered through the building walls. There was no one there. He landed coming right up to the men's rest room door. He told Ra el,

"use it if you have to."

He uncloaked Ra el as he walked through the door. Don stayed outside, cloaked to watch just in case of any security threats. The rest stop was uneventful, and quiet. Don's mind was satisfied for the time being anyway. He had anticipated everything and anything happening even this far away, you just cannot know everything.

Don uncloaked himself, and asked Ra el,

"do you want a coke?"

Ra el responded like an old friend,

"no, I'm good."

Don asked,

"then you're ready?"

"Yea, I'm ready man. This flying stuff is great."

Still Don carried on with telepathy, still Ra el had not noticed,

"good, let's go."

He reached under Ra el's arm and around his chest as if he was carrying a small package. It was the magic of Ra el's life, up into the air they flew. Ra el asked,

"where do you work again?"

Don kept Ra el in the dark again,

"I'm currently unemployed, I just left the FBI, and I guess you might say I'm on administrative leave. No paycheck though, they do not like freeloaders. I do not know if I want to stay with them or not now. I might go back to singing, and playing guitar in bars and lounges again. I'm a musician, vocalist part-time."

Ra el does not say anything. Don cloaked them both again. The flight continued full speed keeping in mind Ra el's safety. As the flight went on further, Ra el heard the whistle in his ears from the wind. It seemed to get louder the further they go. Don heard the complaints Ra el was making to him. Don created sound barriers that were undetectable to the human eye, and could not be felt by the person or being using them. Ra el felt the relief, and immediately asked Don,

"hey man that helped a lot, how'd you do that? You did do that didn't you?"

Don looked at Ra el, and said,

"you're welcome. You would do the same for me I'm sure."

They then start more small talk, and the time slipped by them. Don said to Ra el,

"we're here."

Ra el asked,

"what do you think those Fed's would have done to

me if you had turned me in to them? Do you think they would have killed me, and framed somebody? Do you think they could ever find me here?"

Don felt the desperation when he heard the tone in Ra el's voice. He said,

"no, they'll never find us here.

Ra el replied,

"thank you, thanks."

"Chapter Fifty-Nine: KAWHOCUMDIA"

Don made the landing perfectly, however Ra el had trouble getting his balance. His being in the air for such a long time even had his head spinning. This is what Ra el said to Don,

"could we get something to eat?"

Ra el was trying not to show any impatience with Don but was trying him just a smidgen. Ra el expressed to him trying him further,

"I'm just a little bit hungry."

He looked down at his hands, and saw they were red and swollen. He then said to Don,

"I feel like I've been riding a motor bike all day. You

know that funny feeling you get from the motor's vibrations, tingly kind a, tickles."

Don agreed, and said,

"yes, I know."

Ra el was starting to become curious about what was happening, he said,

"why do you suppose that is? I mean, you weren't vibrating like a motor bike."

Don gave Ra el a sensible answer,

"it's the bad circulation; it came from no movement in your body. It will come back. Why not walk around a while, move your hands and arms to get the circulation going? If you want to, there is a road back into the woods. We can take a walk before dark."

Ra el was pleasantly surprised at Don's response and said,

"yes, that might be a good idea. Then we can get something to eat, right?"

Don almost felt a friendship developing between the two of them, and replied,

"right. Its ten minutes to get back there, and ten minutes back to the house, maybe twenty. I will try to contact mom, she will be happy to meet you if she can get back. We'll just have to see about what she can do."

Ra el was delighted, he said,

"O.K., let's go!"

Don hated the thoughts of letting Ra el down because of his history; he wanted this to work out for the good, naturally. He let Ra el take the lead, and followed him about six feet behind. He called out to Ra el,

"how are your feet, and hands doing?"

Ra el sounded more like a small boy than a grown man,

"fine sir, I think they are doing just fine."

Don not wanting to be the overseer in his voice tried to have his sincerest measure of himself to Ra el, said, "good, let me know if they start feeling uncomfortable."

Ra el, not opposed to good treatment but not used to it said,

"sure, O.K..."

The light from the sun seemed to cast a shadowy orange hue over the trail, which used to be an old one lane logging road. There was plenty of daylight left but something was different. It was just a feeling that Don had, not something, he could put his finger on. Maybe it was just his nerves from the thoughts about protecting Ra el. Maybe it was his new power, and the extra sensory that came with the territory. He was worried about his mom, and Sam, and the rest of the crew. Since he was dropped on this mission, he had worried about many things he had not worried about before. The future had not been looked into that far in advance, so he did not know about all of the events that would take place. For some reason Sam's mind reading entry, kept coming into view on the display in Don's mind but each time deleted after thirty seconds. This done manually sent an alert, and not otherwise specified as the automatic deletions done after each hour. Moreover, if held for a twenty-four hour period, specificity a must by the sender each time.

Don thought it was a signal from Sam and thought,

"why? This could mean trouble, and anything not procedural, was sent as a call for help or a warning of something dangerous."

He readied himself for an attack. He ran an invisible shield just ahead of Ra el. His creations were of his own style. They were his minds plans, his way. He also put an identical twin of Ra el and himself should anything happen. If needed, there would be one of each of them left. If their enemy thought the worst, they would have a better chance of escape. It would only be at the autopsy that they found out. The shields that were up for Ra el could withstand explosions, fire, and gunfire of very high caliber weapons. In addition, of course Don's shield was up as soon as he realized something was wrong. He did this because the messages were not coming through. Ra el asked Don,

"excuse me sir, are we about there? I'm really starting to get hungry!"

That is when Don saw the flicker. He had expanded his view in one section of his screen, and pulled in magnification to pick up reflections, and things that would glitter. The sensors also showed metal objects that were out of place in the forest, the things that would not ordinarily be there.

At that point Don knew there was no doubt about the danger they were approaching. His sensors did not tell him exactly what it was because there was not enough time. The indicator started flashing danger immediately, flashing like a huge red sign in front of them. He jumped through the shield he had put up for Ra el, just barely making it as the released barrier made a pop. Don did it to keep the barrier from trying to destroy them.

He had Ra el under his arm, and was in flight in less than two seconds. His speed was faster than the bullet that hit the heel of his shoe and destroyed it. The shooter must have been trying to calculate his speed, was aiming above his head, and missed his target. There was no harm to his foot or the rest of his shoe but it took the heel off nearly to the sock. He felt the warm sensation as though standing on a heater-vent too long. Ra el yelled out,

"sir, what was that?"

Don called back loud and clear,

"Eba unis fra Tu taeda chee."

Ra el's eyes rolled around in the sockets. He had never heard this before. Ra el asked,

"what language was that? What did you say?"

Don was once again speaking to Ra el through telepathy, and moving his lips with the words, just to keep Ra el at ease,

"Our God help us to escape unharmed, set us free."

Ra el still not understanding it all was searching his memory for some hint of the language, he said,

"and what language was that?"

Don looked at the back of Ra el's head, and put a thought through without Ra el looking at him,

"I'll tell you another time, and place if God be willing."

Ra el tried to turn his head but could not make it all the way around. He looked back again straight ahead, and closed his eyes. He could not stand the speed nor was he hungry anymore. He stayed silent for the next thirty minutes.

Don set down in the woods somewhere in Georgia. He was sure that Ra el had never been there before. It was like that same signal again that led Don to the spot. He thought to himself,

"that's funny; I know exactly where this is. Something else funny, I do not think I have ever been here. This is the sight of the expedition Zadator and his wife Belsha where Samuel their son went missing. Don landed on the rock that was Samuel's favorite place. He helped Ra el sit down. Ra el said to Don,

"thank you man that helped."

He groaned a sign of relief. Just then, a puff of air came from his mouth, and his lips pouched out. Don noticed his letting out the pressure, and chuckled to himself thinking,

"at least it wasn't coming from the other end."

Don knew this location all right from the study of Georgia history. Still, he was not sure of what the signal was regarding. He knew it had to be from someone that had or knew about the power. Don sat down next to Ra el, and crossed his legs in a yoga position. It was time to meditate. He put his head down with his chin on his chest, and closed his eyes. Ra el said quietly,

"what's next? Who will be the next intruder?"

Don was sure that he and Ra el would be safe for a

while. For how long he did not know. Ra el raised his head from between his knees, and asked Don,

"what was that line again, you know the one you said in another language?

Don raised himself into midair, and said,

"Eba unis fra Tu, teda chee."

There was a long silence, and Ra el put his head back between his knees. Don descended back to his original position. His usual meditative position was always three eights of an inch above gravitational hold. He put his head down between his knee, and enclosed himself and Ra el in a protective cocoon, relaxed, and said,

"good night."

"Chapter Sixty: KAWHOCUMDIA"

Time was not always on Don's side before program-ming, now it seemed to be under control. Moreover, this was without too much trouble. The events that would have hap-pened with the FBI would have been easy enough to reverse had Don not stopped before they actually happened. He could have worked through a series of events that would have led him to the agents, now he knew for sure, there were more than a few trying to kill Ra el. His sense was that they had a strong conviction to kill him but Don needed to know how strong, and that was one of the reasons why he ditched the FBI gig, and escaped with Ra el. Alternatively, Don thought, they had started something at the top, way before Ra el was even picked to do the dirty deed. Still, Don had not gotten all of the names involved yet was determined to go back in time until he got every man or woman that was involved.

Don was for just hiding out on top of the lookout rock for as long as he could. However, he knew duty called too. From things that he experienced after going through programming, time travel established to this very spot in the beginning of human civilization. Now, he was capable of time travel himself. Don was well equipped with the powers that Zadator had himself. He wondered if this leader of the Zorvirax might not have more. He was looking for the signal coming from somewhere at this place of meetings, and campsite. He felt he must leave Ra el for a few minutes. Ra el would stay secure in the cocoon. Don had only been asleep for a short while when his thoughts of safety woke him. He took off the shield, and moved away from Ra el. He then replaced the cocoon again. He walked to edge of the huge rock, and jumped down. He helped himself down with his ability to fly, gently, and slowly floating down. Gently, and slowly sinking lower, and lower. He landed in the mulched carpet; the forest had lain for millions of years. This was undisturbed territory. He recognized that this was a place that was not visited by many human beings since the beginning of time.

Don had been in and out of his career, and had put his music on hold most of his adult life. He said it was for one reason or another. His whole idea to keep Ra el with him was to keep him safe from harm. Now it seemed dread was going to follow him wherever he went. Ra el was guilty of the crime, now so were agents of the FBI guilty. He stayed for a while before he walked any further from the rock. When he landed, he just wanted to feel more secure feelings passing through his body before he moved again. The edge he had with his power did not stop his human senses or spirit. Even though programming had changed his strengths, and left his weaknesses almost nil, he still had them. The fact was that

Don had not lost himself in all of these changes. He was sure that Zadator knew he needed these assignments in order to become the allied teammate he should be. Don had always known about being-confident. He learned most of the things he knew about before programming, on his own. His wife was an inspiration, even though they divorced. He had great respect for her, and anyone that had knowledge about the things, which they talked. He said many times,

"I admire those that stuck to the facts of whatever came out of their mouths."

He felt he had to move now to keep his insecurities from creeping in; besides, he had nothing about which to be insecure. In addition, he knew it.

Now, the darkness had set in, and he started his night vision. Suddenly, everything was visible. It was almost like daylight but with a subdued different kind, and amount of light. The feeling it created was it was fake, a false lighting. It was not real.

His first step was not any big deal. He took it, and then several more. What he did not know was that he advanced for the pit that the tribesmen had built centuries ago. This was after Samuel and Peace left earth in the spacecraft that Zadator entrusted for Samuel to find. The crew brought along with Zadator, and Belsha did it under instructions from Zadator. Don being on guard came from the darkness, and his ever-looming suspicious nature, turned on his x-ray vision. He wanted to see through anything from the tips of his toes, to one hundred feet out at a time. He spotted the pit just in time. He said,

"wow, that was close."

He immediately stopped. He was just short two or three feet of the pit. This pit was not a kill pit but a trap for whatever fell in it. He analyzed the hole; it could have kept anyone or any animal until they either starved to death or died from another wild passer-by looking for something to eat. This wilderness jungle was full of mountain lion, bear, wolf, and many other wild things of prey. The wildlife experts assured anyone wanting to come into the jungle that it was still uncharted by man.

When Don looked further down into the pit, he noticed a tunnel that went off to the right of the pit in the lower-right-hand corner. In addition, it had a door which they-shut-tight. From the distance, the structure did not seem to be made of prehistoric architect but was made of and advanced civilizations material, something with power beyond belief. Don thought to himself,

"yes, I think it is from the Zorvirax."

It had the simplest operation to open the door. It had a pull bar that you just pull and it opened. He searched history, and said to himself,

"it was added on; it was built by Zadator, and his son Samuel."

As his search concluded, it revealed that the pit was not built until a future date but here it is in living color.

Don's mind could not believe what it was displaying on his screen. He almost stepped in it, he said to himself,

"wait a minute; this is not for me to see. I am in a space that opens to attack protected by the Zorvirax as un-discovered. It is for someone to find, no wait a minute."

A thirty-second silence split the air.

"Chapter Sixty-One: KAWHOCUMDIA"

"Analysis; code imprint panel originate."

Immediately a hologram with a three-dimensional solid feel to it came up in front of Don's face. His hand went up almost as quickly as the hologram panel appeared. He placed his hand on the imprint panel, and signaled start. Going in all directions, the hologram panel disappeared. As it went out of sight a mechanical, voice said,

"complete."

Don's world started to change, and the whole area turned into a park. He thought to himself,

"this place will be a park someday."

Don brought up the screen again to find out what day

he had just been transported to, and it read, July 4, 3008

Time, 2:28 p.m...

Don started looking for signs of a natural disaster or something that was going to happen. He did not know why being shown this was important to him but was watching, and waiting patiently.

Then, it cracked across the sky with a fiery flame behind it, a huge exploding ball of fire the size of a meteor. Don was protected from any harm but he looked up at Ra el on the rock under the security cocoon. He was covered, and was O.K... It was happening all around Don, and Ra el. The place was now a burning inferno. The explosions were going off all around them. It was if someone planted bombs everywhere. His screen came up again, and told him his time travel visit was up, and immediately he went back to his own time. His formula for getting back to his time he had just left was simple enough. He was standing in front of the pit again. There was still no movement or sound on top of the rock where Ra el lay sleeping. He thought to himself,

"now what?"

Don really needed some time to think.

"What am I to do now?"

He turned and jumped with the help of flight to the top of the rock. He started looking for clues, and really wanted to get to safer ground. Ra el did not move at all or stir the slightest in his sleep. Don thought,

"he must have been really tired."

Don's search for history in his future only revealed the devastation to come but what a significant find. He looked to the edge of the pit from the top of the rock; he was hoping to find the tunnel he had seen earlier. It was only seconds, and there it was, the glowing was unbelievable. He found it, the answer; it led to an underground facility built long ago. He wondered as he thought to himself,

"what stage of development is it in at this very moment?"

He started a search of the place, only visually with his super powered eyes. He started counting the floors that the unit just underneath him had. Two hundred and eight thousand floors was the number where he stopped. He screamed aloud,

"oh my God!"

His eyes were as big as his fist. Don stopped himself, and thought.

"This is the alien complex, and I'm in a time zone where there's no one that can reach me. They're in this building, yet they can't reach me."

It also had a spacecraft hanger just under the ground. It was on the top floor. The ground would open up some way, and they would fly right out. Don said softly to himself,

"what a place!"

He checked for a time on the position that he was in now. He said it aloud,

"what?"

It was not making sense to Don that this was to come on the July 4 picnic. He asked himself,

"how does the world survive? Wait a minute! It is just down the road from here where Sam's place is, the one that enlisted me. He lived there with his family. I hope I am getting this right! It will save me a lot of study, and research.

Now why was Sam from down the road, in the picture? It has something to do with the right person for the job! In addition, it is whom it is that will cause this end to earth! Man, it is hard to think about this. I might be the right person for the job. Am I seeing the true future? I know it is true it is according to the history, and future history provided by the Zorvirax and the programming. This is getting to be quite complicated. There is nothing too complicated for the Zorvirax, or is there something not being told? Will the things that we change make history better? Alternatively, will they cause things to be worse? I mean what made this explosive ball of fire hit earth, and what must we do to save it? I will have to find all of them now. These questions must be answered before I can go on."

He reeled around to, and looked at the rock he left Ra el sleeping on. He was positive he was still standing on it. There was a message on his screen, saying Vortex exit coming, prepare for entry. He then checked for authenticity to make sure he was leaving a place that could get them back to the time that they belonged in. He said to himself,

"this must have been set up for someone else that is coming to learn of the future of earth."

Don's check showed that it was authentic, and he must leave from his point of entry, which would be the top of the rock. He said with relief,

"thank God!"

He waved his hand, and removed the protective cocoon from over Ra el. Ra el's sleepy eyes started to open, he said to Don,

"good morning, I guess. I thought I might have been

dreaming. What's up?"

Don said to Ra el without any hesitation in his voice,

"I'm going to place my arm under your arm pit, and around your chest. Close your eyes, and hang on!"

The only words out of Ra el were,

"oh my God!"

In addition, they lifted off the rock by Don's power, and flew into the air. Don hit the Vortex centered perfectly. Ra el did not see a thing. Don quickly cloaked them, which was for their security. As soon as they hit the other side of the Vortex, they were invisible. They were at the same place as before but in what the Zorvirax called with reentry, *the time of their own age.*

Don thought of himself as a super hero for just a second. Then he said to himself,

"not allowed, not allowed. Signs of human weakness, not allowed."

Just by making, these simple statements made him

feel as if he were back in full control. His sense of humor kicked in, and he made a mouth fart, he said,

"it's quicker than an armpit fart."

How was he going to do that? He was in flight. He said to himself,

"it's not funny but the surprise of doing it is what was funny.

Don figured he had better get Ra el and himself to a safer place. He continued to fly north. He, and Ra el received his cloak check, Don knew if he hurried, he could get to DC before nightfall. He leaned toward the left ear of Ra el, and told him their direction; Washington DC, and would be there before nightfall. He then told him to hang on, and hang in. With the thought of safety, Don started to pick up speed.

Ra el started to feel the sting of the speed on his ears, and yelled to Don that they were starting to sting. With Don's creativeness and in his abilities it became more apparent with each day what he was capable of doing. He told Ra el,

"hang on a minute."

Suddenly, Ra el was surrounded in a harness that completely secured him. Then Don spread his arms like wings, and a wingspan just above each of his arms became shaped. This was the start to help Ra el with his flight. The harness attached to the wings from underneath. Then in rapid succession, the rest of the craft except for the belly, and design was constructed in a matter of two or three seconds, all from the creation in Don's mind. Again, the formulas; brought then to life, the belly of the craft made expressively with a comfortable seat that would far surpass an easy chair. The wings started to form with something like two turbo jet engines under each wing. Don slid in through a passage from the back of the craft. He sat at the control seat, and the uncloaking only took a second. Ra el's eyes opened wide in amazement. His disbelief left him in a shocked state. He found himself in a semi-state-of-consciousness similar to programming sleep. Ra el's eyes closed, and he went sound to sleep. Don could wake him at any time with ease when, and if he wanted to. It would only take a command from Don.

As soon as Don had finished the major functions of the vessel, he assigned the spacecraft with the job of creating all of the remaining features, and accessories. It became the newest and most innovative space ship ever created. History would prove that it was to be the mind vehicle of all time.

Like the mother ship of Zadator, it grew on its own. Don's ship, like a select few, connected to the information given to him by the Zorvirax. Only Don had invented his own formula for time travel, which was different from the one the Zorvirax created. He had programmed it into the ship with codes that only he and the ship would know. This was to keep it safe so that it would not get into the wrong hands.

Don named the ship Artifice. This was especially fitting under the circumstances. His life and Ra el's would depend on the escape tools this craft could quickly invent. Don had no doubt that the ability of the new ship would far exceed any of his expectations. In seconds of his thoughts about his new feelings about the ship, a small young woman's voice came on the intercom created by the ship, and said,

"as you wish sir, the destination's course is charted, and down on record, auto pilot is in the on position. The panel controls will be in halogen at your wish. If there is any question about your need for it visually, I will ask you for the permission to display it. This ship will hover at your destination in cloaked status. This is at a safe distance from earth's touchdown. When you awake, you can take control or call me, I will be waiting.

The voice said, ship Artifice, have a good rest."

Don slipped into sleep, and felt heart's peace for the first time.

"Chapter Sixty-Two: KAWHOCUMDIA"

As Don's eyes opened, he could see the horizon. The large cumulonimbus clouds decorated the blue sky, with smaller clouds to accompany the billowing larger ones. His problem of waking quickly was still there. He rubbed his eyes to try to bring himself to more of a conscience state. While he slept, his mind was still receiving information, and updates relating to formulas that would be an increase in power. He knew that the powers given to him were not of him but as time went on, he was beginning to mesh with the power he had. It was an acceptance thing to Don. He was becoming the man with the power, and accepting the changes that got easier.

Ra el was still sleeping peacefully, so Don left him alone to sleep. He was beginning to feel more compassion for Ra el than in the beginning when they first had their unusual meeting.

After Don had a few minutes to wake, the ship spoke quietly, and said,

"did you sleep well Captain?"

Don then for the first time took in the fact that he was the Captain of his ship. He thought to himself,

"is this ship a complete mind yet, or is it still a machine?"

The voice came back to him answering,

"a machine, but, with a complete mind! And, I do have the means to read your

mind."

Don surprised responded,

"you do? Well, great!"

She answered back,

"but, it's only when privacy is not an issue. You do know about the formula for privacy discernment.

Don now wanting to know more about his ship's new personality said,

"Yes, and you will be called,"

She softly replied,

"since my gender is to suit you, ma'am will do just fine. Alternatively, the name you gave me in the beginning, Artifice. Oh, if in the future you should want to change it to something else, it will be up for discussion. I'm sure though, you will be given the final say, Captain."

Don responded like the Captain on the matter, undirected,

"thank you ma'am."

"Chapter Sixty-Three: KAWHOCUMDIA"

Our story here is about a man who can fly, like the others the gift came from the same source. With this gift came the gift of longevity, maybe thousands of years, maybe even longer. Since the original beings that created the formulas, not all are living now; no one knows how long the receiver of the power can live. Not even Zadator could tell how long life will be. Of the connections with the original Zorvirax, there were some destroyed. The searches for the missing formulas are underway but no one knows how long it will take to rediscover the missing links.

The man of this story started not only flying but got

the nickname Fly. In addition, a man from the past, which also had superpower, gave him the nickname. The same power received by others that exceeded the human imagination. The power, and nickname Fly, was freely given to Lore by Obit a man from earth's prehistoric time. We as human beings know the limits of our abilities to a certain extent, and we can only strive to break the barriers of those limits. It is through much hard work, and many times of trying to reach further, that we can go beyond the records that we set last month or last year. It is then, that the very small becomes the very greatest. Looked upon with much admiration these fractions are celebrated. This story is of the unbelievable, and as for the minds of human beings, the impossible.

It was eleven months past Lore's twenty-first birthday. The year was seventeen ninety, June 4. The earth is a warming place. Many Kings have come and gone, and the phrase, rest in peace was only for the women, and children. Men could never have peace.

The new world called America had won its independence from England, and what they were up against most of the newcomers had no idea. Total independence would be a daily struggle. The wildness of it all kept the faint of heart in constant terror. Kings, noblemen, and pauper alike were in fear about something all of the time.

The town we focus on grew out of sin, and the lust for gold. There were small amounts of gold found in the beginning, and very few really struck it rich. Then, the gamblers, and the barkeeps came. With them came the sex parlors, and harlots galore. In addition, many temptations for men working hard, that did not strike it rich.

The folklore has it that beings with the ability to fly through the air just as if they were birds, they say really exist. They had no wings, and their power source was unseen. In discussions about their existence, some asked,

"Then how did they fly?"

The locals believed it was the work of God, and that

these flying beings were actually angles sent to watch over human souls here on earth. Most human beings in this town, they said, needed watching over.

These people still tell the story of how the town got its name Fly. The old men would say.

"That's Fly with a capital F. You may not see any of those that can fly right now but if you stick around long enough, I sure guarantee you will see a being flying out around this one part of the woods. It's deep in the southeastern part." One old man said,

"you'll like the beauty of the forest though."

Then there was a short pause.

"There's lots of deer back in there."

Then there was another pause.

"Nobody goes huntin' back in there anymore. Folks say no one ever really did."

Another short pause, and then some wicked laughter.

"You will be careful if you go back in there, I hope.

Watch out for snakes."

Then, he said with the most evil sound in his voice,

"I'm not trying to scare anyone, mind you. I guess we'll see you Sunday in Church, right?"

You would think that the birthday of the son born to a well-to-do-leader-of-the-community would be a day of celebration to remember but it was not so. Lore's birth in his father's mind was enough reason not to show any love to his only son. When Anna died, to his father, Lore was at fault for his mother's death. She died in childbirth after the midwife delivered the baby; the midwife cited to have said,

"Virgil kept looking at the baby, and saying over, and over again, let God curse you! Let God curse you!

His tears were not for his wife or their baby but for his own loss in his lusty sickness, nothing more than his selfish pride in the flesh. For what he said to his son, who was just a newborn baby was unforgivable.

"Why did you come into this world to take a life? Why? God will revile you. Why? Over, and over again, he said, God will revile you, revile you."

The midwife then went away into another room, and sobbed for hours.

This being his twenty-second birthday, it was a miracle that he was still alive. The nurse hired to care for the child was the only thing that saved him. She wanted to take him home with her but Virgil would not allow it. She finally became so afraid for the baby boy's life that she moved into the mansion to help raise the child. It was through some manipulation with Virgil's Doctor that she finally got him convinced that it was the best thing to do. She could be his nanny, and his nurse too, even does household chores.

Minnie would not have allowed anyone to harm Lore but as the boy grew, he also became smarter. He became keenly aware of his father's hatred for him. He also learned from his father that it was because of the death of his beloved wife that he hated his son so much. He also learned it would always be this way. Maybe, if he went away, and left this part of the country, things might change.

Since Lore was a teenager, he had dreamed of getting away from this town. Not many people even knew he existed. His father never talked about him the way other fathers would speak of their children. That pride one gets when there is love, and you speak of them with love.

The life of Lore's father now consisted of jumping from one woman's bed to another. The only thing that kept the darkness out of Lore's life was his belief that his mother was watching him from heaven, and that someday he would meet her for the first time. He kept his faith, not only for the father in heaven but also, not to disappoint his mother. She would always be in his heart.

He worried for his father's soul, and prayed for him every night. He thought maybe someday he would change, even though there was little hope. What he saw in his father was a soulless human being. It was sad, too sad but true.

Still, Lore dared not hold on to hope for his lost father yet he did, for we are all sinners, and need forgiveness. Only God's time is the healer, if anything were.

As time came closer to Lore's birthday, he planned a trip to the southeastern forest. He had heard the stories about the legends too. When he was a young boy, he first heard the story when he was seven or eight. Therefore, he wanted to believe the stories. It sounded so exciting, to be able to fly. He used to run to the woods with his arms spread out. And, he would make a swishing sound for his pretending to be soaring through the air. He felt the wind on his face, and believed it was true that they do fly. He would say to himself,

"they do fly, I believe it is so, they do fly."

Then he would grow weary, and stop his pretending he could fly. In addition, he would find a tree to sit down under, and rest. Then he would get back up, and try to run all the way back home, with his arms spread out, still saying, "they do fly, they do fly."

Eventually, he would find another tree before he made it back home, and there he would rest again, and sometimes sleep. His fatigue would leave his small frame but nothing could stop him from flying again, all the way home. He knew he could fly forever, even if it was only pretend.

"Chapter Sixty-Four: KAWHOCUMDIA"

The beginning of what happened to Lore and the new life that was his. Lore's secret observer thought to himself,

"not yet, not yet little one. Not when you are so young."

Lore spied upon from the sky, and he did not know. The child did not know anything of whom was up above him watching with a careful eye besides the Father in Heaven, and Minnie taught him about the Father. In addition, Lore was unaware the sky flier too could see into the child's mind. Obit was seeing his dreams of flying, and knowing of the joy that Lore was feeling because of his help, one small lift for one small boy. It gave Obit great happiness seeing for the first time in this way, how giving the boy the greatest joy of flight was all about giving. That is when he decided to assign the boy a nickname, that name was Fly.

While Obit was flying high in the sky, the super being thought to himself,

"the gift of flying was given to me, and it was only a dream I had, however, it was the greatest gift besides life that I'd ever received. That small boy can fly now, and it will be in his dreams. When he is older, it will become his reality."

The days went by, this is how it started; and Lore waited with anticipation for the trip to the southeastern forest. He had waited a long time for this. Minnie, now his friend, started helping Lore pack his nap-sack. It would be a day's journey to the forest, and Minnie thought, Lore would want to stay at least a day or two, not knowing Lore's intent.

Minnie told Lore she would handle his father, and for

him to go. She said,

"you will have a great time, so go."

This would be a new adventure. Lore had taken two of his father's and his pistols for protection. They were really Lore's anyway. He had learned to use the weapons when he was just a boy completing school. The expert shooter his father hired to teach the lad gave them to him. One thing his father insisted on doing was teach him about weapons. He would say to Minnie,

"a man must be able to protect himself."

The sharpshooter gave the pistols to Lore's father for safekeeping. When the boy was old enough, and became a suitable citizen, his father was to give them to Lore.

He arranged for the expert shooter, one of the best shots in the area, to teach Lore how to shoot a gun. Lore had to learn how to clean, and know of the safety elements of using a gun, the rifle and the pistol. Lore was especially interested in the pistol. He would stand with it hidden under his armpit, and suddenly pull it out, and fire off a shot as the teacher came back from changing the target. His teacher would always say,

"safety first my Lord, safety first."

Lore would reply, respectfully,

"yes sir."

The day before his twenty-second birthday came, and Lore was up at first light. Minnie came into the kitchen where Lore was making his breakfast, and packing his lunch to carry with him. He told her he would kill some game, and have supper this night. She told him to wait for his father to leave; she knew he would be going to the barroom to get an early start with his drink. Lore knew how she disapproved of him going so early but this time she would not say anything, she would hold her tongue. Lore wanted to go before his father got up, so he looked at Minnie, and said,

"please, I must go now in order for me to make it by nightfall."

He grabbed his nap sack, kissed Minnie on the cheek, and said,

"I love you."

In addition, he was out the door. His father would be sleeping for at least another hour, and he could make it quite a distance.

He had never wanted to ride the horses his father had or to use on the hunts, and he seldom went. Now never would. There were stable keeps tending the horses. Lore had a thought about making it farther by riding instead of walking, and decided to go for a horse. When he got to the stable, the men had already saddled a horse for his father. Lore asked one of the men,

"did my father pick this one?"

The keeper said,

"no he didn't, I did. He doesn't care which one I saddle master Lore."

Lore took the horse by the reigns, and mounted him.

He told the keeper,

"this will do me just fine. Would you please saddle my father, another one, and keep it to yourselves?"

The stable keep knew Lore's father would horse whip him if he found out, and defiantly said,

"sure master Lore, I will!"

Lore turned the horse, trotted to the edge of the wooded area, and then took the horse to a full run. It was a very fast run. Lore thought to himself,

"This horse is a fine steed. Father will never know."

Lore had not told Minnie of his desire to leave this part of the country but once, when he was just a boy. Minnie took him aside, and tried to console him for what his father had said to him.

She talked to him with all the love of a mother,

"you must wait until you are much older, when you are really ready. We have to pray that time will heal you father's wounds. You will know when it's time to leave, trust me you'll see."

Minnie was right, and he knew it was time. His father would probably never even miss the one horse out of all of the hundreds he had. Besides, Lore had plenty of money; he had taken all of his allowance, and saved it for years since he was just a boy. When he got to a place where he could buy a new horse, he would let this one go, and he would return home. Lore knew the horse's instincts, so he knew he would. This horse would have been a good one to keep but he just borrowed him for a short trip. Yes, just a bit of a day-trip, Lore knowing all along he was never going to return. He was leaving in the possible scenario that he would return, if his father were to change and call him back. He wished only for a word of praise from his hateful father. Even with his ill ways, Lore still loved the old man very much.

"Chapter Sixty-Five: KAWHOCUMDIA"

Lore came to the most beautiful spot he could have ever imagined. The forest was lush, and filled with green vegetation. The huge rock that was the first thing in sight must have been twenty-four to twenty-five feet high. Lore thought there was something different about this rock. He was about fifty yards away, and he wanted to see it up close with a sense of yearning he had never felt before. He quickly dismounted his horse, and headed in the direction of the rock. He let the horse go, knowing that he would graze for a while. With this much green to eat, Lore would have to stop him or he would eat too much, and founder. He also figured the horse would follow him after eating his fill but he would keep a close watch on him.

As Lore got closer to the rock, he wanted to see if it

was flat on top, and this rock was quite a large rock. Lore thought, if it was flat, it must have a large space on it. He got closer, and when he walked up to it, he put his hands on it. Lore frozen to it, wondered of the mysteries hidden in it. He could not take his hands off. He leaned his head closer, and turned to listen.

He placed his ear up next to a flat spot that was just the right height. He closed his eyes. His breathing became quieter, he listened with his ear pressed against it, and wanted something to give him a sign. Maybe for the rock to share some of its secrets, waiting, thinking each moment he might hear something. How many years had this rock been here?

He listened. Lore was entranced. He wanted to look the whole rock over. He pulled his ear back from the rock. He was sure it would talk to him. Maybe later he would try again.

He went around to the backside of the gigantic stone monolith. This was even more interesting. There were footsteps chiseled out so it was easy climbing. He realized that someone had been here before him. The questions were wildly troubling in his mind. He thought to himself,

"Who was this? Was this the flying beings? Why would they have to build steps to climb up the rock if they could fly?"

He then decided to go for it, and started climbing. He had his nap sack still located on his back. He thought he could climb it with the pack on his back easily. He whistled for the horse and he came running, he stopped right at the rock. Lore told him,

"stay put, and don't go anywhere."

Then talking aloud to himself, he said,

"I wonder who could have been here."

At that moment, he made it to the top. He climbed on up to the very top, and stood up to look out over the terrain. It was a sight to see and more breath taking than anything Lore had ever seen. As he looked down at his feet, he was starting to feel like he was above ground, floating on air. It was true. He was up about an inch. Lore yelled out,

"stop that! What is this that is happening?"

In addition, he came down to solid rock, and firmly stopped. He was standing on top of the rock again. He cried out again in his exasperation,

"who did that? Who are you?"

Then, there was a faint whisper,

"I remember when you were a small boy, and I watched over you from the sky. I lifted you up as you ran along pretending to fly."

Lore did not want to rush to any conclusions but he asked,

"are you God?"

The voice started to take on a form as if it were a vision. He stood there in front of Lore like a gladiator from ancient Rome, when strength ruled in the arena. Nobody would have worn what he had on without that body. He spoke but softly enough not to scare Lore.

"No, and I'm not yet named in my new life but my old name was Obit. I am left here as a proof that the power exist from the future. In addition, that there is hope for the future of our planet. I am from the past, when life first started on this place they call earth. I am not one of the programmed; I am a product of a mistake. I had a piece of one of the Zorvirax's' brain put into my head. It started a process that changed my life into what I am today. I was what they say, only in worse words, mentally impaired. As a small boy, I did not speak but listened. My friends were of the sky. No one on earth treated me as a human but as a subhuman. I felt pain when they would call me names as a child. I did not rebel for who I was. I stayed within what I could understand, and learned many things. That was until one night they put me in for a mystery, in place of my real father. He was too scared to do it himself. Allowed, was a son to stand in for a father.

The captured were taken to be operated on, and a plug taken from their brain, and put into each of a select group of the tribesmen. Some of the others were only affected slightly or so they said. I Obit got the most good out of it. However, then I was the one with the most to gain, with so little to give. It came from the other Zorvirax named Samuel, the son of Zadator. These are great men of the Universe, with knowledge of the beginning of our time, and their time.

Enough! You must volunteer for what I am asking you to do. I will not force you. My thoughts will come to you without vocally speaking. We will use mind reading where I give the power to you. You will understand in a second."

Only a second went by, and Obit said,

"there."

Lore spoke loudly to Obit, with a question,

"you named me Fly?

Obit wanted to have the conversation by using the mind reading, and told Lore, "you have the ability to talk to me without speaking, you know."

The conversation went on silently for about an hour. It was a good visit.

"Chapter Sixty-Six: KAWHOCUMDIA"

They talked of many things pertaining to programming, the formulas created by the Zorvirax, and the new system that Obit had come up with on his own. He was not one of the listed because of the accidental plug operation. No one knew but Samuel that he was the one that had the plug removed from his brain. In addition, each Samuel, and Obit got part of each other.

Obit then said aloud,

"come Lore; let's take a trip to the top of the sky, above the clouds! Let us see what we can see. I've built a protective barrier for your horse, and supplies."

Lore had realized that he was getting information that

he had never even heard of before. He knew he had given Obit the right response to start the process but silently not aloud. In addition, it did not matter. They were communicating and they were hearing each other just as if they were talking. Therefore, the deal was set solidly. The answer was yes.

Obit said to Lore,

"I'm going to lead you up as far as we need to go. You are not complete with your abilities yet but you will be soon. I have a new way of programming that the others do not know about, yet. I use my mind to let you in on what I know. The channel is connected only to me, and no one can tell that you are using my mind for the information you need. Being loaded is your memory. After programming, and when I separate the connection, then you will put it to use. It is actually the same thing except for the use of my mind. We can communicate telepathically now. Follow me.

They both are in such close sync; up they went into

the sky. Fly's only words were,

"my God."

Obit heard him sound off, and looked back at him with a smile. Obit had been alone for so long, he had forgotten what it was like to have a human company. He spoke to Lore with his telepathy in the on position,

"I see you liked that take off."

Lore did not say a word for a few seconds. In addition, even though the information was coming in at a high speed, the questions began to flow out of his mouth one hundred and twenty word a minute. Obit could not stop him, so he fired the answers back at him as fast as he could. It was exhilarating to be in such overwhelming conversation and in flight too. The two picked up speed, and headed straight up. The plan Obit had for Lore had been to show him the future, and actually go there. It would be just another ten thousand feet and they would pass the opening to the year two thousand and ninety-eight, July 4. It would be Lore's birthday, only it would be the surprise of his life.

Obit was watching his speed as he approached the time entry line. He had done this many times before, and always had made it with perfect accuracy. As he approached closer to the line of entry, he told Lore to come along side of him.

Obit said to Lore,

"you must take my hand."

Obit extended his right hand, and Lore did the same. As they gripped each other's hand, it was seconds, and they went through the time hole.

The life Lore had led before now he would be leaving behind. None of the things his father had said or done to him mattered anymore. Lore was indeed amazed. His eyes first went to the skyscrapers he could see in the distance. Then he looked in disbelief at the city that seemed to be hanging in the sky. There was no support visible. Again, Fly did not have enough information. He could see small figures that were also flying and there must have been thousands of them.

Obit said to Lore,

"we finally had a leak. Earth beings have not caught up with us but they did use our formula to teach each other to fly. We believe they have some of the formulas that are in the making that some of them are thinking about trying to do just that, catch up with us. I saw this before I first saw you as a little boy. Lore only listened now, and watched. He started to ask Obit how. He shook his head instead and said,

"never mind."

Lore thought to himself,

"the air is a bit thin up here; I guess we can adjust to it with just a small formula."

Obit started to give him the answer aloud but sent it telepathically and said aloud,

"there!"

He then stopped, turned and with a gesture said,

"come Fly, follow me."

Lore not used to Fly but was sure it was going to be his name. Obit told Lore,

"I'm going to cloak us for security; hang on you'll like it."

It was if he had snapped his fingers, and they disappeared. He told Lore,

"I'm turning on your vision so that you'll be able to see me."

Lore said following,

"O.K., I'm right behind you."

Obit headed for the city in the sky, he said to Lore,

"did you ever imagine this?"

Lore responded,

"no. No, I never did. Will anyone bother us?"

Obit asked him,

"what do you mean?

Obit had not thought of any danger or threat from

anyone in a long, long time. Lore repeated it in a different way.

"You know, is there a threat from anyone? Is there a possibility of an attack?"

Obit said with pride,

"no, not here, not today anyway.

Lore's fear was starting to go away. The thing that he wanted most was to have the programming complete, and at the same time he knew it would mean the connection with Obit would no longer be. It made him sad about Obit having to live for so long. As he reached this point in his mind, Obit spoke to him.

"For all time we will be brothers in the power, it only matters to me, and to you how we got here. My life has been long but I have only just begun to live. I would say you are like a son to me but it is because you are like a friend that I will always remember. We are approaching the city in the sky. This is where I live some of the time. I own a condominium here.

Lore said,

"just a minute, what's a condominium?"

Obit said telepathically,

"a place to live. I just own one apartment. It is very big. There are ten bedrooms, a pool; some of the rooms are for books I've read."

Lore asked suddenly,

"why aren't you married, if I may be so bold?"

Obit quickly responded,

"Someday, I'll tell you all about it. For now let us just say I am still looking. You know, for the right one to come along."

Lore left it at that, and said,

"O.K..."

Lore was thinking of how things could have been at home, and it made him sad to think of his mother not being there. Then there was Minnie. He also thought about the anger he had about his father.

Obit said,

"quickly!"

As the large door opened, he flew in. Lore was right behind Obit, and the door closed instantly behind Lore. Obit said,

"we're here, we made it safely, and I want to introduce you to someone. Keeper say hello to Fly. Fly, this is Keeper."

A voice came out of nowhere.

"Hello Fly."

Fly looked around, and then back at Obit. He said,

"O.K..."

He then gave to Keeper his salutations, and asked,

"hello Keeper, where are you?"

Obit said to Lore,

"turn on your screen man, she's already in your future, she won't be visible until the time comes. I told her about you already. She has seen you and is excited, and wants to meet you now. I told her she should wait, what do you think?"

What Obit already knew was that Keeper had been through programming and they would meet in the next week. He also knew that it was possible for their meeting to be moved-up. Obit needed Fly to come with him to the future so that he could see her, where she has already seen him at the chance meeting, and now waits for his return. Lore not thinking of himself as Fly turned on his screen to see about what Obit was talking.

The minute his screen was up, he saw the messages that were from Keeper. In addition, that she waits every day at the same place they met in her past. Obit had purposely brought Fly back to the place that he had never been in this time, because Keeper was there. As soon as Keeper found out what time period Obit and Fly were in, she transported herself there. Fly looked at her waiting on the steps of the huge building. He glanced back at Obit, and said,

"I haven't met her yet but you've taken me beyond where we did meet. But, she's in a place where she is waiting for me to return to be with her?"

Obit said to Lore,

"yes, interesting huh?"

Lore responded,

"confusing but interesting."

Obit wanted to show the condominium to Lore before he took him to meet Keeper, he said,

"come with me, it will wait."

She did not need to wait any longer. She knew that for Fly, it will be his first meeting but for her she had already met and knew he was the one for her. It will just be up to Fly to realize that he is already in love with her too.

Obit turned to Fly and said,

"you have the power, and the co-ordinance, what are you waiting for man?"

Fly looked at Obit with a half-smile and said,

"see you later, here?"

Obit jokingly said,

"of course, don't keep me in the dark for too long. Moreover, do not make me come looking for you, just a joke. See you later.

Lore disappeared into thin air. Obit clinched his fist in the air in front of his face and pulled it down below his chin, and said with the loudest enthusiasm under his breath he had ever said,

"yes! I knew I was going to play cupid someday. How's that for seeing into the future?"

He listened for a word from God or anybody for a second or two but nothing. He said to himself knowing only God heard him,

"that's alright. I know you are there. I know you're there."

"Chapter Sixty-Seven: KAWHOCUMDIA"

Keeper was born in Canada, just on the outskirts of New York Sky Town. It was started back in seventeen eighty-five, when rebel time travelers from the year thirty-two-eighty-six, went back in time. They decided to build their own town in the sky, long before Keeper was born. The people of the earth never discovered it until Keeper's father found it by accident. That's another story Keeper's father told when he had a captive audience. Keeper became one of the first teenagers of her time to receive the power. Her father thought someone would take him in. However, no one ever did. His wife Sue Lee a beautiful woman from China became a traveler with a crew that had a spacecraft, and they all have the power but Sue Lee. She had the offer to receive the power but turned it down because of her husband. That is another story Keeper's father told too.

Keeper grew up in New York Sky Town, and still has a place there today. She lives at her apartment, which she calls her home. There are eleven rooms not counting the baths. She lives there alone, when she is there. Keeper is only there a few months out of the year, and has a service come in and clean, and keep the place up to date. Her family left her financially independent as far as earthly needs but her power keeps her busy with trying to keep up with the needs of the people. Her interest in Lore came about when she ran into him on a ferryboat ride when he was just seventeen. She knew he was the one from the moment, she saw him. She could not tell him she was from the future or he would have thought she was insane. She had already saved many lives with her power, and programmed most of the ones she had rescued.

When she was on the ferry ride with Lore, she looked into his future and knew he had a guardian angel already,

Obit. She was glad for Lore's sake because she read his fa-

ther's mind, and saw the bitterness he had for Lore because

of his mother. She felt so sad she nearly cried right there in

front of them. However, she was able to hold back the tears

so that she would not give herself away. She knew that Lore

was in her future, and they would fall in love. She was al-

ready in love with him. His long beautiful light brown hair

glistened in the sunshine that day, and she would never for-

get it. She walked to the edge of the ferryboat where Lore

stood next to his father. He turned and looked at her. He

spoke with a very soft,

"hello, nice day isn't it?"

She just smiled and replied,

"yes it is. It's a very nice day."

Lore felt a feeling in his stomach as he had never felt

before. He was not sure if he knew what it was but was sure

it was because of the girl. He asked,

"what's your name?"

She was in hopes he would ask. She said,

"Keeper, Keeper Bans. What's yours?"

Even though she already knew his name, she had to keep up the appearance that she did not. He said,

"it's Lore but for some reason, I think it will be changed when I'm grown.

That is when his father glared down at him as if to say shut up boy, you make me sick. Lore saw the way his father looked at him but that not being the first time, Lore ignored him. They were almost across the river, and near the bank. He heard his father tells him to get his horse and get ready, that they had a long hard ride ahead. Before he walked away, he said to Keeper,

"It was nice to meet you, where are you headed?"

She replied,

"Oh, it's a long way up from here."

She paused and finished the sentence with,

"New York, just above New York State."

She felt sad but knew she would not be seeing him for quite some time. She thought to herself,

"I'll wait for as long as it takes, Lore."

As Lore and his father climbed on their horses, he wanted to find out how to find her later but it was too late. It would not have been acceptable if he were too forward. She called out to him as they walked their horses off the ferry,

"I'll see you later Lore, don't forget me."

Lore's heart fell down in his stomach, and he nearly threw up. He did not let on, and he rode away with his father into the wooded forest. Keeper had made the time travel alone, and just walked into the woods, and disappeared.

As she walked the walkway of her apartment, she thought of what Obit had told her telepathically. She knew she had just left Lore and his father again for the third time. She thought about it, and worried that it would be bad if something happened. She needed to see him again at the first meeting. She was in love, and hoping for the feeling again.

She turned her mind into Obit with her power, and mind reading ability. Keeper was surprised to find Lore connected to Obit's mind. How amazing this was, to be able to see the connection, and to know where they were. Her excitement made her jump and leap into the air. She was almost in flight but calmed herself before her emotions carried it too far. She was still so delighted he was actually here in Sky town. The long wait was almost over.

She was like a silly schoolchild of thirteen. After the calm she started to jump, and leap into the air. This time she was in flight, and back on the ground and started to sing. She was having the most fun she had ever had in the longest time. She did not want it to end. Then, she heard a knock on the door, she screamed like a schoolchild,

"oh my God!" And, after I gave them that vocal introduction earlier, I am a scream."

She knew they must have heard the scream, and spoke in a normal volume but with a seductive voice after the count of three she said,

"come in."

Obit blasted through the door like the infernal regions had just sprung forth. She knew he had just arrived but she was shocked anyway. She knew it was Obit even though she had not seen him in quite a while. She yelled out, with surprised sound in her voice,

"Obit!"

Obit returned the yell,

"Keeper, where have you been? When we talk, you never tell me what has been going on. Stop now, and meet my new and old friend, for real."

Keeper came back with,

"for real?"

Obit started the real introduction,

Fly, I want you to meet my friend, Keeper. Keeper this is Lore, I call him Fly, which is a little nickname I gave him when he was a small, well, wee lad. You'll probably call him Lore, maybe not."

Keeper extended her hand to Lore, and said,

"I think we've met."

Lore replied,

"but not officially. My father, and I were on a ferry

boat crossing the river, if my

memory serves me right?"

Keeper happy to see Lore responded,

"it does, and I'm glad to see that you remember me.

I'm so glad we met, sort of, on the ferry."

There was a pause while they looked into each oth-

er's eyes, and she said,

"I'm so glad we meet again."

Keeper looked at Obit giving him the message she

wanted alone time with Lore, for a while anyway.

Lore spoke up and said,

"you guys do know that I can read minds now, too.

Since my link is with Obit, whoops, I am sorry Obit, was that supposed to be a secret? Anyway, how could I have missed that one?"

His eyebrows wiggle up and down, and a nice smile glowed on his face. He said,

"it's O.K., I'm easy to get along with, and besides, the lady is right. We need to catch up since our last meeting. And, we barely know each other, yet."

He turned his eyes focused only on Keeper and said,

"am I right for speaking up?"

Keeper quickly said,

"yes. Yes."

Obit turned and headed out the door, and as he did, he said,

"see you two later, don't hurry on my account, have a nice time. That's what I brought him here for."

Keeper called out,

"Obit!"

She meant it with light heartedness in her intent, and

Obit had only meant it in the literal sense but Keeper was making it playful. She looked at Lore smiling, and said,

"that guy."

Lore and Keeper started walking away from the front door, and he said answering,

"O.K..."

Keeper told Lore gently,

"follow me."

Lore started walking behind her, and asked,

"do you want to talk or use telepathy?"

Keeper passionately looked back at Lore, and smiled. He then knew her wishes, and silently obliged. They spent the rest of the afternoon looking at each other smiling and making laughter like Lore had never heard before. As they were getting to know each other better, Lore could not stop trying to make Keeper laugh.

After several hours he dug deeper into her mind, and found she was making him think he was funnier that she thought he really was but also found she had a profound love residing inside of her. In addition, it was all just for him. He was so happy with what she was trying to do, he started going for it having more fun with her than before. He left himself as open as he could be, and she laughed at him for revealing how beautiful he thought she was. Him being full of love for her and thinking how attracted he was to her, said aloud,

"I'm in love with you, and you're the most beautiful woman I've ever seen."

After more hours of playful things they did together, she reached over close to his face and said,

"you're not going to go first, so I will."

She kissed him on the mouth. He immediately, kissed her back. He was trying hard to take it slow. Then, without warning, she had him on his back, kissing him passionately. He felt the need to respond, and did, passionately.

He then stopped, and said,

"that was O.K., wasn't it?"

She grabbed him again, and said,

"I'm never going to let you go, never. I have been in love with you from the minute I saw you. I'm never letting you go, never."

She pulled him tighter, and closer to her. Lore was caught up in the heat of the moment and said,

"I've been in love with you too."

He held her tightly kissing her neck, and then back to her lips as they were falling

deeper, and deeper in love as the seconds went by.

Lore felt a slight vibration and heard a rumbling noise coming from quite a distance away, and stopped kissing Keeper suddenly. He leaped for the front door, and up to the window looking out of the front of the place. He saw the huge cloud that looked like a mega mushroom rising into the air from the distance. He spoke softly to Keeper; she had followed him into the front room but was standing back out of view,

"it must be the next state over toward the west. Keeper look!"

His mind was racing, looking for answers on what he saw. He turned toward her to catch Keeper's worried look, and she asked Lore,

"what is it?"

It made him even more apprehensive and he responded,

"I don't know."

As she looked out the window bringing her focus to zoom, she said,

"Oh my God, what have they done? No! They could not have! This must be a trick."

Lore said feeling the frustration of the moment,

"We've got to get to Obit!"

Keeper replied with what she knew had to be done immediately, "no! There is no time! Come with me we have to get to the ship! She grabbed Lore by the hand running toward a door that led through the kitchen and around a corner. She opened the door with her mind just before they got there. Lore said,

"I got that."

Keeper did not say anything but was still heading through the door. As they got out of the door, Lore saw the ship and wondered how they got her inside.

They both felt the rumbling this time, and it was getting stronger. Keeper said to Lore,

"we've got to hurry faster!"

The ship's door opened and the sound of air releasing came rushing into their ears. Keeper said it like a command,

"we'll fly up, I'll go first!"

As soon as she said it, she was in the air and up to the door. She landed on the threshold and was inside in a second. Lore followed her. As she told Lore to take the first seat behind her, she was calling out,

"Obit, Obit! Where are you man? We've got to get out of this place!"

Suddenly, Obit spoke to her and Lore.

"Get out of the building and I'll meet you at the *access-sector-back-space-sufficient*, just before the time travel entrance, you do know where to go don't you? We only have a few more minutes."

They both ring-out,

"yes!"

Obit replied,

"O.K.!"

The sound of the ship was not as noisy as the sound of the roof opening up. In seconds, they were in the air, and Keeper told Lore to hang on to his pants. His silence was understandable. In seconds, they were at the time travel entry. Keeper brought the ship to a hover position exactly at the sector before entry. She opened the hatch, and Obit jumped in. He came straight to the second seat and strapped himself in. He said,

"Let's go!"

The ship blasted through the time travel opening, and they disappeared.

"Chapter Sixty-Eight: KAWHOCUMDIA"

There was not any doubt which direction they were going in time but the direction they all wanted to go was away from the danger. The power to sustain life did not mean for them to walk into fire for no reason. If it were the end of the earth, as they knew it, each being spared is what they wanted to experience rather than having to witness the obliteration. It would be up to them to get past the point of the nuclear explosion that had now destroyed part of earth. If earth survived, they would need to know who made it through the explosion, and who did not.

There would be an assessment of the damage with the power they each had in a particular field. There was always the challenge to go where others would dare not go. This was their bonding between them. They had a choice yet each would follow the other if there were only one that wanted to go into the danger zone. If the risks were great enough they could not let any one individual go it alone. Their safety was in numbers, and the ability to see the future but also their ability of the reconstruction of cells of the being.

Keeper was setting the time travel formula for two years forward in time. Making sure the time was right for an investigation of the results of the destruction. She wanted to have a look just for herself. She cloaked the ship for an invisible reentry. She knew the ship's sensors would pick up any contaminates and report if there was an immediate danger or threat to life on-board.

The ship's feminine voice spoke to Keeper,

"nothing to report ma'am. There is no harm in exiting the ship. If no one needs to be programmed at this time, we all can leave the ship immediately if necessary."

Keeper said politely back to her ship,

"no, no darling, no one at this time. I believe you were planning on master Lore but he was already been taken care of by master Obit. Thank you."

Keeper's unusual affection for her ship did not throw either one of the men but did bring on a flinch in each of their eyebrows, nothing consequential. Obit and Lore each looked at the other just after the statement and shrugged their shoulders at the same time. Obit spoke up and said,

"it is basically the same but I've found short cuts that lessen the time that it takes, and it can be done while they are awake, thoughts?"

Lore took the moment of opportunity to tell them what Obit had done for him as a young boy,

"it seems, Obit started programming me as a young man and kept it to himself. For me to have been able to utilize the power, all that would have had to happen was for me to be in life threatening danger. I would have had momentary use of the power to get me out of whatever danger I saw. Nice huh?"

The ship came down to twelve hundred feet according to Keeper's command. As they glided along; each could see what had happened in the explosion area. There was nothing left but blackened charred remains. It was mostly consisting of black dirt now. There were a few clumps of what looked like molten metal but not in a natural form or order. It was all an eerie horrifying sight.

The ship slowed to a hover, then moved on without words. Devastation for as far as the eye could see, and more devastation…

Keeper tried to break the silence without breaking the mood, which was an overwhelming compassion for the earth, and its people. She asked Obit,

"see if you can get a phone line through to the FBI, or any official sounding group. And, see if you can find out what's going on."

Obit answered Keeper not thinking of her as the one in charge but as a friend,

"not a line there to receive my call as far as I can tell."

Keeper was not sure if she wanted to do what she was thinking of doing next. It may be the only way to find out what they needed to know. She gave the command,

"Obit you take the Captain's chair, I'm going out there. First hand is usually the best hand. I will give you the spot to set her down when I get one. There is no doubt you can fly my ship. Can you not?"

Obit calculated for a second, and said,

"sure."

He did not want to sound too confident but just thought to himself,

"I'm just waiting for you to comment on, that you think I can't, so I'll go ahead and answer your probable question with, yes, I can."

Keeper zoomed right in on it, and said,

"O.K., then it's settled."

Keeper spoke to the ship with her request,

"hover please."

She went to the door; it opened, and without a word, leaped cloaking herself as she exited the ship. Her thought upon exiting and cloaking was for her easy sailing through the sky uninterrupted.

As she settled down to a thousand feet, she started scanning for survivors, hoping that they may have set up makeshift homesteads or maybe small villages. The people may or may not accept her, which was Keeper's thinking. She would come up with something to make it into where she needed to go. Unless destruction was prevalent, the larger cities would be too dangerous and too crowded. She knew she was going to make a stop later in the big city but for now, it was her idea to take it slow and easy.

She had flown over this area a thousand times before

but now it was all unrecognizable. Everything had changed even the air; the smell was still foul. It was almost a blue sky yet something about it was not right. Visibility was still cloudy and there was the funny color in with the blue. It was a shade of milky green. She flew on.

Her speed five miles per hour; she was using her super sight and hearing. She was trying to locate anyone. She had covered about ten miles away from the ship. Still, there was nothing but burnt ground, and mounds of fragmented metal.

Then suddenly, a warning came in her ear. Obit was sending a message from the ship.

"We're picking up something unknown in the air just below five hundred feet. We have been following you since you left the ship, I did not want to leave you out here alone. I have been listening in with telepathy. It was strictly security for you."

Keeper responded,

"O.K. Obit. I am O.K... Besides, I have sensors on, and can produce a breathing device instantly on the spot. I also have a body defense system for anything that might be a contaminant."

Obit felt a need to respond,

"O.K., I'll just listen, and won't interfere, unless I'm needed."

"Chapter Sixty-Nine: KAWHOCUMDIA"

Keeper heard something in the distance, she stopped her reassuring Obit and Lore that she would be all right, and said,

"hang on!"

The pause lingered on to and beyond Lore's breaking point; he spoke up and called to Keeper,

"what is it for God's sake?"

Keeper still not able to identify the sound started a scanner search with memory going back hundreds of year with planned increments in tens. This was a search for any-thing. She may never have heard it in order for her own memory to identify. Maybe she had only heard this sound briefly, or maybe never at all. It could be something in programming memory from millions of years ago. Zorvirax history would have taken her back even further. Keeper assured Obit and Lore that she would find it, whatever it was. She said,

"even if I have to go to the source to find out what it is, I will."

When Keeper followed the sound to its location, she saw an entrance to a cave. It was a large entryway. There was no one in sight; still the sound kept coming from the cavern. She told Obit about the cave, and that she was going in. Obit warned her of the danger that she could be walking into. He then corrected himself,

"flying, I meant flying."

She then told Obit she could handle it.

As she entered the cave, she saw with night vision on and enhancements on, that the mining tunnel was working at one time. She was feeling very anxious but still entered the cave. The sound was now getting louder. She moved her way in slowly.

Keeper was now close enough that she recognized the sound and became embarrassed by what she heard. She said to herself quietly,

"well of all things, a violin, someone is playing a violin, and badly. They must just be learning to play, if it's that bad."

She laughed to herself, Obit in on it because of keeping tabs with their mental telepathy asked,

"are you sure it's a violin?"

Keeper replied,

"I'm not there yet, it's another thirty feet to the corner. I am afraid that if I get to close he might hear or see me. I can say for sure, I do feel his present's for-some-reason without seeing him."

Lore asked,

"how do you know that it's a he?"

Keeper asked Lore jokingly with telepathy still going with both he and Obit,

"when did you become a mind reader, oh that's right you were programmed too?"

Lore quickly answered back to her flirting, and said,

"Obit, she's forgotten already I'm programmed too."

Then switching conversation back to Keeper said,

"this new way of Obit's is really fantastic; I'm able to use the formulas as soon as I receive them. He is still feeding me information. It's still an experimental process, how about that memory formula sweetheart?"

Keeper said to Lore fondly,

"Lore, stop that. I remember now, I've just had other things on my mind."

Obit told Keeper,

"we're out here, be careful."

As Obit finished his sentence, Keeper saw a tall dark figure with a black trench coat, step out from behind the corner, he said,

"are you three going to gab all evening, or are you going to join me? Tell those two out on the ship, I'm tired of being alone."

He stopped, and said,

"hi Keeper, my name is Don. You are Keeper right?"

Keeper's response was not without apprehension but said with relief,

"yes, how did you know that?"

She stopped herself immediately saying,

"O.K., I'm picking it up now. You went through programming too. You give people new lives after helping them. You program the hopeless, murders, lunatics, and rebels like me. Now I know who you are. You are I, only it is in my future. Why is that? And, why do you disappear after you help them?"

Don smiled, and gently laid his violin bow across his chest and said, "that's me. Now, would you tell those two to park your ship and come join us?"

Keeper said,

"just a minute, I can't believe it's really you. Where is your ship? Obit is going to…

There was a short pause,

Keeper started again,

"well any-way, he's going to be delighted to finally meet you. You know that you're like a legend here on earth."

Her sentence finished with a tapering off,

"well, I guess we kind of all are."

Don not wanting to be impatient with Keeper but was getting concerned about the two guy's listening to all of this, said,

"you know I think you're right about that. Would you call them down now? I've got lots of information that they should be dying to get."

Don paused and said,

"not literally."

He paused again, then asked,

"could you please call them down? My ship is hovering just above us. It's repairing."

There is another pause, still she had her eyes glued to Don's, he said again,

"would you call them, now, Keeper right?"

Keeper finally responded to Don's request, she said,

"O.K., O.K..."

Keeper kept her eyes on Don, now he had come closer, she thought to herself,

only parting ways from the other guys, where they can't connect with her private thoughts,

"he is perfect. Oh, stop that, you ninny, Lore's perfect too."

Don did have long hair down past his shoulders. He did not look like he would fit in with the times. His outfit was like something from the year two thousand, that the copycat murders would wear. I guess there were other people from that time that wore trench coats and had long hair.Rock stars, wait a minute he was a rock star. Keeper picked up on the information coming in about Don, and said it without thinking about it, that it might make him blush,

"he is a Rock star! Wow! What are you doing here man?"

Don quietly asked Keeper,

"are you talking to me?

Keeper showed her teeth in a smile, and said,

"sorry. I get carried away sometimes."

Don immediately said,

"it's O.K...

Keeper started calling Obit and Lore aloud, and then switched to telepathy. She told them that Don was asking them to come join them, she said,

"now get down here. He is dying to meet you both, right Don.

He responded,

"right!"

Obit and Lore jumped at the response that Don gave, and got in a hurry. They were at the cave entrance in less than three minutes. Obit left the ship on hover and readiness from an emergency exit. As they, both flew into the cave and the darkness, each switch on night vision.

Their meeting with Don is the highlight of their day, week, and month. They find out from Don that the destruction is even worse than they thought. There were three more bombs set off that week, each two days apart, and 4 more three weeks later. In addition, those were set off two the first week and one for each remaining week later. Don looked at Obit and Lore, then back at Keeper.

"I found out about your trip here, two years after, and only got here ahead of you by an hour. How's that for information finding. I just happen to check on your time; in addition, found out about the nukes, I knew I was going to have to make a mad rush. I found you search trail, anyway long story short, I got here ahead of you."

This was the dooms day event of earth's history. Don had not told them about it being doom's day yet but was waiting for their response to what he had just told them. Neither of the three said anything, just stood there silently looking at Don as though each were in shock. Don knew he was in control so he went on.

"The three continents that were hit with one of the tri bombs were North America, Europe and Africa. There was an expectation for a long time that there would be others. Still, two years after the fear left hope was still in the minds. Every day, more and more are finding shelters and building the underground containers that will protect as many as they can find. The military has become helpless and chaotic. The government as an agency has gone underground somewhere with all its people and they stay in hiding. No one can find an official anywhere. The people that are left must defend themselves. Most have organized, and are keeping it together as well as they can, under the circumstances.

Thank God for the churches and the preachers. Most of the organizing is coming from them and, the workers of the church. All of the food now comes from stores that government programs set up, and developed just in case of such an event. No one ever thought it would really happen. I could not really find out how many people were left. They only have information on..."

Don paused,

"they've found a few more than..."

He paused again,

"three thousand."

Don finished giving what they needed to know. He said,

"there could be more people we haven't found yet, let's hope."

He had held on to the violin the whole time he filled

them in on the information but put it in its case at the finish. Keeper told Don,

"grab some things and we'll head to the ship."

Don replied,

"right."

He picked up a bag and looped the strap over his shoulder, then the violin over the other shoulder, and he said,

"let's go."

They were out of the cave entrance, and flying up to the ship in just seconds. As Keeper reached the ship hatch, the door opened, and in she went then Obit and Lore, then Don. Keeper took the Captain's seat and the others fell in behind her. The command to her ship was for her to head to ground zero of the blast site. The ship responded with,

"yes ma'am, Captain. The ship started to move very fast immediately, Keeper said,

"hold on boys."

She then realized what she had said, and apologized,

"I'm sorry, I'm sorry. You all will forgive me please, I'm sorry."

Lore told her patiently,

"forget about it, it's O.K...

The ship told Keeper the bombsite was coming up. Keeper looked to the front viewer. Keeper cried out,

"oh my God! This is horrible! Give us an analysis of the area, and any danger to life!"

The ship responded,

"yes ma'am!"

Keeper read the report before the ship could give it verbally. She said,

"hover at twelve hundred feet. Keep me up to date on the analysis of the area for bomb fragment. She went to the door, it opened, and as she stepped to the edge to jump, she said turning to the others,

"anyone coming with me?"

They all stood up, and said simultaneously,

"yes!"

Keeper jumped and headed to the edge of the nine hundred-yard perimeter of the hit site. She received the report from the ship of the area.

Don, Obit and Lore land beside her as they all look toward the ground, the burnt chard ground.

Keeper spoke to them confidently,

"it'll be O.K... The ship's findings state that it is safe. I am getting the same results it will be O.K....

"Chapter Seventy: KAWHOCUMDIA"

Following their conversation, Obit said to Lore.

"We can explain the reason no one had found the New York sky city."

Keeper raised her hand as if she needed to get permission to speak, she nodded to Obit indicating that she would explain, and spoke,

"there was a no-fly-zone imposed way back when."

No one said anything about her hackneyed description of the past but she looked to see if anyone objected or wanted to exact time data. She saw no one and continued.

"The United States and Canada weren't enemies but they had a little tiff going on. Air traffic controllers wanted to send special flights out of Canada to the United States and vice versa. The tiff became a dispute that was-settled-in-court. Of course, it was a Canadian court. The United States wanted to keep their Big brother image clean. It was the flip of a coin and Canada won, finally. Moreover, the United States had to give it to them to keep things sweet. In other word's Canada really lost and got huffy at the coin toss and the United States thought it would be nice if they gave it up to Canada. Sky City developed in the no fly zone but neither side was aware. There was a mist barrier created around the city like a ball that allowed cloaking. The city hidden inside the mist barrier, protected if anyone did fly into it, the intruder magically stopped in midair. Then, simply put out on another course and let go again. They would be out like a dozing off, for just a second in their minds and would not know they were not on the same course. We can let them in or we can keep them out. I might as well explain the early developers.

They simply made a whistle stop for a few spacecraft and that was it. A man named Leonardo Pelter later developed it. Do you understand now Lore?"

Lore answered back,

"yes, completely."

Keeper said,

"good, was that you that asked the question, or was it Obit?"

Keeper stared at Obit when she asked the question. Obit looked at Lore and said,

"I don't know why she asked that question."

He shrugged his shoulders and slightly moved his head back and forth. Lore just pointed back at himself as if to say, it was I. He then turned to Keeper and said,

"it was me."

Keeper suggested that they look to see if they can find any clues from the remains of the bomb. She said,

"we can use the ship's scanner to search for metal bits and any small fragments to analyze."

Don and Obit look at each other nodding their head

in agreement. Obit spoke up with,

"all in agreement?"

Everyone said,

"yes."

Keeper started to get a sample from the soil. Obit found a piece of metal and put it in a sample storage bag. He said,

"this one might give us all the information we need. I'll get a few more just in case."

Keeper let him know that she appreciated what he was doing. She told Obit,

"we'll have some milk and cookies before we go to bed tonight."

Everybody got somewhat silly and said,

"yeah team!"

It was so close in unison Keeper looked around at everyone, tilted her head as if she was pleased and said,

"that was great, now, everyone back to work."

Each took their bow jokingly, and went back to work looking for fragments. Lore started to make a comment to make sure he was looking for the right thing when suddenly there it was right in front of him. It was shining like a diamond in the ruff.

Lore thought,

"The name plate couldn't have been missed if a bunch of blind mice had done the search."

It was black from the burn but was undoubtedly a nameplate. Edge parts on the end were- frayed but there were no signs of damage to the inner nameplate itself.

Lore bent down to pick up the piece of metal, it was lying next to what looked like smooth stone three and a half or four inches in diameter. It too covered with the soot and ash that had covered everything for miles around. Lore said to Keeper,

"I think you had better come over here."

He stopped himself before picking anything up, he

wanted Keeper to be the one to do the honors. Lore had involuntarily saved the moment thinking about Keeper.

"She is everything I have ever wanted in a woman. And, I want her in every part of my life."

Obit saw that Lore was waiting for Keeper, and felt his move to get them together was the right one. He waited for Keeper to take flight to the spot, and then he followed.

Keeper saw the piece of metal and jump with excitement causing black dust from the ground to come up in a cloud like smoke. She said to Obit and Lore,

"this might be something worthwhile."

Lore said to Keeper,

"go ahead, when the dust settles, pick it up, it's your find."

She smiled at Lore with an extra gleam in her eye, and said,

"no, it's not.

She bent down, picked up the piece, and put it in her

freshly opened bag. She said,

"now we can head back to the ship."

She asked,

"is everybody ready?"

She looked at each one as they nod with the half grin smile on their faces. She has the thought,

"they're glad to be here with me, someone that is so beautiful."

Don had been waiting and watching them collect their pieces of evidence at the scene, not knowing that what he was gathering was to be the most important part of the collection. While the others were doing their thing, he was scanning to analyze the area. He was doing an age check and a metal density test for things that would have fell to earth after the blast. His gatherings tagged with a formula to area reconstruction. Taken back in time were sections from before the blast. These sections tested and compared to the new that had taken its place. He also did a quick mind trip into the future, covering two life spans of approximately two hundred years. This was to make a check on the development of the earth, and how or if it would repair itself. The longer process that they used took an hour or more but cut to only seconds with the new formulas.

If time were the teacher, and we can say without a doubt that in most cases it is, Don's look this time was significantly farther than any that he had done before. When he checked, there was no one that had ever been this far into the future before. All knew that it was a law to keep the record of how far anyone had gone. What Don found would be the focus of the next project they would have on there to do list. He would tell the others but it would have to be after the events just before the explosions had reconstruction and history changed.

Don already knew from what he had found, which country was responsible and where to look for their location of the missile site. He would tell the others and they would quickly head back to the ship. Don understood that time should not be wasted because of the suffering that was taking place at this very moment.

Scanning through the history of the world was no picnic but with the advances they had each day, there was always something new. Each one of the programmed individuals had the power to find just about anything they wanted, if they had a little bit of information to start. What they had would be enough to get the search going, they would be sure to find the persons responsible for the devastation, and the lives lost on earth.

The events that were to follow were the most unexpected to Don and the population of the world. The other three missiles a confirmed launch, and doomsday was here. Don knew that unless they could save themselves by getting back to the ship in time, it would be too late for everyone on earth. Don knew he had to warn the others quickly.

He rushed to the three with him and said in a commanding voice they had never heard before.

"We have to move now. Fly to the ship as fast as you can, and set the time back to two weeks before the blast. Now move there's not a second to waste."

Keeper started the process as soon as she heard what Don had to say. Before they got inside the door, the ship was already talking and giving them directions of what they each should do. The door closed behind Obit, the last one inside. He could feel the ship in motion. He was in his seat and secured in seconds. They were moving in the direction of a new time space that was formulated by the ship at that instant. According to their calculations, it will only be a few seconds until they reach the time portal. Saving themselves is just a process they go through in the normal. Destruction of their ship or either of them is an impossible thing. No one wants to think about the life ending here on earth. The few survivors could be the ones that were responsible for the bombings. Now, the seconds that it took to get to the time hole had past, and gone…

They are moving through the sky cloaked, setting a course for the desert. Don gave Keeper the information she needed to get them there. He also told the others what he intended to do after his discovery but there was no time; his plan foiled by the culprits. They had to get to the ship to make their exit and even telepathy would have been too slow.

"Chapter Seventy-One: KAWHOCUMDIA"

The crew could see the big city from where they entered the time portal. It was a good feeling. For Keeper seeing the picture perfect view brought tears to her eyes. The bombing that will come two weeks later would leave the city unrecognizable. The possibility of Sky City being severely damage was too high. All four of the super heroes had their minds on the future. Now, their job was to find the criminals and stop them before they got started. Alternatively, at least catch them in the process of setting up, and putting their plan away.

Keeper said to Lore,

"look, what a beautiful sky we have and that great big

old city."

She then turned to look at Lore and said,

"I think I can see Sky City from here."

This did the men well; the voice was so sweet they all chimed in with,

"ah."

The sound was somewhat prolonged, even had harmony. They did not snicker like the usual ten-year-old boys they were at times though. Keeper just said,

"you guys."

Don told her,

"take your last look for a while; we're on our way to Iranian air space."

Obit spoke up,

"yea, we'll be gone for at least,"

there was a short pause. He finished his sentence with,

"whatever."

Don felt some soreness in his back, which he could not believe, he said,

"that last flight to the ship was a rough one. Can we set this baby on autopilot? I do not know about you people but I would like to take a break until we get there. I am so going to miss my music these next two weeks. Maybe, it will not take that long. What'd you think Captain?"

Keeper spoke,

"sure, autopilot, break, cookies and milk, all good ideas."

She told the ship,

"take control ship and only wake us if you need something, until we get there, stay cloaked."

The response from the ship was,

"yes ma'am."

Once the ship takes control, it becomes the responsible party and seriousness is its demeanor.

Each one took their turn saying,

"thank you, good night sweetheart."

Keeper replied to each one because they were saying good night to the ship,

"goodnight."

As the guys get the good night out of their mouths, they look at each other and smile big, holding back the laughter except for the pig snorts. There is something to be-said for the statement, boys will be boys, even if they are the most genius of men. Putting their heads down and closing their eyes, they went off to sleep.

Before drifting off, Don said calling the ship by her name as though he knows her now,

"gentle alarm Emily, on the wake-up."

The ship responded with a soft voice of understand-ing,

"yes sir, and would you like some soft music also?"

Don just asked,

"are you flirting with me Emily?"

The ship responded,

"ooh no sir, I'm not qualified for such a response. And, heaven knows I'm not your type."

There was complete silence in the cabin for the first time in a while. Peaceful silence. Keeper told the ship,

"full speed for us all the way there, and no music to wake us."

The ship answered,

"yes ma'am.

As they lay sleeping, if you were there you might wonder what kept the ship from going off course or from ramming into something. Since they did their cloaking, no one could see them. You might think it was possible for something from earth. Earth's primitive way was nothing to compare to the sophisticated system of this craft. No other spacecraft could match the formulas programming and the individuals of programming. There was no way any individual or group of individuals could ever use the programming for evil, ever. The reality of it was the early creators knew they had to do something about controlling the programming in advance, and they did. We know earth's advancements are the beginning to bring the inhabitance to a higher level but still it does not compare to the programming of the Zorvirax and all with programming.

Keeper's ship was as up to speed with the advances as any ship in the sky. As of today there were only eleven legal. One was stolen once but was recaptured and is now safely in the right hands. Sam, Danny and Jimmy were three people programmed back in the sixties which were the first successful human beings ever programmed. They are working on projects congruently every day.

Obit looked at Lore and told him,

"all of the information that we have, will be available to you as you are programmed. By the time we are through with this project, your part will be complete. From then on only updates will be coming in to you."

Lore's immediate response was,

"great, I'm excited."

Obit smiled and said to Keeper,

"I'll be sending Lore updates for reprogramming if anything is messed with or missed when we pull out of Iranian territory."

Keeper said to herself making a mental note,

"right now, make a mental note about Lore's programming. Done.

While he sleeps, we will take in the sights, if that's alright with him."

Keeper was not feeling the stress the guys were but was seeing them as peers. She really wanted to be one of them. Thinking about the sightseeing tour, she said,

"I'd like to see some things like, <u>The Church of the Holy Sepulcher, Bethany, Golgotha, and all of Jerusalem.</u>"

There is a quite pause, she said,

"we could go cloaked."

Keeper was still talking but was talking and falling off to sleep. She yawned and said sleepily,

"I know how dangerous the area has been but we can work around it with a bit of magic."

She spoke out again more determined this time,

"I know all of the history. I just want to see everything in person, up close. Hey is anybody sleepy yet?"

"Lore spoke to the other guys, you all have fun, and I'll be fine. I am looking forward to getting the programming done. You know, so I will know what to do at every turn. Obit, I thought you said I would not have to sleep during programming. What's up?"

Obit said,

"it just takes longer. Sleeping speeds the process. O.K.?"

Obit said with a look of imposition on his face,

"what's up with the being put out, Lore? I don't hear anybody else complaining!"

Don turned his head slightly looking at Obit, and said,

"nice."

Obit held back a chuckle.

Keeper said,

"that's great."

She had a grin from ear to ear. She was feeling like she was not the Captain but just a girl. A girl with all the men she could possibly ever need. Thrilled she beamed out,

"darling ship of mine Emily, were you listening?"

"Yes ma'am, your course is already set for Jerusalem. We're cloaked and prepared for anything."

Keeper still not ready to sleep said to Emily,

"when we get there, hover for several hours, so that we get enough sleep, and please monitor our sleep. Heart rate and REM sleep before you wake us.

The ship said,

"yes ma'am.

Keeper always took the control with her that kept her in contact with the ship. She can talk to the female personality that she has given the ship, Emily. She felt the bond between her and the ship. In addition, so does the ship. It is just something the ship knew that Keeper wanted and participated. Even though the ship's female personality does really like it, she tried not to get too emotional about it. She knew her part in all of it but the communication with Keeper was the icing on her cake.

Keeper finally said,

"sleep now fellows. I am heading out to dream land. Good night guys."

Keeper listened for a few seconds, and the men all said with telepathy,

"good night."

The space travelers know that all of the talk and putting on about taking time to go shopping was just pretend for Keeper. It is her way of getting through her day. She knew that this matter was to get the person responsible for the bombings. Moreover, find a way to stop him. They would have plenty of time. In addition, even if they have to do a time travel back again, it is O.K...

They had all decided not to go too far back from the time of the bombing. All of the action that would be taking place would be two weeks before the actual detonation. Keeper and all of the men were sure it was at the last minute that the culprits did a lot of moving around with calls to each other, and meeting about the up and coming event.

Obit knew what he found was going to lead them to the maniacs. Keeper had already brought up the information on her visual screen. She was keeping it open to the rest of the crew but not talking about it. She was getting too emotional and thought it would be best if she just did not say anything for a while.

Keeper makes one more statement,

"off to sleep now, you don't want to miss anything

tomorrow because you stayed up late working your brains overtime, again, good night boys."

No one said anything but knew she was upset. The silence among them was not to indicate any dread of the up and coming event. It was just a silence among them all, the last silence of the day before sleep. It always comes, too quiet.

"Chapter Seventy-Two: KAWHOCUMDIA"

The ship hovered over Ahvaz as she called out Keeper's ship name quietly,

"Captain, Captain."

The sound of the ship's voice was so nice and soft, it was mellow to the ear. She called to the Captain with the kindness of a mother waking her sweet young daughter. Again, she called softer,

"Captain, Captain, we're here. Ahvaz, Captain. Do you want to sleep a while longer? We have been hovering for two hours. That's what you said two, hours."

The ship's screen was showing the city below. The trains stopped. Most railroad cars turned over. The rails blown up in different sections as you entered the station. Emily said,

"Captain, I think you need to see this, Captain."

Something had happened here all right, and it had just been a few minutes before their ship arrived. The only thing imaginable that was missing from the scene down below was the sickening smell of burning flesh from the dead bodies strewn around everywhere. The ship's voice said again to Keeper,

"Captain, I really think you need to see this. Quickly now, come look quickly. This brought Keeper to her feet immediately as she woke from her dreams, she said

"Oh my God!"

There were long lines of cars on and off the hi-way. Stopped, and empty. People were fleeing in hordes to the border any way they could get there. There were remains of buildings blown to bits. Bodies pulled in large numbers underneath the rubble of the hundreds of important government buildings. You could see the remains of commercial buildings as well. There were no signs of police or firefighters, and no military uniformed men with the men pulling the bodies out of wreckage and debris. This once a modern Mecca, now a total desolation as far as the eye could see.

The ship's voice said to Keeper,

"Captain you O.K...?"

The silence fell as if some loved ones tomb threw open. Tears were welling up in Keeper's eyes. She heard the rustle of the men moving her way. Obit stared into the screen with the deadpan look of a dying man. He asked,

"is this the reason we're here?"

Don stated,

"this is not nuclear. This is worse."

Don gave the command to the ship,

"check for contaminates."

The ship's response was to Keeper.

"Ma'am?

Keeper quickly replied,

"do what the Captain request."

The ship's voice replied,

"yes ma'am.

Keeper asked Don,

"what do you think we ought to do first?"

He replied with a frustrated look on his face.

"Stay contained in the ship; be prepared in case we have to reach an altitude that is safe for everyone on board, and including the ship's safety, and, one more thing."

Keeper asked with no expression on her face,

"what's that?"

Then Don said something that was profound but wonderful,

"pray. Eba unis fra Tu tae da chee."

I want all of the information compiled from the bombing site and analyzed Ship.

Keeper spoke up and said, wishing they had a better

way to express her name,

"the ship's name is Emily but will respond to Ship.

The ship responded to Don's request with no hesitation,

"yes sir."

Don received the report telepathically from the ship. He now will call her Emily from this day forward he spoke it softly,

"thank you Emily."

Obit did not say anything about her response to him earlier but wondered. He said,

"the great state you live over has just announced its responsibility for the bombing."

Keeper said,

"the city? I do not believe it! The U.S. would not do that.

The next thing they heard was a voice that came from behind the men and Keeper, "that's right they wouldn't do that.

Keeper called out,

"Lore, you're up!"

She jumped with anticipation to greet him. She did
not wait for him to kiss her. Keeper reached his mouth with
the passion of a reunion of many years gone by. There was a
silence from the crew, which was what seemed to be Lore
and Keeper's long separation where they had no contact. Not
so, it had only been a short time span.

Don said to Obit,

"I guess we've got a love story here."

Obit replied,

"yea and I introduced them! Of course, they did meet
before in an earlier time."

When the kiss was over Keeper asked Lore,

"will you be a doll and take charge here? Obit and
Don will be your first mates. I'm going out for a look see."

She headed for the door after another short kiss. She

was out the door quickly as it opened; it closed behind her as quickly as she left. Obit asked Lore,

"can I still call you, Fly?"

Lore looked at Obit with a newfound feeling of admiration. He said to Obit with an air of humor but with affection,

"right now Obit, you can call me anything you want to call me. I am not only flying on air, I am really flying on air. She is the greatest woman I have ever known, ever. How is the air outside?

Don replied,

"not bad, not bad at all."

Lore thinking of Keeper said,

"good, we've got to keep an eye on it for Keeper. Obit would you go and follow her, just to make sure she is safe? We will stay in contact, thank you sir."

Obit answered quickly as he moved toward the door,

"O.K..."

He went to the door, and the second it opened, he jumped into flight. He was not too far behind Keeper. Instead of following her as Lore requests him to do, he called to her telepathically. She turned looking back at Obit. She called back and asked,

"what are you doing?"

She knew that he was coming to catch her, so she waited. As he got up beside her, she looked at him wondering and asked,

"what is this about? He knows I'm capable of handling myself."

She hesitated, and said,

"Lore wanted you to watch out for me, huh?"

As she nodded her head up and down, he replied with the same,

"yes."

She looked at Obit slowly moving out ahead of him and said,

"O.K., let's go."

Moving more slowly, she waited for him to take the lead, and then he got what she wanted him to do. He moved in the direction she was headed. Obit move ahead of her, only a few inches. Then, they both heard the explosion, the weapon going off; the crippling bullet hit Obit in the head. Keeper heard him cry out,

"get out of here."

As he fell from the sky, she could her him calling repeatedly,

"get out of here! Get out of here!"

Her tears started to well up in her eyes as she watched him falling to earth. Her pain almost made her go after him but she realized he was right; she must get out of there immediately. Whoever the shooter was may have been aiming at her and still focused on her, with the purpose of bringing her down now too.

Her sensors were not picking him up anymore, which

meant he was legally brain dead. She cloaked herself and set her super shield. If it were to be, he would naturally restore himself in time. Obit would come to find her when he could. She had to get back to the ship. Keeper was sure the shooter or shooters were wondering how they were flying with no craft of any kind.

The lucky thing would be for them to take Obit prisoner, and his life saved. She knew he would make it somehow. Then, she thought about going in after him, if she had to. She could and would if it meant getting him back. Back alive and safe.

First, she would have to move the time order to change the future. Keeper held out her hand and pressed with all of the pressure she could muster. She reached the place in time where the bomb went off. She then, moved it back in time six seconds, and went on a search that would change the world forever. Time stopped. Her brain was running as fast as it could, her vision check on every avenue done in fractions of a second. Then, she felt the hole she had made for the time entrance was stable. She slipped through and cloaked herself to become safe. No more, crack shot to bring her down. The change of time and uncloaking she did to add to the confusion to the onlooker, if any.

Now, she had the address she needed to catch the culprits that were going to set off the rockets that carried the bombs. She flew just as fast as time would let her fly. She thought of Lore and Don back on the ship, and how they found Don at the beginning in the cave. Lore was the love of her life, and Don was a deeply loved newfound friend and now Obit and the pain he would suffer, all of these thousands of years. In addition, when he was first born and the childhood memories that would never go away. Now, all of these lives Obit had saved. She was feeling the guilt for him coming to watch over her and he was uncloaked because of her. Keeper thought to herself,

"he will survive, he'll be alright."

Now, she thought she would be O.K. they would all survive. The place each one of the programmed always went was the place to survive, which was their insurance they could live to save others and make the Universe a better place.

"Chapter Seventy-Three: KAWHOCUMDIA"

"Every time I see you, when I look in your eyes, I get this feel n' I'm about to cry, over you."

Keeper was singing the song she had heard just a few years before, when it had made it to the top of the charts. It dwindled off with her singing just the one line, repeatedly. The emotions were swelling up inside of her.

She called out loudly,

"ship are you catching all of this?"

Ship responded,

"yes ma'am.

Keeper replied,

"O.K. then."

She was hovering over her destination at that moment, and said,

"keep a close watch now, I'm heading down there."

In addition, with that, in seconds she was on the ground. Keeper made a nice landing, and then the seconds started to take on a new meaning.

She said to herself,

"watch what you are doing now."

Answering herself back, she said,

"I'm watching, I'm watching."

No one was there with her but her second self, which she invented. Then the visual came in clear, and Keeper had her security blanket, an exact duplicate of herself. She had started this after the ship's creation, and was waiting for Lore to come to her. Keeper's duplicate said,

"I'm with you as your helper and only if needed."

Keeper replied casually,

"O.K., I'm ready for some help. Can you fly back up

and keep a watch on this sector?"

The duplicate said,

"yes."

It only took seconds and the duplicate was up and watching over Keeper. She called her Second, and said,

"talk to me Second, and let me know what's going on at all times."

Keeper's duplicate started talking,

"O.K., in the six hundreds, Arab armies conquered Iran and it became a leading center of Islam. In the ten hundreds, Seljuk Kurds conquered much of Iran. In twelve twenty, Mongol armies led by Genghis Khan overran Iran. Keeper suddenly interrupted her, calling her Emily, which was the same as the person called ship, or Emily, or the duplicate,

"hey, hey, hey, could you keep it confined to the present and just in this area? You know this sector."

Emily replied,

"yes ma'am."

There was plenty going on in this neighborhood all right. The demons had a small factory set up with an underground missile site. It was unbelievable what they had done and how they had done it. Keeper was already reading the older one as the historian of the group. His name was Mohammad Mosaddeq; he got his name from an earlier leader that played a part in politics in Iran. This was from 1951-1967. Mohammad mumbled many things when he would speak of history but in his mind, it was clear as a bell on what actually happened.

Keeper asked Emily,

"can you see to the ship getting back to check on Obit and stay here with me at the same time?"

It was more of a statement that a question, and with a touch of command sprinkled in there.

Emily said,

"yes ma'am Captain. It's as good as done."

A noise like a cell phone went off inside of Emily.

She then said to the Captain

"there."

"Chapter Seventy-Four: KAWHOCUMDIA"

The fence seemed to grow higher and higher as Obit looked outside through the crack in the block wall. The cracked wall was a perfect metaphor for a failing justice system. This made Obit wonder why they had chosen concrete blocks. It certainly had an easy to tear down capability. It was not for him to reason why but he always certainly did. For some reason the foundation must have lost its support and the blocks began to give way. The crack was wide enough to have good visibility for some distance.

Obit could see the fence was at least twelve feet high. The loss of the use of his right arm gave him reason to believe his difficulty in getting out of this place would be at least close to impossible, until his injuries were better. He still knew that he had to escape. For some reason his power had been diminished by 90 percent or more. He knew the wound he had was in the forehead, medically speaking in the frontal cerebral hemisphere. His right arm also was wounded. Obit thought this to be minor but it was not. He was able to maintain some of his flight power, which kept him from hitting the ground any harder than he did, lucky break for Obit. Still, his vision was blurry, and his head was about to explode, even before he was actually awake. The pain was so great, Obit tried to stay unconscious, and sleep. It reminded him of the time he was a young boy. He got a blow to the head with a large tree limb. The limb was pulled back and tied to another tree by some of the meanest boys in the village. It was set with a trip string to set free another string that set free the rope. He felt the pain for only a fraction of a second, and then, the lights started to go off in his head. The noises of the forest seemed to get further away until they were completely gone. There was a numbing sensation but it was mostly in and around his head.

As the minutes and hours ticked on, Obit's body started to recoup and was starting to tell him things. This was how he recalled it.

"I looked again out through the small crack. This time I saw the guard as he passed by. He seemed to be very close to the wall. If the concrete blocks had not been there, I could have reached out and touched him.

He must have been walking right up next to the wall. His uniform looked freshly starched and ironed. He was very neat. His weapon was in a holster. In addition, his weapon looked strapped on his left hip with the handle to the outside. If he were right-handed, he would have had to reach across to his left side to draw his gun. There was no sign of a gun except for the handle sticking out of the case. It was enclosed in the case, whatever kind of weapon it was."

Obit heard some yelling as the guard went by and his

head turned back around to his right to look in the direction of the yeller. Obit could hear his footsteps, it sounded like he was walking on rocks. They crunched slowly as he went by on his way.

The pounding in Obit's head kept making him try to loosen up by turning his head around back and to. He had done this before with other headaches. To him, why he was there was a mystery. The last thing he remembered was following behind Keeper. In addition, to make sure she was not in any danger. Obit just wanted to keep her safe.

He said to himself,

"I just wanted her safe."

He started to feel the strength coming back into his body. His brain started picking up things again that he had lost. Obit could feel his right arm healing. His screen came back up in his vision. To explain this he was going to need some time. Maybe the guards that were looking for an escaped prisoner found him. He knew one thing; he was not going to stick around to find out how much time he had left in this prison.

Obit went over to the toilet that was almost in the middle of the small room. He looked at the water that was inside the bowl. There was nothing in it. There was no sign of blood anywhere. He could see there was no sign of him ever having been there at all. Obit could not recall very much of what happened. He said to himself,

"no sign of me. Well, that's a good thing."

He tried to make a contact with the phone line connected to the main office of the prison. As soon as he was up and running, he would use the identity of a man named James Hilton. He pretended he was from the American Embassy to get into the files. Once the phone line made the tie, he was in. What he talked about to whoever answered, did not really matter. He could easily stun the person and have them talk to him as if they knew Obit from a few years back. Then, he would set up a visit. Then, give them a mental picture of him and program a brief history, and that was all there was to it. It did not matter if it was male or female he did it.

Then, all of a sudden, it was all back there as if it had never been gone. His history of the past, even the last few seconds after the shot hit his head. The bullet that went through his head had a fragment that sheared off and hit his arm. It damaged a nerve and caused Obit not to have use of it. He fell from the sky to near death. In addition, because of his cell regeneration that started as soon as he hit the ground, was already recuperating while the guards were examining him. It had just taken it this long because of all of the damage. Total recuperation would not be that long now. The damage to his face was because of the landing, on it, which made Obit look like one of the escapees from a few days before. Not confirmed and prison guards and officials were still in the process of identifying him. He was sure they never would. He would make sure they never would.

Then, there was a connection in his brain from the ship; Emily was on the line. She said,

"are you alright? We are in the middle of something and need your assistance. That is, if it's possible?"

Obit responded,

"I'm in the last few minutes of reconstruction and I'll be right with you, maybe, two minutes or less. I should have set the formula to super shield myself when I left the ship. I just did not think there was any danger especially, involving being shot from the ground. Who would have thought they had a sniper stargazing? It must have been the search party looking for the escaped prisoner or prisoners. That was it, it was coming in now, that there were three of them. When the guards saw Keeper, and then me, they must have had us in their scope. In addition, they nailed me first as I moved out in front of Keeper. Thank God, it was I. Is Keeper alright?"

Emily answered with the happiness you might expect from a human being, "yes, she's fine. However, we need you to get back to her quickly. She is in a very sticky position."

Obit responded,

"yes, you're right. We have to get to her quickly. I am coming out of the top. Are you above me waiting? I had another escape route planned but this is great. I am sorry I am rambling. You are straight up, right?"

Emily responded nicely,

"yes sir, the door will be open."

Obit said,

"nice, thank you Emily."

Emily quickly finished,

"sir, my double is hovering over Keeper's position as we speak."

Obit simply replied,

"don't explain I'll catch up later, unless there is something I need to know.

Or, you can feed it to me as I go."

Emily said,

"feed set to start as soon as you get here. I'll be wait-ing."

Meanwhile, Keeper was in the process of capturing six men in the basement of the factory. She had four of them working on disarming the bombs and destroying the pro-grams used to signal the missiles. Keeper had already shown off a bit with her abilities. The men were terrified of her. When the two that we have left to capture come to the area, Keeper will stun then and force them into an agreement statement. Nightmare situations programmed into their heads and they will start to believe. Keeper then releases them from their stun and she picks up where the nightmare leaves off. There will be names and addresses of others sent to Keeper later.

She was standing guard over the four men and wait-ing. The wait for the other men may be a while. They went for food and supplies. This was to be the end of their contact on the outside, until it was all over. Keeper screamed out a command at the men she had captured, it was unbelievably loud,

"keep working!"

Keeper called out to Emily,

"Emily, are you up there?"

She responded from her watch,

"yes ma'am. There are just a few people that can get through the rubble, it's a mess ma'am."

Keeper called back to Emily in agreement,

"yes, I know. This is getting really complicated. When I get these people in a holding cell, probably somewhere on the outside of town, we will find out if whoever did this is just attacking in retaliation in advance, sounds funny. Someone may have found out about his or her plan and others are trying to stop him or her. It is plain to see it did not work. The bombs here in question were just about on their way if it weren't for us simple folk."

Emily quickly called out to Keeper.

"Ma'am, you have two men coming in the back door now with weapons in their hands! They are dressed in hoods. It looks like they are wearing the women's chador! I'm zooming in on them."

Emily speedily rejects the honest look of the two men,

"ma'am! It looks like there is blood around the chest area in the front of the chador on each of them."
Keeper fired back to Emily,

"O.K., I'll stun them just before they walk in the door. They won't know what hit them."

Keeper used her formulated vision that allowed her to see through the walls. No matter what the walls are made of, she can see right through, no problem.

The men are about to burst through the door and are armed with automatic weapons. They know something is going on inside.

Keeper hit them with stun just before one of the men in the bloody chador reached to open the door. She commanded them to put down their weapons. As soon as they responded, she told them, in their language,

"put your hands in the air sandal maker! You lied to God!"

She then gave them ten commands to perform. They said they were not sure they could remember all ten. Keeper assured them they could. In addition, they immediately began their tasks. She then put a protective barrier surrounding the whole building. No one could come in and no one could get out, not without the barrier first being taken down. If the men did have a way to break the stun that Keeper put them in, they would not have been able to get through the barrier alive. The barrier does give instructions and warnings about what it will do and can do.

Now Keeper had all six of the bad men in this area. The last two were not Iranians but Afghanistani. The other men had finished shutting down the missile site. Now there will not be any bombs hit U.S. soil. These men will have conscience makeovers and will be turned into heroes to work the world over. We wait for these.

Keeper said to all of the men telepathically,

"now this has been a day, *a day of all days*."

It was then recorded in history. Moreover, they recorded all of the events that took place that day; In addition, not just history taken by the human species but history of the programmers' alien and human beings alike. The things that matter to all in the future if there is to be a future are the future. Not now, for now, there will be the unknown changes for most human beings and only a few will know the truth of what is happening, and what is to happen....

"Chapter Seventy-Five: KAWHOCUMDIA"

"The dull plain man with the innocent looks on his face and it seemed to be a part of his visage, had high water pant legs. His brother was of some monsters face to a child, the child in me. Though I loved my brother, as he had gotten older, his appearance had gotten scarier to me and as he was too many others. His top lip always covered with a hairy bandit's style mustache. My brother Roe had started it in the Navy. It became more repulsive each time that I would see him as the years went by. Although it was only a few times that, I saw him, revealed to me through the unceremonious visits that we were never close. The times when I was just a small boy, I remembered it as a pain that I had to endure. He was my brother, and we were supposed to love our brothers.

I remember one incident when we both had to sleep in the same bed. He told me as we were starting to go to sleep, that he was going to spit straight up and, for me to duck under the covers. I was in the first grade I am sure, and like the first grader that I was, I fell for it, and ducked under the covers. I heard him fake a spit all right but then I discovered the smell as well. The laughter coming from my brother was unbearable. I tried to attack him with an overwhelming amount of fist in his face, throwing blow after blow, to no avail. I really disliked him for a long time after that but got over it eventually. Like the heart of all hearts, my love for my brother grew as time went by. He was not a bad looking young man but had some teeth that were crooked and some with jagged points. Even while in the navy, he refused to get them fixed, I did not know why.

The picture of the two middle-aged men still haunts me to this very day that it could be I in the picture. Out of shape, very thin, and even looking like a mental, feckless I had always been proud of the fact that I could play music, and thought that I had done quite well. The plan was to record an album under contract. This would have of course been with one of the better labels. I simply did not understand the workings of life or the workings of a woman hell bent for revenge. Men were her targets I can only say because I am no longer associated with her. In addition, I will never be, and as long as I have anything to say about it. I will no longer put myself through the torture she always will want. Case closed but I have a daughter and a son. I will have to find it in my heart and soul always because of these two people that had nothing to do with their own coming into this world. Case closed except for the grand kids. I have only met my daughter's children by her first husband in her first marriage. Some of this has to be my fault. Guilty I am, carrying around the guilt; I am not going to do.

Again, the dull plain man started running and working out for a few hours, well, a while during the week. It was only after and operation on his back, did he see, no other way for him to survive all-of-this but to do just that. It became his physical salvation. In addition, here we come to the clarifying of the previous sentence. Physical salvation is only in a life or death situation when someone is recovering from an illness that nearly took his or her life or a similar circumstance. Actually, I like the one where Salvation pertains to our Lord and Savior Jesus Christ. I only wanted to explain myself from a point of entry into this life from an earlier time, a time when I was young, grade school or younger.

I remember an incident that my mother said was impossible for me to remember since it was my first birthday. My mother had me down for a nap and I was not going for it. I just wanted to stay up and play. Therefore, I jumped up and down in that old crib repeatedly and again. It was a wonderful time. That I really do not remember because it was marred by what followed. It was the unspeakable happened. I hit my chin on the old railing. That started this noisy racket coming out of my mouth that I did not really understand at the time, called crying. I mean really. It split it open. I screamed my mother came running in to rescue me yet the blood kept gushing out of my chin. Well, that was it, I was a hit the rest of the day. That secured me to be a suckling child for the rest of the week anyway. I guess I learned at an early age, if you want to get attention, you have to get hurt or hurt yourself someway. My philosophy did not last long when I learned I could not stand pain of the severe type. It was really worth it though when I turned six. I had more girls, well as I said; the philosophy did not last long.

Don said to Lore,

"were you listening to that? My brain has been burning to let that out, and now I'll get back to my story."

Obit looked at Keeper and said,

"race you back to the ship."

Keeper was sly when she said,

"that's great but isn't that a little bit childish?"

In the same instant, she jumped as if she were diving into a pool after a long hot day. Her movement was like that of a humming bird but much faster. Obit moved in the same second but after Keeper had already left, he said to himself,

"man, she's fast!"

Keeper was in the Captain's chair; Don and Lore were asleep. On cue, they got their preprogramming and remained positioned in their sleep sites. She said to Obit as he entered the craft,

"don't wake them. Let them get their nap. I'm not breaking any rule here am I?"

Obit sealed them in a sleep cocoon to sound proof their environment. It only took him a second to produce the safe environment that they could sleep in undisturbed. It encased them but was invisible. The conditions for the removal were only for one sleeping in the cocoon to wake, and it would evaporate instantly.

Obit asked,

"where are we headed?"

Keeper said,

"I'm thinking. I want to protect Lore as much as I can at first, so I am thinking.

Obit responded with another question,

"why would you want to protect Fly? He is going to be finished with programming and he will be able to take care of himself?

Keeper got the look of a girl just before she cries, she barely has it out,

"I want us to have the human side of us to share and then become one. I don't want to miss that between the two of us"

In addition, with that, a teardrop trickled down her cheek.

Obit over reacted and said,

"now look what I've done. I have made you cry. I am

sorry. I really did not ever want to do that. Please forgive me. Now my heart is breaking."

Keeper gritted her teeth and pressed down her lips trying to hold back the tears. She was not doing very well when she said,

"it's alright. You see, it's, and I love him so much. Obit, you are the best friend I have. Do not worry about that, I know you did not mean to do anything wrong. It's just that, it'll be O.K., I promise, it'll be O.K..."

Obit regained his composure and gave Keeper a hug. As he bent over, Fly woke up, sat looking at Keeper and Obit hugging. Keeper had responded to Obit's approach to give her the hug and stood where she was facing Lore.

Lore said with a whimsical smile,

"Obit, are you trying to steal my girl?"

Obit answered him with just as much whimsy as Lore,

"right!"

He stepped back out of the way for Keeper to go to Lore's area. Lore stood as she approached. They connected with the passionate kiss Keeper and Lore were starting to expect from each other.

Obit felt the love between his new friend and old one. He said,

"it's good to see what I thought love was when I was a younger man. Someday, she will return to me and my love for her may return.

www.ingramcontent.com/pod-product-compliance
Lightning Source LLC
Chambersburg PA
CBHW051054030726
47504CB00006B/1616